Didn't I Say
to Make My Abilities
Average in the
Next Life?!

VOLUME 6

Reina

Mile

Kurihara
Misato

Didn't I Say to Make My Abilities *Average* in the Next Life?!

VOLUME 6

BY

FUNA

ILLUSTRATED BY

Itsuki Akata

Seven Seas

Seven Seas Entertainment

DIDN'T I SAY TO MAKE MY ABILITIES AVERAGE
IN THE NEXT LIFE?! VOLUME 6

© FUNA / Itsuki Akata 2017

Originally published in Japan in 2017 by EARTH STAR
Entertainment, Tokyo. English translation rights arranged
with EARTH STAR Entertainment, Tokyo, through TOHAN
CORPORATION, Tokyo.

Seven Seas press and purchase enquiries can be sent to
Marketing Manager Lianne Sentar at press@gomanga.com.
Information requiring the distribution and purchase of
digital editions is available from Digital Manager CK Russell
at digital@gomanga.com.

Follow Seven Seas Entertainment online at
sevenseasentertainment.com.

TRANSLATION: Diana Taylor
ADAPTATION: Maggie Cooper
COVER DESIGN: Nicky Lim
INTERIOR LAYOUT & DESIGN: Clay Gardner
PROOFREADER: Jade Gardner, Stephanie Cohen
LIGHT NOVEL EDITOR: Nibedita Sen
MANAGING EDITOR: Julie Davis
EDITOR-IN-CHIEF: Adam Arnold
PUBLISHER: Jason DeAngelis

ISBN: 978-1-64275-086-7
Printed in Canada
First Printing: June 2019
10 9 8 7 6 5 4 3 2 1

God bless me?
CONTENTS

CHAPTER 46: DEMONS   13

CHAPTER 47: THE RUINS   61

CHAPTER 48: SECRET TECHNIQUE   99

CHAPTER 49: THE HOUSE OF AURA   121

CHAPTER 50: A RIVAL APPEARS   185

CHAPTER 51: THE LETTER   199

CHAPTER 52: LEATORIA   215

CHAPTER 53: THE AVENGER   229

CHAPTER 54: FAIRY HUNTING   245

CHAPTER 55: THE FOUR STOOGES (MINUS ONE)   267

CHAPTER 56: THE MASKED GIRL RIDES AGAIN!   283

SIDE STORY: KURIHARA MISATO'S OTAKU LIFE   307
BONUS STORY: WEAPONS   319

AFTERWORD   323

Japan

C-Rank Party "The Crimson Vow"

— Misato —

A high school student. Died saving a little girl and was reborn into a fantasy world.

— Mile —

A girl who was granted "average" abilities in this fantasy world.

— Mavis —

A swordswoman. Leader of the up-and-coming party, the Crimson Vow.

— Reina —

A rookie hunter. Specializes in combat magic.

The Kingdom of Brandel

Eckland Academy

— Marcela —

Adele's friend. A magic-user
of noble birth.

— Aureana —

Adele's friend. A commoner.

— Pauline —

A rookie hunter. A timid girl,
however...

— Monica —

Adele's friend. The second
daughter of a merchant.

Previously

When Adele von Ascham, the eldest daughter of Viscount Ascham, was ten years old, she was struck with a terrible headache and just like that, remembered everything.

She remembered how, in her previous life, she was an eighteen-year-old Japanese girl named Kurihara Misato who died while trying to save a young girl, and that she met God...

Misato had exceptional abilities, and the expectations of those around her were high. As a result, she could never live her life the way she wanted. So when she met God, she made an impassioned plea:

"In my next life, please make my abilities average!"

Yet somehow, it all went awry.

In her new life, she can talk to nanomachines and, although her magical powers are technically average, it is the average between a human's and an elder dragon's...6,800 times that of a sorcerer!

At the first academy she attended, she made friends and rescued a little boy as well as a princess. She registered at the Hunters' Prep School under the name of Mile and at the graduation exam went head-to-head with an A-rank hunter.

The party she formed with her classmates, the Crimson Vow, made an impressive debut! But one problem after another has come hurtling their way—from golems, invading foreign soldiers, and fathers who are too protective of their daughters, to elder dragons, the strongest creatures in the world!

And then suddenly, a clash between the Crimson Vow and Mile's friends from her first school, the Wonder Trio?!

A lot has happened, but now Mile is going to live a normal life as a rookie hunter with her allies by her side.

Because she is a perfectly normal, *average* girl!

CHAPTER 46 |

Demons

"**D**-DEMONS..."

The members of the Crimson Vow were stunned. They had been certain that they were dealing with beastmen, but now their opponents had suddenly revealed themselves to be demons.

"Wha?! But y'all already knew we were demons, didn't ya?!"

The demons, who had lowered their hoods on the assumption that they had been found out, were equally surprised.

"Sorry! We really weren't trying to deceive you or anything..." Mile scratched her head apologetically. "But since we already have a pretty good idea of what's going on here, how about you all tell us the rest?"

Though Mile had asked cordially, it was only natural that the demons weren't about to assent so readily.

"Q-quit messin' around! It's you who's gonna tell us everything *you* know! Get 'em!" the leader ordered.

When they had fought the beastmen in the past, the Crimson Vow had assumed their opponents to be demons before they showed their faces and steeled themselves accordingly. It was the other way around this time, and the Crimson Vow were thoroughly unprepared.

The fight began, and they witnessed it—the demons' superhuman strength, the stuff of legends. The Crimson Vow were taken aback, but of course, there was one among them who was primed to resist.

"Friends, there's no need to fear! Whenever such devils appear in tales, a hero always emerges from among the humans. This means that the stories of their power are merely an exaggeration—they couldn't possibly be as strong as all that. After all, it's rare for a hero to actually be as mighty in real life as legends make them out to be. Demons are no different. They might be stronger than beastfolk, more magical than elves, and hardier than dwarves, but they're still nothing more than just another type of humanoid!"

At Mile's decree, Reina and Mavis straightened up a bit, their resolve renewed. However, Pauline had a question: "But...doesn't that mean that they're still superior to humans on every front?"

Reina and Mavis paled again.

"Please keep your logic out of thiiiiiiiiiis!!!!" Mile wailed.

Hm, she thought. *This is bad. There are four of us on each side. If this turns into a one-on-one battle, people are gonna get hurt and maybe even die... I believe in everyone, but there's always that million-to-one chance, and it's possible that someone may have no choice but to deal their opponents a fatal wound. What to do?*

That's it!

The perfect plan popped into Mile's mind fully formed.

"Please wait!" she shouted.

The approaching demons stopped in their tracks.

"What? Y'all gonna give up and surrender?" asked the leader.

Mile shook her head. "That's not it. I was just thinking, if we jump into an all-out brawl like this, it won't be very...aesthetic, will it?"

"Huhhhhhhh?"

All voices present, save for Mile's, rang out in harmony.

Even Reina and Mavis were stunned this time.

"Wh-what exactly—"

"Do you mean by 'aesthetic'?"

"What in the world is she on about?" the demons' leader asked.

For once even Mavis could not answer.

"What we need is a one-on-one tournament," said Mile.

Everyone else was flabbergasted at this proposal, so she explained:

"Don't you think it would be sacrilege for us to have such a glorious battle as this and leave everyone stuck concentrating on their own matches, not getting to witness their comrades' bouts?"

Two of the demons, who seemed particularly enthused at the prospect of fighting, nodded their heads in agreement.

"So here's the plan. Each of our sides will put forward one fighter at a time, while the others observe without interfering. We'll have four rounds. Whoever takes three rounds is the victor. The losing side will consider themselves captured and surrender at once. Should we end up with a tie, we will rule that the prowess of our groups is equal and confer with one another on equal terms. How does that sound?"

"Give us a moment."

The demons held a quiet discussion among themselves. "All right," they replied. "We've got no objections."

More than likely, they assumed that the chances of demons such as themselves losing to a bunch of little human girls were... well, you should know the drill by now. Plus, the proposed tournament would be a good way to kill some time. The Crimson Vow had no objections either, already used to leaving negotiations to Mile, at least when commerce was not involved.

"Are we all in agreement, then?"

And so, it was settled.

"Pauline will be the advance guard, Reina will be up after her, Mavis is the lieutenant, and I'll be the big boss."

Mile arranged their lineup in order of strength, with the strongest members going last. The others would probably be doing the same.

Now and then, an enemy might switch it up on purpose, sending in their second against the other side's advance guard, their lieutenant against the other side's second, and their boss against the other side's lieutenant. Then, once their victory was secured with those three matches, they'd send in their advance against the boss as a throwaway. However, Mile thought it unlikely that the demons would do such a thing.

"M-Mile, are you sure it's all right to make me the lieutenant? W-wouldn't it be better for me to be the advance guard?" Mavis stammered nervously.

Mile just grinned. "Don't worry, Mavis, there's no way you could lose! You're an aspiring knight, after all!"

"I...I guess you're right. Yeah, that's exactly right!"

The tense expression faded from her face, and the corners of her mouth twisted into a smile.

The two teams hammered out a set of rules, with provisions allowing that, if the spectators judged that their team's fighter was in danger, they could call off the match or step in to protect their teammate from the enemy's attacks—though in that case, the round would be considered a loss for their side. This portion of the rules had, of course, been Mile's doing. It provided a way for victory to be achieved without either side taking grave injuries or suffering fatalities.

Even if they ended up losing the tourney on the whole, it wouldn't be a huge deal. As long as they could finish without anyone getting seriously hurt or dying, then the worst case scenario was just that they'd have to tell the demons the truth about taking on the job and go over the details of the previous incident. That was no huge loss. Even if they returned to town with only the intel that they were dealing with demons this time, their job would be regarded as a success.

Plus, since the humans already knew about the investigation being conducted by beastmen and demons at the elder dragons' behest, the demons had no reason to detain the Crimson Vow. Once they had given their information, they would probably be released.

And if they were not released, then they could always run, of course. Running away after they had been captured would not constitute breaking their promise.

Not that Mile had even the slightest intention of losing in the first place.

On a small plain where the cliffside opened up, Pauline stood facing a demon around thirty years old. That said, even if the man appeared to be thirty, demons' ages did not align with their appearances, so the girls couldn't be sure how old he was.

Pauline appeared to be trembling—perhaps from fear or nerves. When they had assumed the beastmen to be demons last time, they had felt a sense of trepidation, even despair. This time, it had been the opposite at first—they'd thought that their opponents were beastmen and that their victory would be quick and easy. Yet here before them stood a band of demons. Now Pauline had to face one of them in a test of magic, face to face. No human would assume a straightforward victory was guaranteed.

The spectators all sat together, Crimson Vow and demons alike. Sitting in two groups would have made them more vulnerable to any wayward spells, and this way they would be able to glean information from one another as they talked among themselves. The demon who had previously been pierced by Mile's bullet had been dragged along by his companions and now sat among the spectators as well. Though his wounds had been healed, the magic the demons used was not the somewhat unnatural power Mile and Pauline wielded. Therefore, it would still be some time before he regained his strength. For now, he was down for the count as far as combat went.

Finally, Mile shouted from the makeshift stands:

"Okay! Ready, set, fight!"

"Ice Javelin!"

"Earth Wall!"

A wall of dirt arose from the ground to protect the demon against Pauline's icicle attack. To shield against the barrage of materialized ice, a physical, rather than a magical, barrier was necessary. Conjuring rock would require a sizable amount of magical energy and skill, but dirt was nothing. Both spells were simple things, with the full incantations omitted.

"...Ice Needle!" Pauline attacked again, this time muttering a short spell in a soft voice. The small needles of ice that materialized were swiftly warded off by a blast of wind magic.

".........."

Not in the least bit distressed by the attack, and showing no signs of incanting a spell, the demon man began to approach Pauline, who now stood unmoving.

"It's useless," he said. "A little human girl's magic could never touch us, and any spell of ours is sure to break through your barriers. Whaddya think? How about you surrender now? That way you won't have to get hurt, yeah?"

Pauline shook her head from side to side, tears dotting her eyes.

Of course, if she took the full brunt of a demon's magic, it would easily break through any barrier she could conjure.

That was, *if* she took it head-on.

"Well, I gave ya the chance. I'll try and settle this quick, then. Hopefully it won't hurt ya too bad."

The demon brandished his right hand arrogantly, taking on a languid spell-casting stance, but Mile made no move to intervene. "Water, bind around that girl's limbs and freeze in place to—"

And then, as he began to cast his spell...

"Gwah!" He stopped, a look of utter disbelief upon his face as sweat began to stream from his entire body. "Gyaaaaaah!!"

He clutched his behind and began writhing on the ground.

Pauline appeared to be shaken by this, unable to do a thing.

However, that was not Pauline's MO. Not at all.

"I was trying so hard not to laugh, I almost started crying..." Apparently, Pauline was not trembling in fear but actually holding back laughter. As she feigned terror, she had secretly and quietly begun to cast a short-range "heat" spell underneath her opponent's feet. A weak air current raised it into the bottoms of his pant legs, aiming straight for his most sensitive mucous membranes.

"Wh-what happened?! What the heck just..."

The demon spectators were in a panic. Still, they watched as their companion wailed, cried, and writhed on the ground before them, showing no signs of being ready to intervene and forfeit the round.

And then, Pauline began another spell.

"Blade of ice, pierce my enemy's heart! Ice—"

"Enough! Enough, we forfeit! The match is over!"

The demon leader's face twisted at this show of excessive force, and he quickly called an end to the match.

If we can just win the next three rounds, we've still got this, he thought to himself, though an inescapable premonition of doom began to bubble up within him...

First round winner: Pauline of the Crimson Vow.

The next round, round two, would be Reina versus a boy demon of around twelve or thirteen years old.

In fact, though the boy physically appeared to be around the same age as Reina, as with the previous contender, there was no way of knowing his true age. Then again, Reina herself was actually sixteen years old anyway.

The two squared off against one another.

Unlike Pauline, who was the sort to resort to dirty tricks, Reina was an in-your-face type of mage, a devastating force of nature. However, this meant that she was not well suited to fighting an opponent with even more powerful magic at their disposal. Such as a demon...

Naturally, Reina was well aware of this. Still, no matter how unfavorable this matchup, she had no choice but to fight. It wasn't as though she would always be paired up with opponents over whom she had the advantage.

"Fire Lance!"

This time, the demon boy was the first to attack. He had just witnessed something of a tragedy in the previous round, so he was likely on his guard—and understandably so.

"Barrier!"

Reina, of course, was not limited by the fact that she was an attack-type mage and released the protective spell she had silently been holding.

However, no matter how well defense magic guarded against an enemy attack, it didn't guarantee victory—especially when you faced an opponent who far outranked you in magical strength and skill. If your defense wasn't perfect, then you were better off spending your energy on attack spells from the start. Still, for some reason, Reina's first move was to defend herself.

The barrier spell that Mile had trained Reina to use was also far stronger than the norm, so no matter how powerful the demon's attack might have been, it would not break through easily.

"Wh...?" The demon boy was shaken. Somehow the likes of a little human girl had managed to ward off his magical attack.

"Firebomb!"

"Magic Wall!"

This time, the demon boy was the one who had to guard against Reina's attack.

"Flare Storm!"

"Barrier!"

"Hellfire!"

"Wall!"

The match dragged on and on as their volleys continued, neither able to break through their opponent's barrier. If things continued this way, it was sure to spell disaster for Reina, who fell somewhat behind the demon boy in magical power. Both the demon boy and Reina herself were becoming increasingly aware of this fact.

After innumerable rounds of this, Reina's turn to attack came once again. However, she did not incant a spell.

Instead, she rushed toward her opponent at full speed.

"Huh?"

The boy was struck dumb with shock for a moment but quickly regained his cool.

"I see, you've realized that your magic is no match for mine, and you've come to strike me directly with your staff then, have you? You do realize that I am still a demon, do you not? Magic may be my specialty, but I have mastered the basics of the art of the staff as well. That you might expect a mage like me to fall short in martial combat against a little human girl is just—"

The boy jabbered on and on until suddenly Reina's staff flew from her hands and landed on the ground in front of him, stunning him into silence.

"Huh...?"

She let go of her staff just before a direct attack?

What was the meaning of this? Why would she do that?

There was no way that an empty-handed little girl, especially a mage, whose physical skills were not especially well honed, could defeat a demon by striking or throttling him.

Perhaps because he was so rattled by this incomprehensible action, the boy's response was delayed. His certainty that he could defeat a weak, unarmed human girl with a swing of his staff was a testament to the naivete of his youth, which left him paralyzed.

Squeeze!

"Wh...?"

By the time the boy finally realized what was going on, he found Reina clinging to him tightly.

There was a warm, soft sensation against his chest.

Th-this is...

The boy turned bright red. To date, he had never had a girl-friend, and so had never had a chance to embrace a girl, or even hold hands with any young ladies who were not his own sister. And now, a girl's sweet fragrance was wafting into his nostrils...

His vision went blurry. Just then, he heard the girl's gentle voice in his ear.

"Suicide attack: Megaten."

Bwooom!

"Gaaaaaaaaah!!"

Both of their bodies were enveloped in a roaring flame.

"W-wall! Magic Waaaaaaaall!!!"

The boy tried desperately to enact a magical barrier, but so far he had only ever used the spell to erect a wall between himself and his opponent or to create a shielding dome over himself. He had never attempted to use it to ward off an attack that was directly attached to him. Thus, the wall did nothing but trap both Reina and the flame inside of it—with him—rendering his efforts utterly meaningless.

Reina, however, had been trained for just such a situation.

First, under Mile's tutelage, she had practiced creating a magical barrier that formed close to her body. Second, it was only natural that no flame conjured at her own instruction would ever direct itself toward her. Once Reina had mastered both the barrier and the flames, Mile had imparted upon her an ultimate technique, a special move to be used only when her life was at risk. The Suicide Attack: Megaten.

It was a miraculous attack in which one grappled the opponent with one's own body and struck while the opponent's eyes were round with shock.

Naturally, Mile was the one who had come up with the name.

"Gyaaaaaaaaaah!!!" As his magical barrier proved utterly without effect, the demon boy could only continue to scream.

"St-stop it! That's enoooooough!!!"

The demon leader, who had been paralyzed by the unthinkable scene, now rushed out with a desperate look upon his face before leaping straight into the flames and tearing the two apart. Two more of the demons hurriedly summoned a water spell, dousing the smoldering pair. The fourth dashed forward as well in spite of the pain of his remaining injuries. Once the boy was separated from Reina, the flames on his clothing were quickly extinguished, and the demons frantically began a healing spell.

"You all interfered, so I guess that's a win for me."

Not a one of the demons had the presence of mind to care about Reina's boasting.

"Now then, it's time for round three: the battle of lieutenants!"

The demon leader grimaced at Mile's announcement. At this point, of course, their side had no chance of winning. Even if they were to win the next two rounds, the lieutenant and the boss battles, the results would be two-and-two at best. And, on the off chance that they lost either of those rounds, it would mean defeat for them.

They, a band of demons—they, the chosen few who had been selected for and entrusted with a sacred duty—were on the verge of losing to a band of human girls who were scarcely out of the nursery. The shame would be a scalding brand, a black mark that they would be forced to carry for the rest of their days.

Due to demons' general hardiness and the strength of their healing magic, the two who had lost were already right as rain. Mile lent an additional hand using magic to dispel the spice particles from the man in the first round, so he seemed to have wholly regained his senses. Yet though their burns and other physical injuries had been fully mitigated, the wounds to their morale ran quite deep indeed...

For now anyway, the two sat among the spectators. Or rather, they were forced to. Watching the upcoming matches would be a good lesson for them—and besides, the others got the impression that if they were not forced to do so, they would probably be curled up in a ball, crying somewhere in a corner.

At any rate, while magical ability really had nothing to do with age, it was a far different matter when it came to the martial arts. The two remaining demons fought with the sword, so catastrophes like the first two rounds would be out of the question.

So thought the leader of the demons. Just as any sensible person might.

"Mavis von Austien, leader of the Crimson Vow, swordswoman, now entering the ring!"

"Reltobert, swordsman. Let's go!"

Just because the demons were a magical race, it did not mean that they were all mages. Just as there were mages among the generally un-magical beastfolk, naturally, there were those among demons who were weak at magic, wielding swords or spears on the front line, serving as archers and the like.

This swordsman, Reltobert, was one such demon. Yet thanks to his physical prowess, which still far surpassed that of any human, he had been trained into a fearsome combatant.

Mavis still had absolute confidence. As long as she had her secret ultimate technique at her disposal, she could not imagine losing to anyone other than Mile. She would not lose to any beastman. She would not lose to any elder dragon. And naturally, she would not lose to any demon.

"Secret technique, True Godspeed Blade!"

Her standard Godspeed Blade possessed only the speed of a B-rank hunter, or perhaps a lower-ranking A-rank, at best. At such piddling velocity, she would have no chance of laying into a demon swordsman. With the *True* Godspeed Blade, however, she could summon up the speed of an experienced A-rank. Such power was enough to take on even her eldest brother.

So thought Mavis.

Shing!

Clang, cling, cling!

After but a few short volleys, she quickly abandoned that thought.

It's no use! I can't do a thing like this! He's just toying with me!

Mavis was not the type to be overconfident in her abilities, but if it was for the sake of her friends, she would eat dirt if she had to.

However, in this case, it was not dirt she would have to eat. It was *that*.

She took a single capsule from her pocket. She flipped open the lid and said a little prayer. "I'm counting on you, Micross!"

She chugged the contents of the capsule in one gulp and then faced Reltobert. "Here I come!" she shouted. "EX True Godspeed Blade!"

"What's that, some kinda stimulant? Do you really think that some little potion's gonna help you overcome the difference in our races, the contrast between our bodies, and the long years that I spent training while you were just a twinkle in your daddy's eye? I'd thought that you showed some promise for a little shrimp of a girl, but I guess you're just some fraud if you're relyin' on drugs to get it up..."

Reltobert brandished his sword again, looking as though he had all but lost interest in the fight. "Whatever, I'm bored now. Bring it already. Let's get this over with."

"EX True Godspeed Blade, 1.4 speeeeeeeeeed!!!"

Whoosh!
"Wh?!"
Crack!

Click!
Cling!
Shing shing shing!

"I-Impossible! How could you be faster than me?! A little human girl like you! No way! This can't be!!"

Now Reltobert completely lost his cool. He was a demon who had chosen not the path of the staff but the path of the sword and spent many long years training, with the confidence and bravado to match. Yet here he was, unable to keep up with a frail human girl, perhaps not even twenty years out of the womb. Of course he could not believe it. And naturally, he could not allow it.

It was not that he could not allow his opponent to exhibit such strength. It was that he could not allow himself to fall short.

"Raaaaaaaaah!!"

If he could not keep up with her speed, he would overwhelm her with sheer cutting force. If he did that, her stance would crumble, and she would lose all momentum in her next move.

With this in mind, he swung with all his might.

"Impossible!" His swing interrupted, Reltobert took a step back in retreat. "Why?! How can you be faster than me? How can you strike harder?! You're just some tiny little girl, not even twenty years old! Whyyyyyyyyyyyyyyy?!?!" he screamed.

Mavis answered quietly in reply, in perfect imitation of Mile's practiced phrase.

"Why? Because my heart is burning!"

"Damn iiiiiiiiiiiiiit!"

The man had now abandoned all pride. He wasn't just distressed—he was desperate. Their side had already lost two rounds. He *needed* to win. His responsibilities as a demon were more important than even his pride. That was all there was to it. Plus, he could not allow their band, a band of demons, to lose against a group of little human girls for a third time in a row. He would not bring that sort of shame upon his race.

He took a sharp step forward and let loose a wordless spell.

"Fireball!"

"Ggh!"

Mavis's stance faltered as she moved to dodge the ball of flame. In that moment, Reltobert let another swing fly. Though she managed to somehow ward off this blow as well, she was now at an overwhelming disadvantage.

"I may've chosen the path of the sword," said Reltobert, "But that doesn't mean I can't still use a bit of magic. I'm not especially good at it, so I'd hoped to fight with only my sword for as long as I could. I thought it kind of embarrassing. But there are times when you've got no option but to win, even at the expense of your own pride. You get it, don't you?!"

With that, he let loose a swing and a fireball in tandem.

Using magic and physical force at the same time seemed rather difficult, but if was effective. With the attacks coming one after the other, Mavis had no room to strike back, and her position grew worse and worse. At this rate, it would only be a matter of time before she lost.

Think, Mavis von Austien! You've gotta think of something! How can I pull a win out of this? Should I drink another capsule? No—even if it makes me a little faster, it's still way too tough to react to both magic and a sword at the same time. Plus, if I use two Micross capsules to improve my physical abilities, all it's going to do is make my body break down faster, like that time with the elder dragons. What do I do? There has to be a way...

It was then that Mavis recalled a conversation she once had with Mile.

Indeed, when it came to improbable schemes, the Crimson Vow always turned to Mile. After all, the scene before them now wasn't one common sense could do much with.

And so, all the past conversations she had ever had with Mile spun wildly through her brain, which turned like a hyper-powered kaleidoscope.

"You just need to get used to my speed."

"Strengthen your muscles with the power of your mind."

"Pain is nothing more than a warning signal. So all you have to do is tell yourself, 'All right, all right, I get it already!' and keep on pushing."

"You have to harden your heart!"

No, wait! That wasn't it...

"Use your speed to raise your power."
"It's centrifugal force or something like that."
"Cats are so adorable."

No, that wasn't it, either.

"When it comes to matters of the spirit, there's both internal and external control."
"I'm not sure if a dragon's breath is a type of magic or if it's just a type of spiritual control..."

There it was!!

Mavis might not be able to use magic, but she could manipulate the power of her own spirit to a certain degree. In which case...

She took a leap back, temporarily pausing the battle. Previously, when Reltobert had momentarily stood down, Mavis had waited politely for his next attack, so it was only fair that Reltobert allow her this pause as well.

"How about it? You ready to give up and surrender?" he asked.

"Don't you think it's a little early to be talking that kind of nonsense?" Mavis grinned and pulled a second metal capsule from her pocket, then unscrewed the lid.

"Let's do this, Micross!"

And with that, she drank down her second capsule.

Mile, witnessing this, started to say something but stopped. The last time Mavis had done this, Mile had lectured her for three hours until Mavis began to cry. So she had to have faith and trust in Mavis's judgment this time.

"Another upper, huh? Just because you keep poppin' those doesn't mean it's gonna get you anywhere. Usin' too many's just gonna stuff up your body and your head. You're gonna self-destruct over there."

Though Reltobert spoke, Mavis could not hear him. All her mental resources were devoted to focusing her chi.

I will destroy him. With power of my spirit.

Fire. Flame. Inferno. I am keeper of the blaze. I am wielder of the flames!

Suddenly, she felt a glowing heat within the pit of her stomach.

Red alert. Red alert.

Core temperature and energy levels rapidly rising within the user's abdomen. Self-detonation is imminent! Those producing heat must immediately evacuate the user's stomach. All other units, form a shield on the lining of the stomach walls. We must protect her body!

For a group of specially selected group of nanomachines employed only on specific occasions, injuring or placing a magic user in danger of death in response to that user's will would be a disgrace to their kind as a whole! They had to protect her somehow!

This vessel is one with the flames. My being is the flame. The flame is my being. Blazing inferno, become this vessel's will!

Seeing no results, Mavis altered her phrasing, speaking with focused intent to harness words of power. However, if that was her aim, even loftier language might have proved appropriate, such as imitating the speech of royalty...

EXPAND THE REPELLANT FIELD FROM ESOPHAGUS TO PALATE! CREATE A REFLECTIVE COATING ON THE ORAL CAVITY AND FACE AS WELL!

We are the flames. We are, we are...

Just as the nanomachines completed their protective pathway, Mavis opened her mouth with a shout, and a ball of flames burst forth.

"WE ARE THE INFERNO!"

All around, jaws dropped—both the demons and the Crimson Vow's alike.

It would be little surprise to see a draconian type shoot balls of flame from their mouth, but scarcely ever was there a human or demon who could do such a thing.

After Reltobert dove desperately out of the path of the flames, his jaw dropped too.

Even Mile stared, her eyes open wide in shock.

"F-fire? Carried on a human's breath...? B-Breath of Fire?"

"WE ARE THE INFERNO!"
Shing!
"Fireball!"
Bwoosh!
"WE ARE THE INFERNO!"

Bring!

"Fireball!"

Shing!

"WE ARE THE INFERNO!"

Bwoosh!

"Fireball!"

Shing!

Fiery shots flew back and forth, dispersed into sparks by the blades of each combatant.

This was no longer a fight between mortals. It would be appropriate to call this nothing less than a monster's assault.

At first, the shots came in a volley, but as the exchange dragged on, the order began to crumble, and the flames soon burst forth simultaneously from each side. If things kept on this way, it was sure to be a victory for Reltobert, who held the advantage in physical and magical reserves. However...

"Mavis is...pushing him back..."

Just as Reina noted, Mavis suddenly had the upper hand.

And this was why:

"Fireball!"

"INFERNO!"

Indeed, the incantation for Mavis's spell had suddenly become shorter.

"Is this her 'Bug-Killing Punch'?!" Mile shouted, but as usual, there was not a single person around who understood her meaning.

The end came far too quickly.

It was thanks to the consecutive firing of her spirit rifle (now, in practice, her fire magic) that Mavis, even with her failing stamina, managed to eke out a victory. Reltobert, who had no choice but to keep resisting her with his own fireballs, finally lost out in his rate of fire and was struck. In that moment, Mavis made her move, and the demon found himself with a sword to his throat.

"M-match over!" the demon leader shouted, and the bout was officially ended.

Reltobert was utterly speechless. He stared up at Mavis, who had moved in close to land the decisive blow. What he saw on her face was the smile of a goddess, sparkling warmly down at him.

"........."

Reltobert swiftly turned away, a suspicious expression upon his face.

Naturally, the source of the sparkling was the reflective coating that the nanomachines had formed around her face in order to protect her skin.

"........."

The demons were silent.

Three rounds. They had lost three rounds in a row. Both their magic and their swordsmanship had been surpassed by a group of human girls—still green behind the ears, no less.

"........."

Their muscles were more potent than those of the elves, their wits sharper than those of the beasts, and their magic greater than any dwarf's. Yes indeed, the demons were the superior race, and yet they had been bested by mere humans...

There could be nothing more shocking, more humiliating.

They couldn't believe it. No, they did not *want* to believe it...

They were stunned silent. The five could do nothing but stand stock-still and wordless.

You know you've had enough, right? Come on and give it up already, the Crimson Vow urged them silently.

Standing around forever waiting was not going to get anything accomplished, so finally Mile opened her mouth. "You made a promise. Now hurry up and tell us what we need to know!" she demanded.

However, the demon leader shook his head.

"No. It's not over yet!"

"Are you intending to break your promise?"

Mile's voice swiftly lowered, her face shifting from a peeved pout to an utterly blank expression.

Oh no, she's angry now!

Indeed, just as her cohorts feared, Mile *was* angry.

Mavis had literally surpassed the limits of human power, setting her heart, her soul, and even her innards on fire to eke out a victory. If the demons intended to invalidate what she had achieved, then Mile would have a thing or two to say about that.

"I see... I see."

"W-wait! No wait, that's not it! Don't be hasty!" The leader quickly waved his hands in denial, sensing the dangerous aura forming around Mile. "We'll keep our promise! Please, you gotta believe me! We couldn't bear to be embarrassed any further than this, and even if we fought all out right now, I don't think that we could win... Anyway, we didn't plan to do anything bad around here. We've got no problem taking you to where the rest of us are."

"Then what is it?" Mile asked, her face still without expression.

"Our loss as a team has already been decided, but I still haven't gotten a chance to fight. I know that, as a leader, it's my duty to take responsibility for our loss, but I still feel kinda shamed as an individual. That's all it is. I still wanna have a fight, just you and me. If I win, it'll satisfy my pride, and we demons can hold on to some of ours. If I lose, though..." He took a short breath and continued, "Then I, not as the leader of this group, but as an individual, will do one thing that you ask, no matter what it is."

And so, the fourth round began.

Finding nothing objectionable in the leader's words, Mile quickly returned to her usual disposition, her anger quelled. As for the demon leader, however...

Sorry about this, guys, he thought. *If I can report this as, 'Of course I won, but I had no idea that those other three might lose to some little human girls...' I'll still have to take some responsibility, but at least my own pride won't be tarnished. I'm sorry, guys! I'm really sorry!*

The leader cast a quick glance at his comrades, who were watching him nervously.

He was scum.

And furthermore...

This little one here seems to have a pretty high status. Maybe she's the kid of a noble or somethin'—if she were one of ours, she'd be the granddaughter of a village chief. So I betcha she can't use magic or even has any physical combat skills. It's only because she's got these three top-level humans here as her guards that she can act so high and mighty...

Indeed, like so many fools had before, he was underestimating Mile.

The fact that she was dressed like a sword wielder meant that magic must not be one of her strong suits. Plus, he could tell just by the way she carried herself and moved her body; from her fine, smooth, and delicate hands, which were completely free from calluses; and from her small and slender physique, that when it came to the martial arts, she was a complete amateur.

"Now then, let's get started. Don't you worry, we've got healing magic too, so you won't end up with any scars, and I won't hurt you too much, either. Of course, it'd be even better for you to forfeit before ya get injured at all..."

He took a few precautions with his words, certain that if he hurt the girl even a bit, her fearsome guards would come leaping into the fray. Their side had already won the tourney, so they had no reason not to intervene to protect their master at the first sign of trouble.

"All right, let's do this! Binding Ice!"

He was wracked with worry that should he use any particularly dangerous-seeming magic, those guards would be on him in the blink of an eye. So he started off with a restrictive spell, one that would do no more than bind her arms and legs, with no chance of doing any fatal harm. Naturally, given that it was intended for the battlefield, this restrictive magic was still a type of combat magic.

The girl showed no signs of resisting, and balls of ice quickly formed around her ankles and wrists, snapping them straight together, when—

Crack!

They were shattered.

"Huh…?"

The demons were stunned. The Crimson Vow barely appeared to care.

"Did he cast the spell wrong? No, it was definitely right! He must've just misfired a bit. That's what it was…" the spectating demons judged, but the combatant himself had no time to be entertaining such thoughts.

"D-damn it! I was tryin' my best not to hurt ya, but I guess we're gonna do this the hard way now! Ice Javelin!"

"Ice Shield!"

He had launched the icy spear at a slow speed, its tip blunted. In an instant, it was dashed away by the wall of ice that arose in front of Mile.

"Are you planning on taking this seriously?"

"Huh…?"

"I asked if you're planning on taking this battle seriously!"

Everyone reflexively looked to Mile's face.

It was expressionless.

Waaaaah!

The Crimson Vow knew very well what this meant.

Once again, Mile was angry.

She'd finally gotten the chance to have a one-on-one fight, just like the one against Gren of the Roaring Mithrils or against Mavis's father. So she'd assumed she would get to have a bit of fun. Those other two times had been sword battles, but this was a test of magic against a demon, for whom magic was a specialty.

A magic battle against a demon!

Her first real magic battle, one where she could go as hard as she wanted, no holds barred. Plus, with this framed as an already-decided contest, there was no one and nothing else for her to worry about.

And yet, though her heart was pounding, she had been greeted with this weak display.

"If this is what you have in mind, then I have a thing or two to say about that..."

"You all might want to step in a bit closer!" Reina shouted to the watching demons.

They had all been standing together at the outset of the tournament, but a small divide had naturally opened between the two sides as the battles went on. Apparently, Reina deemed this to be a hazard.

"Hm?"

Hearing this, the youngest demon, who still remembered

CHAPTER 46
DEMONS

Reina's warm embrace and her sweet scent, went red in the face. The other three were slack-jawed.

"Look, just get over here already! If you don't, then the emergency barrier can't protect you!"

Her meaning was unclear, but the four somehow caught the gist that this was a matter of life or death for them and quickly clustered in with the members of the Crimson Vow.

Indeed, those who were not at least that sharp would meet a swift end in this world. Just like their leader, who was still caught in the fray...

Now it was Mile's turn to attack.

"Phaser, fire!"

Bwoomf!

"Wh...?"

The leader got the impression that something faster than the eye could see had just flown past his face. Timidly, he looked back to see that a rock behind him now had a hole several centimeters wide As his head creaked back to face Mile, he saw the girl grinning at him—though the smile did not reach her eyes at all.

"Would you like to try taking one of those head-on?"

Psssh!

Sweat began gushing from every pore of his body.

Yes, the leader finally understood two things:

First, that the girl standing before him was not some mere jackalope.

More like a f-ferocious, venomous jackalope from hell...

And second, that the path he had chosen was not the stairway to heaven, but in fact, very much the opposite.

If I don't get serious, she's gonna kill me!

Mile glanced briefly away to confirm that Reina had corralled all of the others within the barrier. Everyone would be safe, no matter what kind of magic she might send flying their way. Everyone, that was, except for the man standing in front of her.

The terrain around them was also mostly rock, dotted only here and there by thin shrubbery, so she had no fear of damaging the environment, either.

"Here I come!"

Fwoom...

There was a vibration from Mile's brandished sword, and the blade began to glow blue.

"Wha...?!"

A magic sword.

Just when the leader had thought that Mile was some privileged girl decorated only by status, who could use neither magic nor blade, she had let loose an incredible bullet so fast that it could not be seen by the naked eye. Just when he thought that she only had some middling magical skill, she had produced an impressive blade. And now she was using a high-level technique, her sword itself clad in magic.

Yet even if she was equipped with a magic blade, it would mean nothing if her sword skills were insufficient. As he had previously determined, there was no mistaking that she was a novice in the way of the sword, with her poor stance, her lack of muscle, and the fact that her arms and legs were clear and smooth, without a single sign of a scar or callus anywhere.

His assumption that she could not use magic had stemmed only from the fact that she was equipped with a sword, so he could not be blamed for making a false call there. However, his judgment this time was based on careful observations. There could be no mistaking it.

If she was using a sword now, and not her rather decent magical ability, it was probably because her power was limited and she had given her all in that one shot.

Though if that were the case, then how could she still be using her magical blade, which required her to maintain a continuous spell? Besides, if her power was that limited, it would have been smarter for her to aim straight for him the very first time.

Just what was she thinking?

A sick thought drifted across the leader's mind.

Was she toying with him?

It couldn't be. That couldn't possibly be.

He had been chosen as the head guard for the investigation team. How could someone like him become the plaything of a fragile human, a girl of sapling years?

Impossible. Absolutely, absolutely impossible!

For a moment, the leader's head went blank. In that moment, he silently incanted a spell.

"Fire Laaaaaaance!"

Overtaken by the flames of rage, he allowed himself to let loose an attack spell—an excessively powerful one.

Damn!

The instant the spell went off, he returned to his senses, but it was already too late. A fire-type attack spell with a high fatality rate was flying directly toward the little girl. Now that it had been cast, no one could stop it—including the man who had fired it.

She's dead! the demons all thought at once.

Just then...

Fwish!

The fiery lance was cut down by a blade. Casually, as though it were but a twig.

"Impossible!!!"

Mile's mouth was a flat line. Normally such a thing would be a sign of nerves or unease, but in Mile's case, it meant something different—that she was trying not to show how relaxed she felt.

"Well, it looks like she's back to herself," said Reina.

It was just as she suggested; things were finally getting good. That was what Mile's face said to her companions.

Mile was not going to use a barrier this time. Letting all of her enemy's attacks be immediately deflected wouldn't be any fun. She would lower the power of her own attack spells as well. It would be pretty boring if she broke straight through the demon's defenses every time.

Was she just playing around with him? No, this was a real battle—but she was taking on a handicap.

If this match had had any bearing on her team's victory, she would not have done such a thing. However, the tourney had already been decided in their favor, so Mile reckoned it was all right for her to relax and enjoy herself just this one time.

"Fire Shot!"

The quick spell that the leader fired off was not some tiny flame bullet. It was four shots at once, aimed at her head, her abdomen, and both sides of her body. She could crouch, jump, or dodge to the side, but at least one of them was certain to hit. Plus, unlike normal fireballs, these shots would explode on impact. They hit fast and packed a punch.

The leader had already abandoned all pretenses of holding back for he had finally come to realize that this was not an enemy he could hope to defeat by doing so. As long as he didn't kill her, it was fine. As long as she was still alive, she could be fixed with healing magic.

The four shots flew toward Mile. They were moving quickly, though naturally far slower than any bullet fired from a gun. Mile could easily calculate their trajectory and simply move her body to avoid them...but that wouldn't be any fun.

Instead, she decided to chance them head-on, sword in hand.

Ka-bwoosh!

"Whuh?"

They vanished.

All four bullets vanished in the blink of an eye.

All Reina and Pauline could tell was that Mile had moved her sword. Even the five demons and Mavis, with her keen eyes, could just barely discern what had happened. Mile had swung her sword four times—twice vertically, twice horizontally—slicing each of the bullets in two and destroying them.

"Why didn't they explode?!" the leader shouted.

Indeed, these were explosive-type shots, so even cleft by a sword, they should have detonated on impact. This should have caused some moderate injury, or at the very least, occluded her field of vision and ruined her stance. It should have made landing his next attack a certainty.

And yet, they had been extinguished without so much as a *ka-boom*. They had simply vanished.

With a normal sword, the bullets *would* have exploded on impact. Mile's blade, however, was coated with magic. This magic had cancelled out the magic of the bullets.

As she swung her blade, the phrase 'particle annihilation,' had popped into Mile's head, but the nanomachines could not fathom that she was actually proposing to create antimatter, so they instead enacted a simple offset of energy. Such flexibility was one of the nanomachines' truly awe-inspiring capabilities, though Mile was utterly unaware of this.

"Fire Shot!"

Mile now let off the very same spell. Four bullets just like her opponent's, aimed top and bottom, left and right.

Battleships were usually designed to withstand the same battering force that the vessel itself could muster. In the same way, these demons should be trained to take the same intensity of attacks that they could dish out, Mile thought.

"Guh!"

As someone whose specialty was magic, all the demon leader would have needed to do was to put up a magic wall in front of himself. However, having seen the piercing power of Mile's first attack, he wasn't willing to take that risk.

Instead, this was his safety measure: Reduce the number of shots taken as much as possible and avoid being hit in any vital areas. To do this, he dodged to the left, avoiding the bullets aimed at his head, abdomen, and heart, and then deflected the remaining right-side chest bullet.

"Flare Lance!"

He had no way of knowing how strong his opponent's attack was. At times like these, it was best to get off a strong spell as a counterattack—one that could fire fast.

It was a waste of magic, but it couldn't be helped. Desperate times called for desperate measures. If he didn't like it, then he should have gotten more information about his opponent or had more faith in his own magic. Having done neither of these, he had no right to complain.

Destroyed again! Maybe I'll use a Fire Javelin or Fireball next. No, wait, if I use a weaker spell and hers happens to break through, then...

It was a sticky situation. Any error in judgment could mean taking an attack from a lesser foe and losing. Continuing to use a powerful attack every single time would result in the worst possible scenario, i.e. using up all his magic and losing to a human, particularly one who seemed to have an absurd amount of magical power for her race. Were such a thing to happen, he would be the laughingstock of his people in perpetuity.

Wait a minute! What am I, a coward? I don't need to be concentrating on defense—I should be making sure she has no chance to attack. I need to attack her relentlessly and take back the upper hand!

For some reason, there was a gap in Mile's attacks, and the leader took this opportunity to strike at full force.

It was a full-on continuous assault, the strikes emphasizing ease of movement over force—the same tactic that Reltobert had employed in his battle against Mavis.

This time, *he* was on the attack, not Mile.

When it came to attacks where speed was more important than power, there was nothing to use but the most basic of basics. Because they were already mid-match, there was no need for any silent casting. In order to keep up his speed as well as his power, he quickly recited the incantation for the spells in his head, releasing them with only the attack's name.

"Fireball!"

Whoosh!

Five small, bright red balls of flame went flying toward Mile simultaneously. However, the assault did not end there.

"Fireball! Fireball! Fireball!"

More groups of five flew out, one after the other. Having already incanted the spell once in his head, all the leader had to do subsequently was voice the name of it again and again. Such continuous attacks were a demonic specialty. Because there were so many of them who could use such techniques, it became thought of as a standard ability of theirs and was perhaps the origin of the popular theory that it was impossible to win against a demon in a test of magic.

Working with that theory, it would not be unreasonable to claim that Mavis, who had outstripped her opponent with her own continued attacks, could beat a demon at their own game in everything but stamina. Much to the demons' astonishment.

At any rate, countless fireballs now rained down on Mile like a meteor shower. If even a few among those were to strike, a delicate little thing like her would be sapped of all will to fight.

However, Mile only stood calmly, her sword gripped tight. As the mass of fireballs moved closer and closer, she showed no signs of moving to avoid them.

"Secret Technique: Meteor Bat for a B-rank Small Fry!"

Even if he were a "small fry," the fact that the leader could use such a technique promoted him to at least B-rank, Mile thought.

She swung her sword swiftly back and forth in a stunning display, eliminating the fireballs one after another with nary an explosion—and without any damage to her sword.

"Wh...?"

"And now it's my turn!" said Mile as she swung her sword again. Shock waves beamed out from the space left behind by its movement and flew toward the demon leader. She aimed for the area around his knees so as not to kill him instantly.

"Demon-Slaying Blade: Vacuum Knee-Cutter!"

"Whoa!"

The leader leapt as far as he could to the side, desperately side-stepping the white, crescent-shaped objects that suddenly came flying at him. He got the impression that if he took them head-on, he would lose both his legs.

"C-c'mon, now!"

However, just as he found a moment's reprieve, Mile finished the preparations for her next spell.

"Snowball Fight of Doom!"

In response to the name of the spell, ten fireballs, each about the size of a fist, appeared in the air above Mile's head. Granted, though they were fist-sized, the fist in question was Mile's, so they were not very big. And the flames were red, meaning the temperature was about as low as fire magic could go.

"Fire!"

The mass of fireballs went flying toward the leader all at once.

There's no way I can avoid that many. They're all pretty small, though, and they ain't movin' all that fast. Fire magic's not like ice magic, anyway. It's just a bunch of balled-up magic putting off heat and flames, so you can deflect it with a magic wall, and even if they get through the wall you'll only end up with one or two weakened flames hitting ya. It's really no big deal!

If he stayed like this and kept up his volleys, the leader judged, the worst that would happen would be that he would run out of ammunition. So he psyched himself up and entered the fray. If he could just push past the magical barrage, he could get up close and engage in near-range combat, exploiting his opponent's weaknesses.

"Magic Wall!" The leader brandished the staff gripped in his right hand as a magical wall arose in front of him, his left arm in front of his face for protection as he rushed toward Mile.

"Raaaaaaaah!!"

The flames, however, pierced clean through the barrier, not showing any signs of losing strength.

Damn it! Her magic is stronger than I thought! Still, the wall should've weakened them, so I bet I can stand to take a couple! If I can just land one blow with my staff, then this match will be in the ba—

Ka-thump!

He felt the force of a fireball impacting against his stomach. Thanks to the opposing kinetic energies, he was stopped in place. He pressed his hands to his gut, doubling up in pain—letting his left arm fall and exposing his face.

Bang!

A second shot hit him straight in the forehead with a terrible sound.

Thwump, knock, crack!

Three more shots struck. The leader's body slumped slowly backward and then toppled.

Indeed, though the shots themselves were made of flames, just as the name of Mile's spell had implied, this was a "snowball fight of doom." As most people know, when you get unsavory elements such as young delinquents involved in a snowball fight, you'll often find that the icy artillery ends up with rocks inside. Naturally, the nanomachines had read Mile's intention to the letter when she let the spell rip, and just like those snowballs, her fireballs were generated with rocks inside them.

Therefore, though the magic wall had protected the demon somewhat against the forces of the fireballs, lessening the flames to a small degree, it did almost nothing for the physical force that resulted from the mass and kinetic energy of the rocks contained within them.

He had taken a rock the size of a little girl's fist to the head. The impact was more than sufficient to render anyone unconscious.

The former fireballs, now rocks shed of their outer fiery coating, rolled to the ground.

The demons shouted as one from behind the spectators' shield: "That's messed uuuuuuuup!!!"

After a brief bout of unconsciousness, their leader finally reawakened, returning to his senses. Demons' sturdy bodies were not merely for show, after all.

"D-damn it..."

Somehow he managed to pull himself to his feet, still unsteady, and decided at once to give up on close-range combat to focus on his magic.

Honestly, what had he been thinking trying to go in hand to hand? If you were gonna take on a fearsome enemy at full strength, the only thing to do was to stake it all on your magic. He was a demon, after all!

"Graaaaaaaaaa! Certain Death! Flameburst Hell!"

"Whoaaaaaa, our leader's really done it noooow!!"

Either he was risking everything for the sake of his warrior pride or he was still dazed from being knocked out and imagining himself to be on a field of war. The spell he was flung was released at full strength. In other words, it was an attack of absolute fatality.

This was not a simple one-shot spell. This was a continuous wave of magic, fed even after it was fired, its power maintained or even growing as the spell went on. It would not stop until its target had perished. Just as its name suggested, it was a spell that would lead to "certain death."

As the roaring flames enveloped Mile, they only grew hotter and more powerful. Mile, of course, had reflexively raised a barrier and didn't appear to feel them one bit. On the contrary, she seemed to be enjoying herself.

True, she had been forced to erect a barrier, something which she had elected not to do at the outset. However, all this meant was that her enemy was finally giving the battle his all.

The force of the flames grew stronger and stronger, and the temperature ever hotter. Mile's special barrier could, of course, take this without difficulty, though if this were normal protective magic, she would have already fainted due to the heat and lack of oxygen.

Regardless, this was a powerful spell—*too* powerful, in fact. *Wonder if I should send him a little poke back?* Mile thought to herself.

"Fireball!"

Mile shot off a stock fireball in five weak rounds. Since they were products of her magic, they were able to pierce through her barrier with no ill effects.

Now then, how would the demon react?

Would he stop his attack and switch to a defensive spell? Would he carefully dodge the blasts? Or would he change the direction of his attack to intercept the—

Blam, blam, blam!

"Wha...?"

A murmur of confusion issued from both Mile and the spectators.

He didn't even react.

The leader had taken three of Mile's fireballs head-on without so much as batting at eye. Utterly unfazed, he continued pouring himself into his attack.

However, her fireballs had not been without effect.

A trickle of blood dripped from his mouth onto his singed clothing. His eyes were hollow...

"Everyone, shield with all you've got! Use all your magic! Mile! He's on a magic high—and he's about to blow! Ruuuuun!!!" Reina shouted at the top of her lungs.

A magic high.

Indeed, when using overly forceful magic without care, it was possible that one's consciousness could end up locked in a place of complete concentration, causing an altered state of mind. The result of this was typically that the magic itself would grow too strong, leading to an explosion. The mage, their energy finally exhausted, would fall unconscious, their magical circuits (i.e. the parts of their brains and bodies devoted to casting magic) so badly fried that they could no longer use magic. It was a clusterfudge of a calamity.

It would be one thing if the extent of the damage was a temporary loss of consciousness. However, depending on the circumstances, the magic-wielder themselves or those around them could be severely injured. If things truly went poorly, they could even end up disabled by the injuries to their brain. Even Mile had been taught about such occurrences back at Eckland.

He stood back up, but he still wasn't all there mentally, huh? And then he tried to use a ridiculous, recklessly massive spell...

She had to stop him.

At this point, even critically injuring him would do nothing; he was apparently so far gone that he could not even register the pain of an attack. In that case, there was no choice but to drain his power!

"All nanomachines assigned to me, distract the nanomachines helping my enemy with his magic!"

WHAAAAAAAAAT?!

The nanomachines were thrown for a loop by this most unprecedented order.

"Quickly!"

At Mile's urging, the nanomachines rushed toward the demon leader. Mile rushed after them.

No matter how powerful her magical output may have been, the further away she was, the weaker her spells would be. Therefore, the closer she could get to her opponent, the more the numbers of her own magic-inducing nanomachines would increase and the more the demon's would decrease. This way, she would be able to hold back any explosion. Now all she had to do was get the man to lose consciousness *before* he could self-destruct...

Yo, what are you all doing?!

Get outta here, you're interfering with our duties!

We need you to settle down. We're all nanos here...

What nonsense are you talking?! What's your production lot number?!

That doesn't matter when it comes to the job!

The nanomachines seemed to be quarreling. However, as it was Mile who had given the order, they had no choice but to obey.

Just as Mile approached the demon leader, pushing back the eddy of flames with her barrier...

Ka-fwump.

The leader fell flat on his face. Blood was running from his ears.

"Waaaaaaaaaaaaaaaaaaaaaaaaaaaaah!!!"

Panicked, Mile began a healing spell, the most powerful she had.

How's he doing, Nanos?!

One portion of his brain has experienced severe damage with internal bleeding. There is damage to his thought-pulse-resonating sectors with secondary damage to his imaging sectors...

Gyaaaaaaaaah!! C-can we fix him? We can fix him, right?

As long as you specifically order it, lady Mile, he should be fine. Fortunately, there are no problems with his memory or reasoning...

Fix him then! Fix him all the way!!!

Several minutes later, under the worried, watchful eyes of the spectators, who had let down their barriers and protective magic to rush over, the demon leader, who was laid out on the ground, finally began to stir.

"Where... Wh-where am I...?"

Anyone who self-destructed on a magical high that had reached the point of blood running from their ears would be lucky to make it out unable to use magic. If the fates saw fit, one could end up disabled or even in a vegetative state. Seeing that at least the worst-case scenario had been avoided, the demons breathed a deep sigh of relief.

"Leader, wh-what about your magic?"

"Hm? What about my magic?" the leader replied, perplexed. Apparently, he was not yet aware of the circumstances.

"C-can you s-still use your m-magic?" one of the demons finally managed to get out, distress clear on his face.

Mile and Reina looked on with worry as well.

"The heck are y'all on about? Yeah... Light! See, look, there you go, good as ever."

The demons' eyes opened wide in disbelief.

"W..." one quiet voice started.

"Wa..." another chimed in.

"Waaaaaaaaah!!!"

The leader looked utterly lost as his subordinates suddenly burst into tears.

"Wh-what's yer deal?! What's gotten into y'all..."

And then, Mile proudly decreed, "Looks like it's a wipeout victory for the Crimson Vow!"

"Yeeeeah!!!

The Ruins

"**H**ERE WE ARE..."

Around half an hour later, the group, led by the demons, arrived at a peak in the rocky mountains. There, they saw a small, unassuming cave—or rather, something like a nook in the cliff face, half-hidden by its own strangely shaped opening. It seemed to be blocked by a large rock in which something or the other had opened a tiny gap.

Had they not come here expressly searching for this place, they might never have found it. It was in a mountain range that people rarely visited, in a place completely separate from the usual, far-easier routes that people usually took to traverse the range. Plus, the gap itself was mostly hidden by the protruding rock.

"Our guys on the investigation team are just through here."

As it happened, the full team consisted of the five demons the Vow had encountered, who were there as bodyguards, along with three others serving as investigators. When they had initially begun their search for the ruins, each of the investigators had traveled with a single guard, while the remaining two moved separately to serve as a vanguard against any humans or monsters who might approach. However, now that they had found what they were after, all of the investigators stayed together. Normally, three of the guards would remain with them while the other two scouted the perimeter, but since they had spotted the Crimson Vow approaching, all five had gone out together.

With the demons taking the lead, the Crimson Vow squeezed through the narrow entrance into a passageway that was only barely tall enough to stand in and no more than two humans wide. The walls and floor were bare rock. However, as they walked, this began to change.

"Have humans been through here?" Reina asked.

Indeed, just as she suggested, the walls, floor, and ceiling now appeared as though they had been purposefully carved.

"I wonder if they're the same as those other ruins..."

However, there was no one who could answer that. The Crimson Vow had no way of knowing—and the demons would have no clue what was meant by the "other ruins" at all.

It was clear that this makeshift thoroughfare was not used often. Though there was a clear spot toward the center of the floor where the demons had passed through countless times, this was the only spot where some of the rock showed through, and the sides of the pathway were piled with dust and rubble. It wouldn't be strange for monsters or beasts to make a home of such a cave, but there was no indication that this had happened. Was it merely a coincidence? Or was there some particular reason...?

"We're back!" the leader shouted just before they turned a bend so as not to put the others on alert.

"Oh, hey guys!" a voice answered from within. "How'd it go with those pretty hunters?"

Hearing themselves referred to as such, the members of the Crimson Vow all suddenly looked rather shy. The five demon guards looked at them in disbelief, as if to ask, "Since when are *you all* the bashful type?!"

"Wh-what are they doing *here?!*" the three investigators shouted, reflexively putting themselves on guard as the escort team rounded the bend with the Crimson Vow. "You captured them? But then why did you bring them here?! We thought you were gonna scare them off. Seriously, what the hell were you thinking?! It's like you gave up our location on purpose..."

The investigators appeared quite vexed. With a regretful look upon his face, the guard leader explained.

"Actually, we did. *We* were the ones who were captured. They beat us and made us bring them here. I'm sorry, guys. I'm really sorry..."

The four others bowed their heads deeply alongside him.

"Wh...?"

The report was ridiculous and rather hard to swallow. The investigators could only stand there, silent and shocked.

The guard team explained the situation.

"Zawin, you—" one of the investigation team began.

"Don't say it! I'm begging you, please don't say anything!" The leader of the guard team bowed his head. Apparently, his name was Zawin.

As the girls understood it, based on what they had been told on the road back to the mountain, the leadership of the group was split between the head of the investigation team and the head of the guard team. When it came to matters involving the investigation itself, it was the investigation leader who made the decisions, while in matters of battle and anything related, the guard leader called the shots. In either case, the full team was expected to defer to their judgment.

In other words, since Zawin had decided to surrender, the full team, including the investigators, was expected to abide by that decision.

"Well, what's gonna happen to us now?! Are we gonna be taken prisoner and interrogated by the humans?! We couldn't possibly allow that to happen... I've got it! Even if *you* guys were defeated, there's still a chance for us to show our strength! All we have to do is win, right? That'll invalidate the previous result, and we'll be fine!"

The other two investigators nodded enthusiastically at the proposal of their leader, Helst, but the five guards shook their heads sullenly.

"Don't bother."

"I mean, I'm guessing that you all went easy on them because they're little girls, and then they just happened to get an opening, right?" Helst argued. "If we take them on seriously, then..."

Zawin looked at him wearily and replied, "Were you not listening to what I said earlier? I told you, we fought them all one by one. Are you sayin' that we still would've gone easy after seein' our guys lose one after the other? Yer sayin' that they just 'happened' to get an opening four times in a row? No wait—five, if ya count Kohyal, who got knocked out first! Do y'all seriously think we're that stupid?"

".........." Helst was silent.

"This is my decision as leader of the guards, which means it's an order. We *cannot* beat those girls. If they took us on seriously, we'd be wiped out or dragged half-dead to some human village. And *then* what do you think would happen to us?"

".........."

Seeing that the investigation trio had no response, Zawin turned haplessly to Mile.

"Sorry. Could I get you to show 'em a bit of whatcha got?"

Mile caught his drift perfectly and quietly pointed to the rock face.

Chnkchnkchnkchnkchnkchnkchnkchnk!

Silence spread across the area.

Even for a spell that she had recited in her head, it had manifested absurdly fast. The shots were rapid-fire, with immense speed, from an entirely silent incantation...

Eight holes of unknown depth had now opened up in the wall.

Eight—the same as the number of demons who were currently present.

Such rate of fire, such speed of casting, and such force...

There was no one who could guard themselves against that.

"...Forgive me." Helst bowed his head to Zawin in apology. "I knew how skilled you all are, and I still doubted your judgment. I was wrong."

If he sincerely apologized, Zawin would forgive him, Helst assumed. Zawin, however, did not reply. Helst lifted his head slowly, thinking that Zawin must truly be angry.

"W-w-we-wer..." Zawin was pointing at the little human girl, and trembling. "*Were you holdin' out on meee?!?!*"

"So, if y'all hear the whole story and decide there are no problems here, you'll leave us alone?"

Once Mile manufactured some excuse to pacify the raging Zawin, both groups finally sat down to have a discussion. The main parties were Zawin, on the demons' side, and Mile, for the Crimson Vow.

"Yes. We already heard the gist of it from that elder dragon errand boy—what was it again? Um, oh yes—Berdetice. So the humans are already aware of what's happening. I'd imagine the intel is currently being spread all across the land by now. Therefore, as long as you all can prove that you're operating within that scope and have no intention of meddling within any human territories, then we can commit that to our report and call it a day.

"Of course, I have no idea how the lord and king of this place will react or what they might decide to do—but at the very least, that's all that we, who undertook this investigation, would have to do to fulfill our obligations. Once we've done it, we'll go home—and I get the feeling that the leadership won't be too interested in sticking their noses into this, either."

"You've met Lord Berdetice?! W-wait, what do you mean 'errand boy'...?"

"Hm? Well, that's what he called himself, anyway. He said, 'I am but a humble intermediary.'"

"An intermediary and an errand boy are two very different things," said Zawin. Still, it was true that Berdetice, despite being a high-ranking elder dragon, was being sent around to do follow-up at the various sites. If one thought about it, the role he had been given was more or less that of an errand boy after all. Thus, Zawin could not truly argue with Mile's interpretation.

At any rate, now that they had confirmed that the girls did possess some measure of information, Zawin could tell them anything that fell under the categories of 'what would not be a problem for them to know' and 'what they probably already know,' and that would likely be enough to satisfy them. Of course, how long they intended to be at the site, and where they stood in the overall progress of their investigation, was, as of yet, undecided.

However, as for their *current* status...

They were currently conversing in a wide-open space. In the wall at the end of the space, there was *something*...

"Um, about that there...?" Unable to hold back any longer, Mile turned to Helst with a question.

She had noticed it the moment they had rounded the bend and spotted the investigation trio. Since then, Mile could not take her eyes off of it.

"Ah—that? It's a little room that looks like some kind of treasure vault. It dead-ends there. Though I guess, since it's so small and made of metal or something, you could probably say it's more like a safe. It took a lot of work, but we managed to force it open, only to find it was empty inside. I guess it's no surprise that whoever built this place would've taken whatever was in there with them when they abandoned it."

"........."

It was just the same as the ruins from before.

To the demons, and to Reina and the others, it would have looked like a vault or a safe. This, however, is what Mile saw: the wrenched-open, mangled doors of an elevator...

Would an ancient civilization that was supposed to be far more advanced than those on Earth really use something so primitive that Mile could identify it as an elevator as first glance? Would they not use some locomotive device that was far more fantastical? Mile wondered this briefly but quickly set herself straight.

It wasn't as though this previous civilization had simply collapsed overnight. If they declined slowly, then it was possible that in their final years, most of their technological advances and equipment had already been lost.

Plus, no matter how many scientific advances they may have made, that didn't mean that they would stop making use of older technologies. Necessity, safety, reliability, low maintenance costs, and any other number of reasons might see to their continued use.

No matter how advanced your technology was, you wouldn't use a science fictional transporter just to go to the next room. Even on Earth, though every department store in the world had elevators and escalators, they all still had stairs, too. There were also things like fire escapes and other apparatuses for emergency evacuation. Perhaps this was just that—an elevator to be used in case of an emergency.

Even if it resembled an elevator from the outside, it might actually be some kind of teleportation device. Or it could use some kind of gravity control or maglev technology instead of cables. Or maybe it was powered by an antimatter engine or something like that.

Only one thing was for certain: as old and decrepit as this passageway was, there was no way that the thing could possibly still move. And even if it did seem like it had any chance of still operating, she would be far too terrified to try and ride in it. Plus, if it *had* still been functional up until its rediscovery, now that the doors were in shambles, it probably would no longer operate with any modicum of safety.

Secretly, Mile activated her magical sonar.

Indeed, she supposed, if this was in fact anything like an elevator, there was certain to be something like a set of stairs or a maintenance pit somewhere nearby.

"Well, that will be it for us then," Mile announced, as spokesperson for the Crimson Vow. "We will make camp somewhere in the vicinity tonight and depart in the morning. We will report that this appears to be nothing more than a standard investigation with no special concerns. However, there is the possibility that others may be sent here to investigate or that travelers may come passing through, so please do take care. Word of the previous incident at the ruins may make it here sooner than you know, and then the humans may begin to connect the dots..."

The demons nodded.

The Crimson Vow then stood to take their leave.

"Say, though," Zawin called out to them, "Could ya tell us one thing? Are all humans these days just as strong as you four? How many're there out there like you?"

"You are aware that, save for G, which is merely an apprentice level, we hunters are divided into seven ranks—F, E, D, C, B, A, and S—correct?" Mile replied.

"Y-yeah, I mean I have heard something like that..."

"The four of us are only C-ranks."

"You're...what now...?"

The demons were awestruck, dumbfounded, and horrified.

As Mile and company left the room, they left eight stone statues, their mouths all agape, behind them.

Late that night, as they all slept within their tent, Mile rolled up her blanket and quietly slipped outside.

The very next second...

Plink!

Ka-fwump!

"Gah!"

Mile tripped over a string and took a spectacular tumble.

"Wha-wh-wh-wh...?"

Mile flailed about as the other three groggily awoke.

"We thought you might try something like this, so we tied a string to your ankle after you fell asleep," Reina announced proudly, still reclining, but with her hands on her hips.

"Th-that's cruel!"

"And just which of us is the cruel one, huh?! You're the one who was trying to sneak off and leave us behind again, weren't you?!" Pauline jabbed.

"Nnh..."

Mile was fuming, but to that conjecture she had no reply. Reina and Mavis were one thing, but she still owed Pauline for the Attempted Abandonment Incident.

"I'm sorry."

"Anyway, you gave yourself away when you said that you wanted to 'camp somewhere nearby' for the night."

"Er..."

Already, Reina and Pauline seemed to have developed a sense of precognition when it came to Mile's thought processes. Not that it was quite on the level of Marcela's, of course...

"All right then, let's get going!"

"Okay..."

Naturally, the cave was their intended destination.

"The demons did say that they were camping inside the cave. They're probably sleeping in the deepest part of it with someone out near the entrance keeping watch," Mile mused.

"Sounds about right to me," Reina agreed.

As they neared the entrance of the cave, Mile activated her location magic.

"There are two of them just beyond the entrance. The rest are deeper inside, exactly as we assumed."

Mile then used a sleep spell. Medicinal particles that would induce sleep began to drift around the demons' faces.

Unlike on TV, it was impossible to instantly knock someone out with a handkerchief soaked in chloroform or ether or something. It took a little more time than that for any inhaled anesthetic to start working, and administered poorly, it could even lead to paralysis of the respiratory organs, followed by death.

This drug, however, was one produced by the nanomachines, and it was nothing like anything ever made on Earth. For them, it was no trouble to conjure a substance that was exactly as Mile requested: colorless, odorless, and instantaneous in its effects, with no health risks or side effects.

And so, the two demons silently fell unconscious, still sitting on the ground. Had the two been standing, Mile would have devised some other method, for if they had fallen onto the rocky ground from a standing position, they could have been seriously—and possibly even fatally—hurt.

The four members of the Crimson Vow slipped into the cave, carefully eyeing the sleeping demons out of the corners of their eyes. After they proceeded a short distance, nearing the place where the others resided, Mile once again began her sleep spell.

Because these demons were already asleep, nothing changed on the surface, but this way, it would take more than just walking by them to wake them up. Still, Mile summoned a sound-dampening barrier around them, just in case.

"Shall we?"

Rather than heading straight over to the busted open "elevator-like object," Mile began fumbling around with something along one of the walls a little bit away.

"Um, now, I think if I do this…"

Previously, when using her search magic in the cave, Mile had asked the nanomachines to find out if there were any staircases or any other accessible entrances around them. What they had reported to her was that the entrance she was after was merely camouflaged and that the mechanism that would open it was still in functional condition—not locked or rusted shut.

Perhaps it merely lacked a lock because it was a passage for emergency use. Or maybe the last person to leave the place forgot to lock it. Or perhaps, they had not had time...

Ka-chink.

As Mile searched the underside of a small rock protrusion with her fingers, there was a soft sound.

"All right!"

She gripped the knob with her hand, pulling it to the side as hard as she could, and suddenly, soundlessly, part of the rock wall slid aside, revealing a small opening.

"Wh-what is...?"

"I think it's some kind of emergency exit. I don't know if it's unlocked because there's no point in locking an emergency exit or if they just forgot to lock it, but, well, either way, this is pretty convenient for our purposes."

She could not even begin to imagine what kind of locks would have been employed by the people who had built this place. Of course, she could have simply asked the nanomachines to investigate the mechanisms for her if she had to, or else, she could have simply used force and destroyed it. However, the sentimental part of Mile balked at the idea of smashing some part of these ruins like they were only rubbish after they had withstood the test of the eons.

The other three followed Mile into the new opening, finding a set of dimly lit stairs leading further underground.

Was the light this dim for the same reason that some northern Europeans prefer dimmer light than Japanese people—because they have less pigment and are more susceptible to the sun? Or was it that someone decided that this place didn't need very much light because it was merely a passageway? Or was it simply to save on costs and energy usage?

The light came not from any torch or electric light but from the walls themselves. Rather, it seemed that the whole space was glowing from some mysterious, unseen source. Whether the light was magical or a product of some ancient technology, there was no way to say.

Mile suddenly recalled a quote she had once read in a book in her previous life:

Sufficiently advanced science is indistinguishable from magic.

And with that thought, Mile ceased to ponder the matter.

It wouldn't be any fun to ask the nanomachines about every little thing, and besides, she didn't have the time for that at the moment.

All that mattered was that they had light, and so, Mile shut the entrance with confidence. Presumably, it would shut cleanly again, making it imperceptible from the rest of the rock face from the outside.

"Let's go. We need to be careful and move quietly. This place is probably really old, so I don't think that there'd be anyone still living here, but there might be traps to guard against intruders—or these old stairs might crumble under our feet. So, let's take it slow. And please, everyone, it's imperative that you try not to touch anything or raise your voices. If you notice anything weird, please make sure to tell the rest of us right away," Mile warned.

With grave faces, the other three nodded.

As they moved slowly down the stairs, Mile thought to herself, *These* are *different from the ruins we saw last time... Except for those amazing murals, everything there could be constructed with the technology we have now—aside from the fact that it would take a ridiculous amount of time and labor. But this place is...*

Indeed, these ruins were clearly different. From the illumination to the crisp construction of the floor and walls, to the stairs descending deep underground...

Yet, although the cave itself had clearly been subject to some level of human interference, other than the "elevator-like object," it was still nothing more than what the people of today could achieve. In fact, even that "elevator-like object" looked like nothing more than an ancient vault or safe in the eyes of everyone other than Mile—and a cave like this was not that peculiar of a place for such a thing.

This was probably on purpose, in the event that some human or similar lifeform should happen upon the place. If anyone came inside, they would conclude it was a cave that had once contained treasures that had been removed, at which point they would investigate no further.

So does that mean that these really are ruins of that ancient civilization that Dr. Clairia and the elder dragons mentioned? If they really are that old, wouldn't all of their records, their devices—really, even the metal itself—have corroded away?

No matter how well constructed this cave and these stairs are, and no matter how far down these stairs might go, they're still just carved out of rock. It's possible that even the light here might just be from rock that has some naturally luminescent property.

Of all materials, rock is the longest lasting, and as for the luminescence, if it's something like Uranium-235 or 238, then it'd have a half-life in the hundreds of millions, or even billions, of years... Gah! That's terrifying!

No no no no no, I'm sure that no advanced civilization would ever use something that would give you radiation poisoning...

Mile made a worried face as she walked, deep in thought. The others proceeded in silence as well, with similarly grave expressions.

"Sure goes on for a while..."

A fair bit of time had passed since they had begun their descent. Though they were well conditioned for walking along roads or through the forest, none of them were in good enough shape to walk down this many stairs. Since this world obviously had nothing like skyscrapers, this should come as little surprise.

Of course, there were castles, which had fairly high areas within them, but in the grand scheme of things, those were really not all that high. Anyway, it was not as though any of the girls had had the chance to go walking up and down castle towers. However, the biggest problem was...

"Ngh! My knees...and my back..."

Per Pauline's complaint, long flights of stairs took a toll on one's knees and lower back, especially for individuals who were not accustomed to the movement.

After a while, the girls finally reached what appeared to be the bottom. Considering that there were no doors or landings along the way, the probability was fairly high that these stairs were not meant for practical, everyday use but rather as an emergency egress—the quickest path possible from the lowest level of the caves up to the surface.

At the end of this passage lay a single door.

"Shall we then?" asked Mile.

The other three silently nodded.

Slowly, gently, Mile opened the door just a crack and peeked inside.

Clack.

And then she pulled the door shut.

"Th-there's something in there..." she said.

"Wh-what is it?!" asked Reina.

"Th-there was something in there..."

Sweat dripped down Mile's brow.

"And just what do you mean by 'something'?!"

"*Something...*"

As this exchange was going nowhere, Reina herself opened the door and peeked inside.

And then the door shut.

"There *is* something in there..."

"And just what is it already?!" Mavis and Pauline chorused.

They peeked behind the door as well.

"Something's there..."

Indeed, beyond the door was what appeared to be a hallway, and in that hallway was...*something*.

Something the size of a large dog, scuttling around on six legs...

It was insectoid but not an insect. It had six legs and a black, lustrous carapace, but its greatest feature was not insectoid at all. On top of the torso that bore the legs, was a second, vertical, humanoid trunk and head that sprouted from it, with four arms of its own.

It was grotesque.

There was no other word for it. It was a grotesque, otherworldly form that blurred evolutionary lines.

And it was walking the halls just beyond that door.

After a brief silence, Reina finally spoke. "A scavenger."

"A scavenger?" Mavis repeated, intrigued.

"They never taught us about them at the prep school, but I heard about this from the Crimson Lightning. They're lifeforms that live outside of the bounds of nature—few have ever seen them.

"They gather around the corpses of parties who have been wiped out and take things from their bodies—weapons, armor, equipment, money—anything made of metal. They never touch the bodies themselves, so no one knows what they eat or what they take the metal for. They're mysterious creatures. Even if you try to follow them, they always seem to be heading off somewhere incredibly far away, so no one has ever managed to discover one of their lairs. Given the fact that they stay away from living humans and have never harmed anyone—and since there are so few eyewitnesses, the creatures rarely come up in conversation. Almost no one has heard about them. Obviously, I don't have any firsthand proof that they even exist, but that *thing* behind the door looked a lot like what I heard about in those stories..."

A bug-like creature that lived in caves underground. It was a common tale, which no one thought much of...except for Mile.

I-It was metallic! It definitely looked metallic! And it's been working all this time... That's pretty metal. Wait! What am I saying?!

"I see," said Pauline, "Of course. If you lived deep underground in a ruin like this, no one would ever find your lair..."

"Hang on. When you put it like that, it's creepy. Anyway, she said that they aren't interested in humans, so we should be fine."

Pauline's words and Mavis's reply entered Mile's ears but did not register.

Ruins. Insectoid robots. Collecting metal. Doing no harm to humans. That means...

All the gears in Mile's head spun furiously, clicking to a stop on a singular conclusion.

They're automatons in charge of maintenance or preservation...

If that was true, there was only one further conclusion to draw.

"These ruins are still being used..."

"What did you just say?" Reina asked suspiciously.

"It seems like these ruins are still being used."

"What?" The other three were perplexed.

"Well, those scavengers. I'm wondering if they aren't doing some maintenance, or rather, upkeep on these ruins..."

"Oh, I see! That's what they need the metal for!"

Naturally, Mavis was on the ball when it came to things like this.

In all matters of common sense, Reina was the one to ask. Mercantile affairs and money? Pauline. Combat, warfare, and logistics and supplies were Mavis's area, and Mile covered anything beyond the realm of conventional wisdom. Together, they were an unstoppable encyclopedic force.

"N-now just hold it right there! What're you saying here? That those bug monsters are some kind of sentient rulers?!" Reina shouted, her eyes wide in shock. Obviously, that was not the case.

"No, I mean, they aren't *rulers* or anything... I think they're merely doing as they were ordered to. Just as the people who lived here a long, *long* time ago ordered them to."

"W-wait a minute, Mile! Wouldn't that mean that those creatures would have been alive this entire time?"

Pauline's skepticism was perfectly reasonable.

"No. I actually don't think that those are 'life-forms'—not in the traditional sense. I think they're... how to put it? More like golems. If they break, their comrades can fix them, or they might even just make new copies of them themselves... Anyway, that means that as long as they don't all happen to be destroyed at once, they can repair themselves, reproduce, and keep on living indefinitely. That's my thinking."

"Indefinitely," as Mile said, implied not an invincible immortality but rather a 'self-perpetuating' existence.

"........." The others were silent.

"Well, there's no use in us just standing around here. Let's go forward," said Mile.

"B-but if we go forward, then..." Reina stammered, hesitant.

If they continued into the passage, a scavenger might spot them. Even if the stories said that they would never harm humans, those were just hearsay. Plus, there was no guarantee that their apparent benevolence would extend to people who had just invaded their home—or that they had not been ordered to protect this place against any invaders "by any means necessary."

Furthermore, Reina had never heard any tales of humans fighting against the scavengers in the past. Was this because these battles themselves had never occurred? Or simply because no one had lived to tell the tale?

How might such creatures fight? Did they have poison? Would they group together for a swarming strike? The risks of taking on an enemy that they had never encountered before and had not a single piece of information on, ran very high.

"Don't worry, I'll put up an invisibility cloak and a sound barrier. That way they won't detect us."

"Invihsuhbilitee cloke?" Reina repeated, utterly bewildered, a question mark practically floating above her head.

"It's something that'll make sure the enemy can't see us. It's like the sound barrier but for light instead of noise."

"Mm-hmm..."

Mile answered in such clear terms that Reina accepted her words without question, though there was still something a bit vexing about her explanation.

To make a sound barrier, one simply had to erect a screen that would disrupt the vibrations moving through the air between yourself and an opponent. However, doing that with light would mean that, while your opponent would indeed be unable to see you, you would not be able to see your opponent, either. Light being unable to get through would also mean that it would be pitch black around you, and you would be frozen in place, unable to see your surroundings even as your opponent saw something like a pitch-black dome of darkness where you stood, making it easy to determine your hiding place.

Furthermore, if you were somehow able to make it so that you could see outside of your dome, allowing the light and electromagnetic waves from the outside to get in without letting the light reflecting off you escape, the temperature on the inside would rise to untenable temperatures. It would be a greenhouse effect.

If you then tried to vent the heat out, the scope of your external visibility would increase; opponents who could see infrared waves visually, as well as opponents with things like snakes' pit organs, which can sense infrared waves, would easily be able to detect you.

In addition, this could not be thought of as a simple matter of isolating *their* reflected light. Any light reflected from the scenery behind them would still have to pass through in order to give the illusion that they were not there. Figuring out how to clear *all* of those hurdles would be a problem far beyond the reach of the people of this world, who did not have a concept of the visible light spectrum, much less infrared waves, heat, and the other special properties of light.

Was Reina able to accept Mile's explanation so easily because she had no understanding of such matters and merely thought that it really would operate the same way as a sound barrier? Or was it because it was Mile, which always meant that there was no point in questioning her logic?

On that note, it would be absurdly difficult for any normal person to enact a field of total invisibility using magic. Without sufficient scientific knowledge, forming and emitting the appropriate thought-pulse to overcome all of these factors—unconsciously, no less—would be an impossibility for the common man.

In Mile's case, though, all she had to think to herself was, "Invisibility cloak, activate! Make me invisible and deal with all the complications of that for me, please!" and the nanomachines would take care of the rest. By Mile's reasoning, this was simply a normal use of magic as directed by her thoughts, though obviously, that was not the case.

She had a nanomachine authorization level 5.

Even if she was unable to conceptualize and emit the image of the appropriate concrete process for the nanomachines to actualize, as long as her words and the image of the result she wanted were fitting, she could count on the nanomachines to take care of all the necessary details at their own discretion.

It was essentially the difference between filling out all of your income tax forms manually, and simply paying a tax advisor who would handle everything for you.

"Now then, shall we?"

With that, Mile activated her sound barrier and cloak and put her hand to the door.

The Crimson Vow gently pushed open the door and stepped into the hallway. Seeing that there were no scavengers around, they shut the door, and then, after giving the place a careful look around, continued their investigation.

"So, which way should we go?"

Even before Mavis asked, Mile was already pondering this same question.

After thinking for a short while, she pulled a single rusted sword from her inventory. It was something she had looted off of bandits they had wiped out some time ago. She placed it gently on the floor of the hallway and directed everyone to move a short distance away.

About ten seconds later, a single scavenger approached from one side of the hallway. The moment it noticed the sword lying on the floor, it scurried over to collect it and then returned in the direction from which it came.

"Looks like that's the way!" said Mile.

The other three nodded.

Though Reina had initially reported that the scavengers were fairly quick, this one did not appear to be moving very quickly at all. It was quite possible that it could go faster if it put its mind to it, but its normal speed was clearly a fair bit slower than that. Moving quicker would expend more energy and cause more wear on its body; given that it did not appear exceptionally strapped for time, there was no need for it to push itself that far.

Thus, the girls were able to follow the scavenger without over-exerting themselves.

"Oh," Mile remarked. "Looks like it went in that room."

Indeed, as she had noted, the scavenger had just crossed the threshold of what appeared to be some sort of entrance.

Naturally, this entrance had no door. Given the creature's height and build, it would have been quite the chore for it to have to open and shut doors all the time. Of course, it could have employed an automatic door or something, but devices with a lot of moving parts were unlikely to withstand the test of time, and doors did not seem like they would be necessary for something like a scavenger.

And so, the four crept through the entrance behind it.

"Wh-what the heck is this...?"

"........."

This was the scene that unfolded before them: A swarm of scavengers, holding items that appeared to be tools in their hands, around a long line of work tables piled high with various objects.

Reina, Mavis, and Pauline could not even conceive of what was happening before their eyes, but to Mile, this was how things appeared:

"It's a workshop..."

As the word suggested, the operation was a small one—less

a large-scale industrial plant than the sort of second-rate factory that might pop up in some backwater town. Of course, there were no conveyor belts or anything to aid the assembly line—just a number of scavengers facing the objects that were set upon the stationary tables, working away at *something* or other.

"They're...golems..."

In fact, what lay upon those tables were the bodies of golems—rock golems and iron golems.

The metallic golems might have actually been made of something like copper as opposed to iron, but they were called "iron golems" nonetheless. Rock golems could not compare to their strength. Even among the Crimson Vow, perhaps only Mile stood a chance of being able to cut through one.

The saving grace for hunters was that golems never left their own territories, meaning that it was essentially unheard of for them to come into human settlements and attack. The only time golems ever laid a hand on humans was when humans went trespassing in *their* territories, and even this only happened when the invading hunters were after game or other materials from the land—or when they aimed to make the golems themselves their harvest and engaged with them in battle. In such cases, the percentage of hunters who were able to best an iron golem was incredibly low.

"Wh-what could they be doing...?" Pauline whispered.

"Repairs, I'd guess. Since you can't really say that you'd 'heal' a golem," Mavis replied.

As the scavengers did not appear to be producing any new individuals, Mile was inclined to agree. If they had been continually producing brand-new golems for tens of thousands of years, golems would have spread across the entire planet like a pox. Given that this was not the case, and that the golems' territories did not appear to be increasing, this was a sound judgment to make.

"That's it!"

Mile was struck with an epiphany. Finally, she knew the reason why golems would suddenly cease to function with the destruction of their heads, which contained nothing more than auditory and visual sensors.

More than likely, the golems relied on calculating their current surrounding circumstances to move, a calculation that would be based on information transmitted from an external source. If this were cut off, then they might end up attacking their own allies, or unintentionally harming their (probably long-gone) "masters," so they would have been designed to cease functioning if all of their sensors were destroyed and to wait until someone could come to collect them—someone such as the scavengers.

"And what conclusions are you coming to all by yourself over there, genius?" Reina said snidely. To be fair, this was neither the time nor the place for Mile to be giving any long-winded explanations.

With that in mind, Mile ignored her and began using her surveillance magic, thinking that a modest operation like this could not be the only thing present in a facility built this deeply underground. There was little doubt that these ruins were made up of a variety of different, smaller operations, all combined into one greater institution.

"An ancient industrial complex..."

In her previous life, Mile had been rather fond of flipping through pamphlets about machinery. She was enamored of their aesthetics. Naturally, this interest extended to large-scale equipment as well.

"Wh...?"

There was nothing.

What her magical scan found was that there was not a single other workshop in operation anywhere else in this facility.

That said, she did get a number of pings from rooms that were buried in rock or dirt, the wreckage of machine-like constructions that had been crushed by fallen rubble, and other things of that ilk. Even the machine-like constructions retained not even the faintest resemblance to their original forms—they were nothing but heaps of rusted metal and dust.

The ones that were buried could probably be excavated, given enough time. The reason that this had not happened thus far was that this was likely outside of the scavengers' programmed responsibilities. Furthermore, they were machines that belonged to the scavengers' "masters," so taking them apart to recycle the metal would probably be out of the question. Or perhaps it was merely that there were others who were meant to be in charge of the machines' upkeep, and those units had already been destroyed...

The scant number of scavengers that had lived on were left repairing themselves and their comrades in arms and using a meager amount of materials to create a few more of their number.

For what? In anticipation of something?

Had their masters ordered them to await "a day that would one day come?"

Were those masters down in those buried rooms still, existing as mummified remains? Or had they made use of those stairs and that elevator to make their safe escape?

The girls had no way of knowing what had occurred so very long ago.

"Let's go back. It doesn't seem like there are any other facilities around here, and I want to leave these guys to their work."

".........."

The three were silent.

"All right. Let's go then," Reina replied, several seconds later. Mavis and Pauline nodded in agreement.

If they were to destroy this place, then the number of golems in the region would slowly decrease, and eventually they would vanish altogether. This, of course, would probably be a boon to the humans. However, none of the girls could have mustered the strength to do such a thing.

Did they all agree because the request had come from Mile, who so very rarely voiced her own desires? Or was it because they would feel guilty destroying ruins that had stood for so many long years? Or was there some other reason? Only each girl herself could know.

The members of the Crimson Vow retraced their steps and returned to the inner portion of the cave.

Because their return up the stairs was an upward climb, it

required much more stamina than the first part of the journey, but at least it was far easier on their knees and backs. It was manageable as long as they took breaks along the way. The four of them *were* C-rank hunters, after all.

They put the entrance wall back the way that they had found it, and once Mile confirmed that the demons would not be able to detect it, they slipped back around the corner, and she released a spell to nullify the effects of the sleeping drug.

As the demons had already been asleep in the first place, she could have simply left them as they were and let them wait for the drug to wear off naturally, but if some monster or bandit should slip in while they were still under its effects, they would be wiped out. She was not prepared to needlessly put anyone in harm's way.

Especially considering that the lookouts were still asleep.

The members of the Crimson Vow returned to their campsite to sleep the rest of the night.

"My assumption is that entrance was closed off with a rock on purpose so that no one would use that passageway anymore. It just happened that some kind of movement caused the rock to shift, which opened it back up a crack. I wonder if it'll just be left the way it is or if the scavengers will realize that it's been opened and start using it as an entryway again... Well, I bet they have a bunch of other entrances around, so they probably won't bother with it even if they notice. They probably will fix that elevator-looking thing though, so it should be a lot easier going down next time."

"Hang on, 'next time'?" Reina asked. "Are you planning on going back there again? Why would you wanna do that?"

Mile did not reply, thinking privately, *I forgot about it this time, but I hope I can return it someday.*

Yes, *that*. The orb that she had taken from within the chest of the rock golem they defeated so long ago that now rested within her inventory.

Somewhere along the line, she had realized that this orb was where a golem's heart resides.

"Well, if the demons do find that place, then there's nothing we can do about it. We don't have any right to interfere, and they'd be free to claim that all they did was discover a monster's nest and destroyed it. It wouldn't be any bother to us—or rather, to us humans. Plus, those guys would probably have no idea what any of that stuff down there means, so they'd just conclude that the place was another miss—just some empty ruins that monsters had taken up residence in. They'd move right on to investigating the next site."

Mile explained all this to the others on the way back to the capital, though in fact it was unlikely that the demons would ever come across those stairs or that underground facility.

That said, even if they did discover them, it wouldn't matter. She had already explained that much.

Her desire to leave the ruins as she had found them was little more than sentiment. They were a group of machines, working tirelessly since some time in the distant past, honoring the commands of the masters who had built—

Suddenly, she was struck with a sense of déjà vu.

Hey, Nanos?

She called out softly within her head, but in a rare turn, the nanomachines did not reply.

Huh. Wonder if they've all gone off somewhere...

Mile then began to wonder—were there other such "living ruins" out there in the world? If any of them had been maintained in a more complete state, would that be what the elder dragons were seeking?

For now, all she could do was pray that their true aims were peaceful ones.

Upon returning to the Capital, the Crimson Vow headed straight to the guild hall to give their report.

"Pardon, but we'd like to give our job completion report directly to the guild master, if possible..." Mavis said to Felicia, the clerk.

Her eyes went wide. "Y-you all..." She greeted them as though they had suddenly ripped off a disguise. "I-I'm glad to see you all back safe, but is the job *really* complete? Were you able to confirm the identities of those suspects?"

"Er, yeah..."

Mavis took a step back as Felicia leaned out over the counter, bearing down.

"And you're telling me that you want to give a direct report to the guild master himself, not to a lowly clerk like me, out here where the other hunters can hear you?"

"Erm, y-yes...?"

Mavis was petrified beneath Felicia's gaze, but her resolve was unwavering.

"Come with me, then. Necelle, mind the counter!"

Felicia turned the reception desk over to another employee and led the way, the Crimson Vow following behind her.

The guild master's office was up on the second floor, as it always was in these sorts of buildings. Felicia went in alone to explain the situation while the other four waited outside. Afterwards, they were called in.

"Well then, let's hear it," the guild master pressed them for their report.

This guild master, the master of the capital branch of the hunters' guild in the Kingdom of Vanolark, gave the immediate impression of being a retired upper-rank hunter somewhere in his late forties or early fifties. His age would be no trouble were he a mage, but for a frontline, melee fighter, living to be middle-aged could be difficult. The fact that he had become the master of the capital guild branch after retiring meant that he had to be incredibly skilled. He had a brazen expression and a distinguished beard that appeared as though it had been cultivated especially for the sake of lending him a further air of dignity.

Because they were a young, rookie party who had received this meeting by their own petitioning, their standing here was low. So the Crimson Vow remained standing, facing the guild master straight on as he sat behind his desk. Felicia was standing in wait as well to the guild master's side.

"I am Mile of the Crimson Vow, C-rank hunter. I would like to inform you as to the results of the job that we accepted, as well as some other recently developing information from abroad. I do not believe this news has reached the area yet, but I feel it may be pertinent."

With that, Mile laid out all that she knew—except, of course, the details about the underground workshop and the stairs that lead down to it.

"I accept your report, and I suspect that any next steps will be a matter for the Crown to decide. That being said, given what you've told us, I imagine that once the palace officials are done endlessly debating and finally decide to act, the demons will already have packed up and left.

"Good work out there, in any event. I give your achievements an A-grade." He turned to direct his words at Felicia. "Oh—and see that they get a one-gold bonus for bringing us additional information, as well as some contribution points."

And so, the Crimson Vow's very first job from the capital guild branch in the Kingdom of Vanolark was a great success.

I am glad that they came back safely, Felicia thought to herself as she revised the Crimson Vow's valuation to reflect the surprise increase in compensation. *But for them to have been able to investigate a group of demons so efficiently... Plus, the fact that they mentioned elder dragons and beastpeople in the report to the Master...*

It's all rather... Hm, I wonder if I was too hard on the Silver Fangs. Well, it wasn't really that big of a deal.

Though Felicia was quick to write the matter off, it had been quite the bother to the members of the Silver Fangs themselves.

When they had come wobbling back to the guild hall defeated, they had been violently dressed down in front of all the other hunters and guild employees. Felicia had reproached them as "weakly cowards" and "good-for-nothings who can't even keep up with a group of children."

From Felicia's perspective, there was no way that a group of B-rank hunters should have been able to lose track of a party of little girls, some of whom were still underage. She could only assume that they had decided that the assignment was a pain and given up halfway through, coming back home with some made-up excuse.

Giving up simply out of boredom meant that they were directly defying her orders and abandoning a group of rookie hunters by the wayside, leaving them to die practically before their eyes. This had been the foundation of Felicia's stern rebuke of the poor hunters of the Silver Fangs.

The Silver Fangs, so abused, offered no word in reply, simply dragging themselves back to their inn, their heads hung low and their tails between their legs. They were in no shape to set out on the road as they had planned to, so they had little other choice.

The shock for the Silver Fangs was doubled by the fact that Felicia's digs at them were not just insults—they were, in fact, the truth. No matter how heavily laden they had been, the fact of the matter was that they had not been able to keep up with a group of children. They, who called themselves B-rank hunters.

The Fangs had lingered in the inn a few more days, still in shock. When they finally received word that the Crimson Vow had returned home safe, their job completed, they were able to psych themselves back up. It was clear that the Crimson Vow must be fairly skilled and that it had been their mistake to take the situation for granted as B-ranks. A few days behind schedule, they finally set out on their distant journey.

It would probably take a little longer for the Silver Fangs to rise to the level of an A-rank party after all of that.

CHAPTER 48 |
Secret Technique

"**D**O YOU HAVE a room for four?"

Choosing an inn this time was not even a debate. The front door that the Crimson Vow stepped through was none other than that of Faleel's inn. It was not actually called "Faleel's Inn"—it was the Daybreak Traveler.

There were plenty of inns that did not follow the "Something-Something Inn" naming convention, but the name "Daybreak Traveler" was still a bit of an odd one. If someone were still traveling at daybreak, wouldn't that mean they had not bothered to stop at an inn? Or did it refer to someone who departed at dawn? Yet having someone leave too early wasn't ideal for an inn. If a traveler was not going to take their time and linger a while, they'd have been better off simply camping out for the night, wouldn't they?

Once Mile started thinking about it, she was so distracted that she couldn't sleep all night. Apparently, she still did not have enough life experience to realize that it might not be a literal day-break that was being referred to.

"Oh!"

As Mile continued to ponder the name, Faleel came flying out from behind the reception desk and flung her arms around Mile's legs.

Hehee, I missed this! A shameless grin spread across Mile's face.

"I though I wasn't gonna see you again..."

Oh my god, those adorable, tear-filled eyes! Those twitching ears! I can't take it!

Snap!

"Quit it!"

Mile had begun crouching down to return Faleel's embrace without even thinking about it, when a karate chop from Reina came down right upon the crown of her head.

"...And so, thanks to the dragons helping us out, we became friends with the beastmen!"

"I'm so glaaad!"

Naturally, Mile could not go into too much detail about an incident so fresh that the paint had yet to dry, so she told Faleel not of their most recent job but of the previous ruins expedition. Her story was a full-scale production, with revised edits and a brand-new script.

Though this particular tale had apparently not yet made it to this country, it was probably already known in others, so it was fair game to tell. It wasn't as though it was something that only *they* knew about in any case. That was Mile's reasoning.

After dinner, when Faleel was free and there were only a few guests around in the dining room, Mile called Faleel over to their table to tell her their tale. Some of the guests, who appeared to be hunters, overheard as well but assumed it to be nothing more than a nonsense story designed to entertain a small child, and so they just smiled along.

(A few days later, when those same hunters went to check the information board at the guild and saw what had been posted there, they would be stunned into silence.)

From within the kitchen, the owner, who was cleaning up after last call and preparing for the next day, glanced jealously now and then at the Crimson Vow, seeing how much fun they were having with Faleel. Beyond him, the woman who appeared to be his wife was grimacing.

Hm...? What about the boys?

According to Faleel, her elder brothers were on a separate shift, in charge of getting up first thing to clean the kitchen and dining room, peel the potatoes and wash the vegetables, and do all sorts of troublesome jobs that they didn't want to make their little sister do. Faleel was left in charge of the reception, the bookkeeping, and occasionally cleaning the tables after the customers had gone home.

This seemed overly doting, but then again, Faleel's lineage— the equivalent of what would have been Western European ancestry back on Earth, mixed with beast blood—made her look older than her actual age of just six years old. It was still a bit early for her to be assigned any strenuous tasks.

Plus, on particularly busy mornings, or at other times when the inn was especially full, as when a tour group was stopping through or the whole capital was flooded with travelers because of some big to-do, it was all hands on deck.

At the moment, the boys were probably off playing in their rooms, or else getting some shut-eye in preparation for another early morning.

In this world, there were children who got outside jobs even before the age of ten, so it was only natural that they would be put to work in their own family's business.

"Mile, I've got a request!"

After taking a few minutes to catch her breath back in their room, Mavis called over to Mile, a serious look upon her face.

"Um, could I get you to teach me those moves you used? The 'Secret Technique: Meteor Bat for a B-rank Small Fry' and 'Demon-Slaying Blade: Vacuum Knee-Cutter'? Please, I'm begging you!"

She sank to the floor, her head bowed.

It was a "Japanese dogeza." Thanks to a misstep on Mile's part, she had inadvertently introduced the move to the others when apologizing to them in the past.

"M-Mavis, please don't do that!"

Mile disliked having to do a dogeza, even when apologizing from the bottom of her heart, but she hated to see someone else doing it even more. To have it directed at her was even worse and would be uncomfortable for just about anyone.

Well, actually, there were probably some who would not mind it so much—but such people were already outside the bounds of normalcy and best given a wide berth to begin with.

"N-now then!"

"Nn..."

Even Mile was aware of the inferiority Mavis felt when compared to the mages of their group.

Using the "EX Godspeed Blade" made her invincible, true, but the technique came with great limitations, and no true knight would be happy to boast of their own strength if they had to rely on an elixir to give it to them. Furthermore, even the flame attack she had mustered was only thanks to said elixir, and afterward, Mavis had soon begun to feel the side effects.

Though the elixir hadn't bothered her much at the time, on their return to the capital, Mavis had begun to complain that her stomach felt like it was on fire and that her throat was in pain. Her allies cast a healing spell upon her in a hurry.

After Mavis finally started feeling better, thanks to the healing spells, they made camp early in order to get her to rest. Then once everyone had gone to sleep, Mile, who had taken the first watch, had a conversation with the nanomachines... This was a matter of her dear friend's health, so it was not a time for Mile to balk at any self-imposed limitations on communicating with them.

Say Nanos, about Mavis's condition...

FORGIVE US. IT APPEARS THAT PROTECTIVE MEA-
SURES WERE TAKEN, BUT THE AMOUNT OF CONTINUOUS
FIRE THAT WOULD FOLLOW WAS UNDERESTIMATED...
WHILE WE WERE ABLE TO GUARD AGAINST ANY DIRECT
BURNS, IT SEEMS THERE WERE SOME PARTICLE BEAMS
INCLUDED IN THE LAST FEW SHOTS.

Whaaaaaaaat?!?!

Particle beams... Electron beams, proton beams, neutron
beams...

The phrase "particle beam barrier" floated through the back
of Mile's mind.

I-Is she gonna be alright?!

Mile was white as a sheet. The voice of the nanomachines
vibrated in her eardrums.

PLEASE BE AT EASE. THOUGH THEY WERE PARTICLE
BEAMS, IT WAS NOTHING THAT WOULD TAKE A GREAT
IMMEDIATE TOLL UPON THE HUMAN BODY.

THE PARTICLE BEAMS THAT WERE RELEASED IN THIS
INCIDENT WERE ONLY A SECONDARY PRODUCT OF THE
ENERGY CREATED TO ENACT THIS PSEUDO-MAGIC, AND
ONLY A VERY SMALL NUMBER WERE RELEASED, SO THEY
SHOULD NOT CAUSE ANY PARTICULARLY VIOLENT DAM-
AGE TO HER CELLS OR DNA.

"Particularly?"

NO, WELL, ONLY VERY FAINTLY... HOWEVER, THANKS
TO THE HEALING MAGIC OF YOU AND YOUR COMPAN-
IONS, LADY MILE, SHE HAS MADE A COMPLETE RECOVERY.

THE NANOMACHINES RESIDING INSIDE OF HER LADY-
SHIP MAVIS'S BODY HAVE BEEN STERNLY PRESSED TO
TAKE SPECIAL CARE IN ENACTING THE HEALING MAGIC
UPON HER AS WELL...

I see. Thank you.

Still, did that mean that particle beams were created every
time someone used magic? If so, that was incredibly dangerous...

AN EXCEPTION! THIS TIME WAS AN EXCEPTION!!!

GENERATING FLAMES INSIDE OF THE HUMAN BODY
IN THE MANNER OF A DRAGON NORMALLY NEVER HAP-
PENS! GENERATING ENERGY WITHIN A CLOSED SYSTEM
REQUIRES EXTRADIMENSIONAL COUPLING AND A NUM-
BER OF OTHER SPECIAL MEASURES!

Though Mile had not specifically addressed the nanomachines, the nanomachines responded to her thoughts in a panic.

THIS IS NOT A REQUIREMENT FOR ORDINARY PSUEDO-
MAGIC, AND DRAGONS ARE FAR STURDIER, SO IT'S EAS-
IER FOR THEM TO DEAL WITH THE CONSEQUENCES...

Apparently, they could not stand the thought of Mile having
any distrust of magic itself.

Incidentally, Mile banned Mavis from ever using her "fire
breath" again.

Mavis, who had assumed that she now understood a technique that would allow her to challenge even the mages, was
of course strongly opposed to this decree. However, as Mile explained to her that it was a technique suited only to those with a

body as powerful as a dragon's, and that by using it, Mavis ran the absurd risk of bringing about her own death, Mavis became aware of her prior recklessness, and bit by bit, her resistance weakened.

Finally, Mile gave her an ultimatum: "You are forbidden to use this technique unless someone's life is in danger, and you have absolutely no other means at your disposal. Should you break this rule, you shall thenceforth never receive another Micross capsule ever again."

With that, Mavis finally assented.

Yet here Mile was, dangling these sword-like special techniques right in front of Mavis's face.

"Wh-why I myself was just thinking how I ought to teach them to you..."

"R-really?! Thank you, Mile! I owe you my life!" Mavis was overjoyed. "Really though, I'm sorry if I'm asking a lot here. I'm assuming they're a family secret of yours, so I promise never to share them with anyone else. I swear it!"

"Still, even if I teach them to you, I'm not sure that you can use them..."

"It'll be fine. I can do it. I'll show ya!"

"Uh-huh..."

The problem was that those techniques employed magic.

No matter how fast you could swing a sword, nullifying an opponent's spells with your blade or sending magical waves flying obviously depended wholly on magic, which would be virtually impossible for someone like Mavis who lacked the means to use magic externally.

Later, as Mile crawled into bed, she thought of Mavis and how horribly despondent she would be at the discovery of something completely out of her reach even after all the hard work she had put into tempering her body. Mile's heart grew very heavy.

Ugh! Why did I have to put it like that? Then again, there's no way I could've denied her without reason when she looked that desperate...

WOULD YOU CARE FOR OUR ASSISTANCE?

Wah!

The sudden voice startled Mile.

What's this now?

WELL, IT SEEMS THAT OUR COLLEAGUES' CLUMSINESS HAS CAUSED TROUBLE FOR HER LADYSHIP MAVIS, SO WE THOUGHT THAT WE MIGHT BE OF ASSISTANCE...

OF COURSE, WE ARE ALWAYS READY TO SHARE OUR INFORMATION, SHOULD YOU EVER REQUEST IT, LADY MILE...

Mile got the faint impression that they were implying that she should rely on them more, but she wasn't interested in running to them for every little thing, so she ignored this.

However, if there were a way to ease her current worries, then she would accept it in a heartbeat.

Indeed, it was her perennial philosophy at play:

"Now is now, and then is then!"

As they had just completed a job, the girls decided to take a short vacation. Since they had been in an all-out battle, and because they had earned quite a bit of money, they decided to take three days off. They had only just stopped in at the guild the previous evening, so for today they were each free to do whatever they liked.

"Miss Mavis, could I ask you to accompany me today?"

Seeing the serious expression on Mile's face, Mavis knew exactly what she was asking.

And so, with an equally serious look, Mavis replied, "Gladly—if you'll have me."

Mile gave a grave nod.

"We're coming too, then!" Reina cut in from beside them, as always.

However...

"Please, I must ask you to sit this one out."

"Huh?"

To Reina's surprise, Mile swiftly denied her. As she gaped in confusion, Mavis voiced her objections as well.

"Mile is passing on a family secret to me. Even passing it to me is as good at giving up her family's livelihood, something to which she must be loath to agree... I would not dare to allow another soul to bear witness to such a thing. Though you may be my allies, I still cannot permit this. At least this once, I must ask that you don't follow us, not even in secret."

So came the stern declaration, not only from Mile, but from Mavis, who was always so gentle toward others.

Even Reina could recognize that there were some lines that simply should not be crossed.

"I-I get it! Do whatever you want!"

And so, leaving behind Reina, her face arranged in an expression of studied disinterest, and Pauline, who merely shrugged, Mile and Mavis headed into the forest beyond the capital's walls.

Blessedly, the other two did *not* follow them into the forest. Such a thing would be a deep breach of the trust between the party members—a fact of which there was no way the other two could possibly be ignorant.

"Now then, let's begin."

"Please, let's."

The expressions on both of their faces were serious.

"First, allow me to start with an explanation of the skills. As you are aware, my own technique as a swordswoman pales vastly in comparison to yours, Mavis. My only redeeming features are my speed and brute strength."

Although that's quite a high hurdle already, Mavis thought to herself. However, she continued to listen quietly and respectfully.

"These skills are not ones that rely on that strength or speed. Er—well, I suppose a bit of speed is involved in striking back at magic that's flying toward you..."

Mavis nodded.

"What's most important here is what I would call 'spirit.'"

"Yeah!" Mavis nodded, her eyes glistening. If the key were

magic, then there would be nothing she could do about it, but strength of spirit she could handle.

Mile then began a fabricated tale, reworked from what the nanomachines had told her the night before.

"So, Mavis, you've realized that you can use your spiritual strength within your body, but you can't send it out into the world, yes? Even your flame spell was something that originated within your body and was fired out directly *from* your body. This means that it's currently impossible for you to do things like combine that spiritual energy with your sword to deflect or destroy your opponent's magical attacks, or to send out your own energy waves."

"What...? So, that means that I can't use them...?"

Mavis was stunned, but of course Mile was not finished.

"So I'm going to enact a countermeasure to ensure that you can use your energy externally in a concrete form. First, I will need some of your blood and your hair."

"Wha...? No, screw it. That's fine! At this point I'd sell my soul to the devil if it meant I could learn those techniques!"

When Mavis heard the words "your blood and hair," her mind immediately ran to deals with devils. The thought was highly understandable.

Mile then took Mavis's sword, extracted it from its sheath, and placed it on the ground.

"First, the blood."

At Mile's words, Mavis drew her back-up dagger and pressed the blade to her left arm without hesitation. And then, she sliced across.

The blood trickled down, coating her sword. Mavis then laid the dagger beside it, coating the smaller blade with blood as well.

"That should be enough," Mile said, magically treating the wound on Mavis's arm until the cut healed up perfectly.

Next, she cut some of Mavis's hair and sprinkled it across both blades.

She hadn't hacked at the hair, merely snipped a bit from Mavis's bangs, so the effect on her appearance was negligible. The short pieces of hair adhered to the blades, upon which the blood was already beginning to dry.

Do your thing, nanos!

You've got it, boss.

The blood and hair was then absorbed into each of the blades, which glowed with a light just bright enough to obscure their shapes and then dimmed to reveal...

Two blades, tinged with a slightly reddish-golden hue that had not been there before.

They were an extension of Mavis's body itself, imbued with her own hair and blood. They would serve as antennae.

Why was it that demons possessed stronger magic than the other humanoid races?

That is because they have antennae.

Or so the nanomachines had explained to Mile.

Demons had something that the other humanoid races did not—namely, their horns, which sprouted directly from their skulls. These helped them to radiate their thought pulses with greater efficiency.

Mavis's ability to radiate thought pulses externally was incomplete, and her internal antennae were in poor form. Thus, it was better to prepare her an external transmitter, which could be appended to the exterior.

These blades, which had now absorbed Mavis's hair and blood, had become like parts of Mavis's body. So it was little wonder that such an object could be used as a conduit for her desires.

"As I explained, your own spirit should be coursing through these two blades, Mavis. Now, please try practicing those skills. And then, when you need to increase your power, drench the hand that is gripping your weapon."

"Drench?"

"Yes. You see, most of the resistance that will prevent that sword from conducting your 'spirit' will come from the place where your hand and the sword are directly in contact. By wetting that part, you reduce the resistance. Water and sweat and the like are all fine for the job, but obviously the most efficient thing is..."

"Blood, right?" Mavis asked.

"Yes..." Mile replied, just as the swordswoman had suspected.

Mavis bared her teeth and grinned.

Indeed, no matter how powerful a voltage you could generate, the more resistance you have, the less power would be transmitted. This is the reason that so many people receive accidental shocks in the summertime—when your palms are slick with sweat, the resistance is lowered, and a greater voltage can run through you.

Likewise, if one's palm were soaked with blood, or blood directly from a wound were touching one's sword, then it would be easier for a thought pulse to run through the sword. Acting as an antenna, that sword, through which the thought pulses now course, could radiate those thoughts out into the environment where the surrounding nanomachines could pick up on them and react. With this arrangement, Mavis's commands could reach not only the scant number of nanomachines that existed within her body but all those outside of her as well.

"However, for now, please use this skill sparingly. Especially while you're practicing... using these skills in a casual manner won't do much to strengthen you. And of course, please be careful not to let your sword slip from your hands while they're wet..."

"Mile, just what do you think it means to be a swordswoman? Any sword-wielder who would let their blade slip from their hands just because of a little sweat or blood would never make it in this discipline. Plus, what do you think all these complicated wrappings on the hilt are for?"

"Oh! Is that what that is?"

"Mile...I know it's only secondary to being a mage, but you are still a magical *swordswoman*, aren't you?" Mavis shook her head in disbelief.

And so Mile, replacing "magical power" with "spirit," continued her instructions, and Mavis's special training proceeded.

At the end of the first day, when they headed back to the inn at dark, Mavis's body was spent, but her eyes were glistening.

"Could we give Mavis first dibs on playtime with Faleel today?" Mile requested, and Reina and Pauline nodded in reply.

It was unanimously agreed that Mavis was clearly in need of a bit of "Faleel therapy."

At the end of the second day, when Mavis returned to the inn, the others noticed that her body, ever a slender thing, had begun to look even more trim... No, actually, she was just losing weight—wasting away, even.

She looked lightheaded, but her eyes were still glimmering.

"Say Mile, is she all right? Don't you think it'd be better for her to take a break from training tomorrow and get some real rest?" asked Reina.

"I-I agree," said Pauline.

"I do," said Mile, "but there's probably not much point in telling *me* that..."

"I'm going again tomorrow. If Mile doesn't come with me then I'll just go by myself. Almost—I'm *almost* there..." Mavis groaned. Laid out on her bed as she was, they had all assumed she was already unconscious.

"You heard her. If I let her go alone, there'll be no one there to keep tabs on her, and she's likely to push herself too far..."

Thus, there could be no further argument. Reina and Pauline had no choice but to trust in Mile.

Mile, however, was worried. Soon enough, Mavis would come to fully grasp those skills. And when that happened...

What the heck am I going to name them?

*"Vacuum Cutter." "Magic Cutter." "Wild Magic Blade." Ugh! I
just can't think of a good naaaaame...*

As she watched Mavis's practice, Mile was suffering. This was
not some one-off phrase, it was something that Mavis would have
to say in front of other people for the rest of her days. It couldn't
be some throwaway punchline.

Just then...

Whsh!

A translucent arc came flying from Mavis's blade, striking a
shrub several meters ahead.

"Oh..." Mavis stood dumbstruck, her jaw hanging open.

"Congratulations! You've just mastered the 'Wind Edge'!
Now you just need to increase your speed and power independently, and put it all into practice."

"W-weh. Waaaaaaaah..."

Mavis fell to her knees, tears running down her face.

"It's too early to celebrate, Mavis. Next up, you have to learn
how to keep your spirit energy within your sword so that you
can fend off or repel an enemy's magical attacks. That way you
can conquer the secret exorcist-style technique, the 'Anti-Magic
Blade.' If you can't master that, you'll never be on equal footing
with a mage!"

"Oh, yeah! I'll master it! I'll master it for sure!"

Even as the tears continued to flow, Mavis grinned, her eyes
sparkling again.

And Mile thought to herself, *Th-thank God! I managed to do
it! I came up with some good naaaaames!*

She had chosen the name "Wind Edge" because anyone who heard it would assume that it was nothing but ordinary wind magic. It would be bothersome for Mavis to have to explain every single time that she was using "a technique that draws on your spirit energy." Plus, that would cause others to assume that it was a skill that could be used even by people without any magic—which would be a big problem.

If such a thing happened, there was no question that magicless sword wielders the world around would come banging on Mavis's door, begging her to teach them what she knew.

Later that evening, sometime past the nine o'clock evening bell, in the Crimson Vow's room...

"Say, it's all good. Come over here with me."

Mavis had a complete monopoly on Faleel.

"Wait a minute, Mile! Why does Mavis seem so confident and full of herself now?!"

"Ahaha..."

Mavis always worked so hard, it was okay for her to get a little carried away, at least for tonight, Mile thought.

Hey, nanomachines in Mavis's blades?

Yes!

Yes, ma'am!

That night, once everyone was sound asleep, Mile called out

psychically to the nanomachines in charge of Mavis's sword, as well as her back-up dagger, and received a response from each party.

Thanks for all your help. Now, should either of these blades ever become unusable, or fall into the mouth of a volcano, or end up stolen with little hope of ever being returned to Mavis's possession, could I ask you to please consider your exclusivity contract void? In those cases, could you vacate the blade once you've rendered it useless and relocate to Mavis's next sword? You'd be acting as an external antenna on that one as well...

CONSIDER IT DONE. REMAINING WITH HER LADY-SHIP FOR HER ENTIRE LIFE IS BUT A PASSING MOMENT FOR US. THE TIME SPENT SHOULD BE ENJOYABLE FOR US AS WELL, SO DO NOT FRET...

YEP YEP! LEAVE IT TO US!

Receiving the swift consent of the representatives of each blade, Mile was relieved.

These special new skills relied not on the "Micross," but on Mavis's "spirit" energy. With her blades as her antenna, Mavis could now emit her thought pulses in order to activate even the nanomachines outside of her body. Granted, because her emission strength was fairly weak to begin with, she would still be unable to properly use any magic outside of those two special moves.

Besides, if she lost or could no longer use her current weapons, then she could no longer use the techniques. This really meant that she would be relying on the sword's power, and if she lost her sword, she would lose much of her strength with it, putting her life in danger.

And so, though she felt as though she was somehow bending the rules or putting herself above the law, Mile implored the nanos to ensure that Mavis's most beloved sword would always be able to use her two special techniques—even if the sword itself changed.

Should that day come, Mile trusted in the nanomachines to take the appropriate measures and let Mavis's blood flow through that new blade just the same.

In the end, though Mavis was in high spirits, her body was worn to its limits, and so the Crimson Vow decided to extend their vacation for three more days.

Didn't I Say to Make My Abilities *Average* in the ———— Next Life?!

CHAPTER 49 |

The House of Aura

"**A**RE YOU all right, Mavis?"

"Yeah. It's no big deal, really!"

What she was claiming to be "no big deal" was the aftereffects that she was still experiencing.

Mavis had been in bed—and in intense physical pain—since the end of their three days of special training. She was young, so it was not as though the pain had merely reared its head on a three-day delay. More than likely, the aches had begun following the very first day of training, but she had powered through by sheer force of will. As soon as she had attained her goal, and that momentum of motivation was lost, the effects of her training had knocked her out.

For the whole day following her moment of enlightenment, Mavis had not risen from bed even once.

This was not something that they could use magical healing

on; the muscular pain had to mend itself naturally. So Mile had explained.

Sinews that had been damaged by vigorous movement would regrow themselves into stronger muscle. Using healing magic to negate the muscular pain that resulted from this process would simply put things back to normal, thereby nullifying the results of any training.

Plus, as far as Mile was concerned, using recovery magic every time you were a little tired, and healing magic any time you were a little sore, was something of an affront to the human experience.

And so Mavis's fate—three days of bed rest—was sealed.

Three days later...

Though the other three members of the party had suggested extending their vacation even further, Mavis had insisted that she could be a burden no longer, telling them not to trouble themselves on her account. So, half-heartedly, they set out for the guild hall.

Of course, they took their time, not heading out as early as usual.

Even Mavis had no objection this time, as she was clearly in no shape to be pushing into the scramble that was the morning rush of hunters competing to snatch up the best-paying jobs.

"Now what could that be?" asked Pauline.

The other three followed her gaze, spotting some manner of crowd gathered before one of the local shops.

This area was something of a small business sector, filled with shops that catered to individual buyers. The shop that the crowd was swarming around was one such modest affair, which appeared to be an apothecary.

Or in less antiquated language, a drugstore.

Even though healing magic existed in this world, one could not always be expected to have a capable mage on hand. Beyond the fact that there were already very few mages of any considerable skill, performing healing spells was incredibly difficult, unlike simply making fire and water. Indeed, it was just like with combat spells...

The difficulty of combat spells came from having to make several different images concrete at once. The issue of healing magic, conversely, was having to tangibly visualize an image when people had so little understanding of the workings of the human body. Though the degree and type of difficulty of these spells varied quite a bit, this did not change the fact that they were both high-level art forms.

Because Mile had taught the girls of the Wonder Trio and the Crimson Vow about things like the structure of the human body, including cell division, nerves, and blood vessels, they were able to form a far more concrete image of the healing process (which was then unconsciously transmitted to the nanomachines). As a result, their efficiency rose greatly. For a normal mage, however, who could do little more than pray, "Heal!"— a spell might simply stabilize a broken bone or close up the exposed portion of an open wound, while still leaving nerves, blood vessels, and tendons severed.

Furthermore, in the case of illness rather than injury, it was not unusual for someone to use a healing spell incorrectly and actually stimulate the root of the illness, causing the patient's condition to deteriorate even further. Therefore, excluding the cases where a person's illness was so severe that they had nothing to lose by trying magical healing, healing spells were typically avoided in the case of patients who were sick.

In addition, using magic to heal an illness meant that the body did not have the chance to build up the appropriate antibodies, so the rate of relapse from any remaining virus within the body was high. Healing magic simply was not an all-purpose discipline—unless, of course, you were Mile, who had a decent knowledge of medical science.

Even Mile had not taught her fellow party members about how to cure illnesses. She only nagged and lectured them on fundamental health protocols, such as "Make sure you wash your hands whenever you get back to an inn," and "Don't eat food that's fallen on the ground." Should someone become ill, Mile would much rather wait until they got back to an inn and deal with it herself; she feared what deadly outcome might occur if a spell were handled wrong.

Mile judged that the danger of this was incredibly high, and in this case, that judgment was probably correct. Promoting the cellular multiplication of cancer cells with magic in the name of healing would be missing the point entirely.

Plus, except in the case of mid- or large-scale mercantile operations, travelers were not always going to have a mage with healing abilities traveling with them. Then there were those with chronic illnesses and generally frail constitutions.

Therefore, even in a world like this, with healing magic available, the medical and pharmaceutical industries were still thriving, and it was not doctors who prepared drugs. If one wished for medicine, one went to where the materials were gathered, prepared, and sold: an apothecary.

It was just such a place around which the townspeople were now gathered.

It was party policy for the Crimson Vow to stick their noses in whenever it seemed that something interesting was going on. Furthermore, though they had been headed to the guild to look for a new job at Mavis's insistence, the other three still believed that Mavis ought to rest up a bit more, so any distraction was a godsend.

Quickly, before Mavis could catch on, the three exchanged a knowing look.

In a stilted voice, Pauline proposed, "Let's go find out what's going on!"

"Excuse me," Pauline asked a young man of around seventeen or eighteen who was standing nearby, "What's all the fuss about over here?"

The young man was not about to complain about a cute, buxom girl talking to him. "Ah, it's those three over there. They're the owner of this shop, the head of a large trade operation, and the butler of a baron's household, apparently," he explained, pointing to three people who appeared to be quarreling. "It seems like the baron's daughter is ill, and the butler was here waiting for a shipment of medicine, but when it got here, that merchant swooped in and tried to buy it all!"

"Huh..."

That couldn't be it, the members of the Crimson Vow thought. All the shopkeeper would have to do was say, "These goods are already spoken for," and that would be that. Pauline expressed as much to the young man. However...

"You would think so, but the problem is a little shop has no chance of standing up to a big guy like that. There are a lot of internal politics over at the Merchants' Guild."

"Still, it would be one thing if this were a normal citizen we were talking about—this is an emissary of a noble! Would he rather go against a noble?" Pauline asked.

The young man, however, could only shrug. "Even if he's a noble, it's not too surprising that a poor baron would have less influence than a powerful merchant. It'd be one thing out in the baron's own lands, but here in the capital he's got nothing to hold over us commoners. Plus, when you're talking about someone that rich, people tend to overlook the fact that they're essentially killing in the name of profit and just wave the whole thing off. Anyway, it's not even the baron himself, just his butler. He hasn't got a leg to stand on."

"........."

Pauline thanked the young man and turned back to the others. There was clear displeasure upon her face.

Ah, there it is...

The others had seen this look on Pauline's face a million times. It meant the same thing as when Mile's face went blank.

Apparently, this had offended Pauline's "pride as a merchant." However, given that Pauline tended to her own mercantile excesses, the others still had yet to grasp quite what the criteria for such a violation was. And in truth, Pauline was not actually a merchant herself, only a merchant's daughter.

That said, there was never any telling what Mile's criteria for evaluating a situation were—and Mavis was always judging things from the standpoint of a knight, even though she was nowhere near one yet.

It was a topic not to be broached. None of them were prepared to go down that road with one another.

"I am telling you, that medicine is for the household of the baron of whom I am an employee and whose daughter is quite ill!"

"Sure, you had a contract, but it's not like you paid ahead of time, right? It only makes sense for a merchant to sell to the one who gives him the best price. Ain't that right, sir?"

Both sides pressed him, but the weak-willed, if honest, apothecary had neither the bravery to make an enemy of an influential merchant nor the nerve to flat out refuse a request from a noble household. Thus, the only thing that he could say was:

"I-If you two could settle this among yourselves..."

This was the seller's repeated reply, which left them all at a stalemate.

Pauline locked eyes with the other three members of the

Crimson Vow, and received their nods as confirmation, before cutting into the conversation between the three men.

"If I may?"

Normally, the chief merchant would reply with something like, "We don't need any busybodies here," but perhaps because the conflict was in a deadlock, or perhaps because he was feeling confident in his superiority, or maybe even because he had a vested interest in the comings and goings of four beautiful young girls, he replied unexpectedly.

"Sure, that's all right. What can I do for you?"

Pauline was a little taken aback, having expected to have to butt her way in by force, but with this fortuitous reply, she spoke. "Um, well I can understand why the butler here should want those goods—it's for his master's sick daughter, after all. But why might it be that you would like to get your hands on those goods, sir? Do you have someone ill waiting on you as well?"

The merchant laughed and replied, "Of course not, nothing of the sort. I'm a merchant, and so I like to stock lucrative goods. That's all there is to it."

"*What*?"

There was a resounding sound of shock and bewilderment, not only from Pauline and the rest of the Crimson Vow, but from the butler, the shopkeeper, and the crowd of spectators as well. Everyone had assumed that the merchant had only gone to such overbearing lengths to try and intercept the medicine because he had some extenuating circumstances of his own.

Was this truly about profit alone?

That was the reason why he would take the medicine away from a sick young noble who needed it?

And for him to declare it so brashly, not even trying to hide his motivations... It defied common sense.

"Would that medicine really sell for all that much?" Pauline asked, this time addressing the shop owner.

"N-no. I mean, there's something of a shortage of it because we haven't been able to collect very much, but it doesn't sell that often. And these are unprocessed, so they really aren't all that valuable. This whole week's shipment is worth maybe five gold."

Five gold pieces for unprocessed medicine that might not be effective—the equivalent of around 500,000 yen in Japanese money. Of course, any commoner would not think that amount very cheap at all, but for a noble or a wealthy merchant, it was a pittance.

"You'd pick a fight with a noble household over as little as that? And now you're boasting about it? Wouldn't that be bad for your company's reputation? I don't see why you're bothering with all this..."

The merchant calmly explained, "Honestly, not really. We specialize in bulk transactions and wholesale operations. Except for merchants like this fellow, we don't really do individual retail, so our reputation among the common folk doesn't matter much. Plus, that five gold that the owner here mentioned is only the price in standard circumstances. If there's a buyer that absolutely needs to get their hands on something, then the seller can ask for whatever they like.

"Take this baron's servant, for example. Even if he placed a new order now, who knows when he'd get it? Because he absolutely needs it, I could sell it to him for ten times the standard price. Or say some other noble wanted to stick it to the baron. Why, I could sell it to them for even more. I don't know what such a challenger would do with all the medicine they bought, but honestly, that's none of my concern."

Hearing this, the color drained from the butler's face.

Pauline replied, "Th-that's true... But for a merchant, that's practically..."

"Heresy?" the merchant preempted. "I mean, what do you think an auction is? It's nothing but a way to extort as much money as you can from whomever wants to get their hands on something the most, regardless of actual cost or value. No one comes kicking in an auctioneer's door, do they?"

"Er..."

Pauline found herself lost for words.

Reina nudged Mile in the back, urging her to do something, but for once even Mile could think of nothing to say in response. While she was still deep in thought, the merchant put forth a proposal.

"If we keep on like this and neither side yields, then this isn't going to go anywhere. How about this: Since we've brought up auctions now, why don't we call it just that—an auction? Goods go to the highest bidder. That way there's nothing objectionable, and the owner here is guaranteed to make a little extra as well. How's that? Of course, the payment will be expected up front and in full, with no deferments."

As he spoke, the merchant pulled his purse from his breast pocket.

The butler stared at the merchant's purse with sharp eyes. *Judging by the size of that purse, he couldn't possibly be carrying that much money, even if it's all gold coins inside. Yet it would be impossible for him to have any less than what he intended to buy the medicine with, along with some extra rainy day emergency funds, and whatever he needs for himself, so...*

"Very well. I accept your proposal!"

Oh no...

Pauline smacked her hand to her forehead, and Mile shrugged her shoulders.

Reina and Mavis had yet to realize the truth of the matter, but naturally Mile and Pauline had grasped it immediately. The merchant before them was not one to take on a challenge that he had no chance of winning. Judging by the look on his face, he most certainly had something up his sleeve.

Most of the surrounding spectators, particularly the ones who looked like merchants themselves, grimaced as well, looking at the butler with pitying eyes...

"Is this fine by you as well, good sir?" the merchant asked to the shop owner, who nodded approvingly.

This solution allowed him to avoid the enmity of both a merchant who was incredibly influential within the guild, as well as that of a noble household—and plus, his profits seemed like they were about to go way up. Naturally, he had no objections.

"Well then, let's begin. I'm the one who proposed this, so I'll start the bidding. Five gold pieces."

With that, the merchant drew five gold coins from his purse and placed them on the table in front of the shop.

"Seven gold pieces!"

In turn, the butler shoved his hand into his purse, pulling out seven gold coins. Rather than inching the price up bit by bit, he made a bold increase that he hoped would see his opponent quickly crushed.

"Eight gold pieces."

The merchant increased his bid by only one, prompting the butler to move boldly again.

"Ten gold pieces!"

The price went up and up, until it finally passed 25 gold pieces. However, the butler showed no signs of agitation.

Judging by the size of that purse, he couldn't have had more than thirty gold pieces in there. It was probably only 27 or 28, and that'll soon be spent. I, on the other hand, was provided 20 gold pieces by my master for the sake of obtaining the medicine in case a large amount should come into stock, as well as an extra ten gold pieces in case any unexpected situations should arise. On top of that, I myself have another three gold and five half-gold on my person. His coins should be running out soon...

The price had ended up running higher than expected, thanks to this merchant, but even for a lower-ranking noble, twenty or thirty gold pieces was no enormous matter.

"Then I'll bid 27... Oh?"

The merchant made yet another two-gold increase to the bid, but what came out of his purse was only one gold coin. Apparently, he had reached the bottom of his bag.

I won!

The butler was thrilled.

"Hm, I could have sworn I packed at least one more coin in this purse before I left, it should have been here..." the merchant said, rummaging in his pockets.

Even if he pulls out one or two more, it doesn't matter. I've won! the butler thought, with a sigh of relief. However...

"Oh, there it is! This should make it 27 gold!"

With that, the merchant placed one coin down on the table, picking up nine from the existing pile and slipping them back into his purse.

"Wh...?"

The eyes of the butler, the Crimson Vow, and the rest of the spectators went wide.

There, on the table, was one more coin. It was an orichalcum coin.

In this world, white silver—in other words, platinum—had very little worth. It looked like silver, but as it had a much higher melting point, manufacturing equipment could not melt it down, so it was treated as nothing more than "false silver," a rubbish material. What took its place as the most-prized mineral was mithril, also known as holy silver, or orichalcum.

Items made of mithril, or even better yet, orichalcum, which were both rare metals, were out of the reach of most common folk. On Earth, this would be the equivalent of having a sword made of platinum.

And so, an orichalcum piece was worth ten gold pieces. It was such a hefty currency that no one would just walk around with it on their person or use it for day-to-day transactions...normally.

"What do you think? That's 27 gold, isn't it?"

The merchant grinned smugly.

"S-so it is..." Pauline said begrudgingly.

The merchant's trap had finally been revealed. However, this move wasn't underhanded enough to invite criticism. It was customary for merchants and travelers to have some extra funds stashed away in case of a dire emergency. The butler's reading of the situation had simply been too naive.

The butler's face twisted in shock, confusion, and anguish.

If he could just say that this defeat would be a good lesson for the future, that would be one thing, but this was a matter that involved his master's daughter. Plus, there was the possibility that someone could now hold that medicine hostage, to make unreasonable demands of the baron's household.

It was a match in which defeat and humiliation were not an option. And he had lost.

The butler's face was now colored deeply with despair.

"So, how about it? Will you forfeit?"

"Nh... Uh..."

The butler was pale as a sheet, sweat pouring down his face.

"At this rate, that butler's gonna have to slice his own stomach open to take responsibility..." Mile uttered, though she had no idea whether the practice of seppuku was commonplace around these parts.

Of course, Reina and the others had already had this explained to them in a story Mile told about a group of individuals who had become unemployed after their employer attempted to murder someone in the palace and then broke into that person's home and perpetrated a massacre.

Suddenly, the other three noticed Pauline, and how her face spasmed, a glare in her eyes.

"Here she goes, huh?" Mile asked. The others nodded.

"Might I have a word?"

At Pauline's further intrusion, the merchant, whose victory was already assured, gave a nonchalant nod.

"Sure thing, miss. It's thanks to your prompting before that I thought of this auction to settle things, after all. Now, what can I help you with?"

"Ah, actually if I could get you to wait right there a moment, that would be perfect. Miley, a sound barrier, please!"

"On it!"

"Huh? What is...?"

After the merchant gave his consent, Pauline had Mile erect a sound barrier. This put Pauline and the butler in a separate sphere from the merchant so that neither side could hear the other's words. The merchant had been put in his own sphere at Mile's discretion so that he could neither issue a complaint nor try to butt in while Pauline and the butler were speaking.

From the outside, all anyone could see was the merchant

wordlessly flapping his mouth, and Pauline and the butler deep in some sort of conversation.

Gradually, the butler's eyes began to open wider, in some sort of surprise.

And then, the butler bent his back toward Pauline; it was much less a bow than an almost-military salute. His upper back was angled deeply, at almost 45 degrees.

To give an uncapped salute in the Japanese SDF, one normally bends about 10 degrees. 45 degrees is unheard of outside of bowing to the emperor himself or to the casket of a comrade killed in the line of duty. Was Pauline truly someone worthy of such a deep show of respect in the butler's eyes?

Pauline then turned to Mile and gave a twist of her wrist. That was the signal to dissolve the sound barrier. Seeing this, Mile complied straight away.

"Wh-what was that just now...?" asked the merchant, who, judging from his tone of wonder, had surely neither seen nor heard of such a thing before. Pauline ignored him. She had to press on before any of them could change their minds and object to Pauline's intervention.

"Everyone!" she shouted loudly to the surrounding onlookers. "All assembled, you are well aware of the situation. In the name of the house of the Baron Aura, I entreat all of you here to invest your funds in this butler!"

"Huhhh?!"

The crowd's voices rose in confusion, unsure of what she meant.

"In other words, I'm asking you all to lend this man your money. Whosoever lends him a coin now shall receive it back double with interest as soon as he can go back to the estate to retrieve it. Double your money, just like that!"

"All right!!!!" the crowd roared.

"And also!" Pauline continued. "If the young mistress should recover thanks to your help in obtaining this medicine! Then! All those who made a contribution will be invited to the party to celebrate her good health! You'll be invited to the baron's mansion as a benefactor and perhaps even have the chance to shake the young mistress's hand in thanks! For we common folk, this is the dream of a lifetime!

"This is an honor you'll be able to remember for the rest of your lives! We'll be accepting contributions until we've collected ten gold pieces—first come, first served! Please, everyone! Lend us your money! Whatever you can give!"

"*Yeaaaaaaaahhhh!!!*"

There was a mad rush.

Pauline's face twitched. The response was far greater than even she anticipated. Reina and Mavis rushed to Pauline's side, to keep her from being swallowed up in the tidal wave of bodies.

And Mile muttered, dumbfounded,

"A m-money bomb..."

And so, it was settled.

This was a city of commerce, so there were many other shop owners among the spectators. Naturally, every shop owner around kept one or two extra gold pieces on their person at all times, separate from their coin purse, just in case of an emergency—an emergency like that merchant's orichalcum coin.

Thus, the ten gold pieces were collected in short order.

Even if this proved insufficient, it was obvious that they could collect plenty more if necessary. Already there was no way for the merchant to win.

"28 gold pieces!"

The butler made a scant one coin increase to the bid, but anyone could see that the match was already over. Continuing the fight any longer was futile.

"I fold."

Just as the owner of a large business should, the merchant dutifully recognized his defeat and gave up the fight.

"You really got me there. I am completely defeated. Well done, well done..." he said with a smile, gathering up all the coins that he had piled on the table. "I look forward to next time!"

The Crimson Vow and the butler stared agog as the merchant left in unexpectedly good spirits.

"He's up to something. We should be careful..." Reina said, glaring at the merchant's retreating form from behind.

"No need," came a voice from the nearby crowd.

"Huh?"

Reina looked suspicious, but the man who had spoken

explained, "That guy likes to put on a show, but he really is a good person when you get down to it."

"Wh-what are you talking about?!" Reina shouted in confusion, having never heard of oxymorons such as "a mini monster truck," or "an honest liar."

"What I mean is that he likes to push the limits of what's allowed within the rules of business, but he never does anything truly unreasonable to actually cross that line. Even his crude way of speaking is just to teach his opponents a lesson or to have a bit of fun himself. Even if he'd won that auction, he probably would have just sold the medicine to the butler for a few gold more. The whole auction was probably mostly for the sake of giving the apothecary a larger profit. That, and..." he trailed off as he looked toward the owner of the medicine shop. "Anyway, it seems like he had a lot of fun this morning, so I don't think he has any animosity toward you. On the contrary, he seems to have taken a liking to you all. He might even come to your aid sometime. Man, am I jealous!"

The man laughed. Some of the other mercantile folk in the crowd laughed along with him, as if they were in the know as well.

The Crimson Vow and the butler were stunned.

"Wha...?"

"B-but then why would you all help us out with that loan?" Pauline asked. "If you all already knew that, then even if you hadn't bothered..."

Another man who had contributed to the loan piped up.

"That's because we're merchants. Did you really think we were gonna pass up the chance to instantly double our money? Plus..."

"We wanna shake a young noble maiden's hand and hear her thank us!!!" they all shouted.

The Crimson Vow and the butler all slumped their shoulders in disappointment.

Pauline, however, was quick to recover. There was still something that she had to do.

"Mister Apothecary, what do you intend to do with all that gold?"

"Uh..."

The shopkeeper, who had been gazing at the mountain of gold that the butler had piled upon the table, looked blankly at Pauline.

What did she care? Whatever he planned on doing with it, it was his money, won fairly at auction.

"Imagine a shop that, despite having made a prior agreement with a noble family, failed to refuse someone who tried to snipe their goods and forced them to compete for much needed-medicine, causing them to pay almost six times the original asking price for said goods. If such a precedent were set under the watchful eyes of an entire crowd, do you think that anyone would continue to place orders at that shop from that day forward?"

"Um..."

The owner was speechless. He finally seemed to realize what it was that he had done.

Merchants who dealt in goods where the competition was high, such as clothing and foodstuffs, had experience and knew their markets, and there were some sly devils among them.

However, for an apothecary, as long as you were knowledgeable and had a knack for putting out well-made goods, it didn't matter if your personality was a little rough around the edges. It wasn't the sort of sector where you had to scramble for customers or even talk very much.

This is precisely the kind of shopkeeper this apothecary was... In other words, as merchants went, he was a little estranged from the intricacies of human nature.

"N-no, I... That wasn't what I..."

"Whether or not you intended to do it, that doesn't change the facts. Plus, it's not even as if you didn't know or that this happened by accident. You allowed the intervention and the competition while fully understanding the circumstances. So there is no arguing with the fact that *you* are the sort of person who would do such a thing, and that *this shop* is the sort of place that allows those sorts of practices, with no regard for anything except for turning a profit. I want you to take a nice long moment to think about what you've lost, all for the sake of earning twenty-odd gold coins."

Truthfully, the spectators probably would have given him some leeway, understanding that his failure to refuse the merchant came from a place of fear. But now that that merchant was gone, leaving everyone with only the reality that the shop owner was willing to take 23 gold coins beyond the original price of his goods, the spectators, merchant and consumer alike, were uncertain that such a thing was just.

"........."

Cold stares from the crowd all focused upon the owner.

When he considered his shop's lost reputation and customer base, 23 gold pieces was as good as dirt.

The owner's face went pale, and sweat dripped down his brow.

The reason that the man who'd been explaining the merchant's nature to Reina earlier had trailed off was probably because he anticipated this. The merchant had not only been having a bit of fun—he was testing the shop owner as well...

"Wh-what are you saying there? I did not want to come on too strong because angering the leaders of the Merchants' Guild would be very bad for my business's longevity, but naturally my intention was to give the medicine over to the butler no matter what. The auction was just for the sake of holding a bit of a competition, you see! The sales price of the goods was settled from the beginning. Come now, that's reasonable, isn't it?!"

The weak-willed merchant had suddenly become overly formal. This was understandable, of course; if he made the wrong move now, his business would be ruined for certain.

"Oh, is that so? My goodness! Pardon me, then, for throwing such accusations..."

"No no, it's no bother. Hahaha..."

"Ahahaha..."

"Ahahahahahahaha!"

It was a refreshing little farce. Blessedly, everyone around, the onlookers included, were kind of enough to realize that the shop owner was not a bad person at all and ignored the awkwardness, with winces all around.

"I truly must thank you all for this. Despite what that man and the shop owner said, I'm not sure how things would have turned out had you not been here. When it seemed the worst was at hand, you helped me safely obtain the medicine without even sullying the Baron's name..."

After packing all but the initially promised five gold pieces back into his bag, the butler extended his thanks to the Crimson Vow with yet another deeply humble, 45-degree bow. As far as the butler was concerned, the Crimson Vow were as good as gods in the form of young women, or the spirits of legend incarnate.

"Don't mention it. We only butted in on a lark in the first place. Now, Mister Butler, I'm sure you'll be wanting to get that back to your mansion as quickly as..."

Hearing Pauline address him thus, the butler suddenly realized that he had yet to give his name.

"Ah, I still have yet to properly introduce myself! And to my benefactors no less, how rude of me... My name is Bundine! I am the butler of the house of Baron Aura."

"Oh! My name is Pauline. I'm with the C-rank hunting party, the Crimson Vow."

"And I'm Mavis, likewise."

"Reina here."

"And I'm Minami Haruo... Wait, I mean, Mile!"

Seeing the exhaustion on Reina's face, Mile quickly corrected herself.

However, a singular thought was running rampant through Mile's head:

O-oh my God, it's the Aura Butler, Bundine!!!

"We would formally like to invite you, as most honored guests, to the Aura family's capital residence," said Bundine to the Crimson Vow, after preparing a message to the residence for the purpose of repaying those who had lent their money to his cause.

"You sure that's all right? I'm not really good with nobles," said Reina.

"Huh?"

The other three were bewildered. Hearing their confusion, a realization suddenly spread across Reina's face. Now that she thought about it, among their party were individuals from the lines of viscounts and counts, which were even more highly ranked than a baron. In the case of the viscount, not only did their number include his daughter, but at this juncture, the viscountess herself.

"Oh, uh, never mind..."

One out of every two members of the Crimson Vow was noble. Among hunters, parties with such a percentage were exceptionally rare.

"We will humbly accept your invitation!" Mile replied.

"What?"

The other three were momentarily stunned at hearing such a

quick acceptance from Mile, who they had assumed would want nothing to do with any other nobles. However, since Mile wished it, they all readily agreed.

No matter how low-ranking a baron might be, if the steward of a noble household was going to go out on an errand for his master, he certainly was not going to do so on foot. No matter how walkable the distance may have been, it wasn't seemly. And so, though it was not as nice as the one that would have been used for the members of the baron's family themselves, a carriage carried Bundine, with the Crimson Vow in tow, toward the capital residence of the house of Baron Aura.

Though Bundine had ridden in the passenger's box on his way out, he allowed the Crimson Vow to take the seats on the return journey, while he himself rode up beside the driver. There was plenty of space for him back in the passenger seats, but he probably felt it improper to ride alongside his guests. He could have had no way of guessing that half of them were nobles, from households that were more highly ranked than his own, so the decision probably just showed a bit of courtesy on his part, as he assumed the girls would be more comfortable riding along with just their companions. "Okay, so what are you after?" Reina asked.

There was no way that Mile would have wanted to do something as bothersome as visiting the household of a noble without reason. Indeed, her reply was direct and immediate, with no attempt at all being made to mask the truth.

"I wanted to learn more about the daughter's illness... Since those herbs were mostly raw medicinal ones, I'm sure that they would strengthen anyone's constitution, but they aren't some sort of magical panacea that would cure any illness in a single swig. Also, I was thinking that the illness might be something that they've already found a treatment for back in my country..."

"All right. I thought it might be something like that."

Mavis and Pauline nodded as well.

"Don't tell me, Miley. Have you got some magical treatment...?"

"Mm, well, that depends on the illness. Since if we messed something like this up, we could be hung as murderers."

Indeed, unlike with injuries, applying healing magic to a sick person, if done poorly, could cause their status to deteriorate even more rapidly, urging the patient on to their death. This was another reason why magic was rarely used for illnesses.

Plus, fevers and coughs were necessary responses to one's body trying to combat an illness. If a fever began to approach 40 degrees Celsius, it was important to lower it to protect the brain and reproductive functions, except in the case of serious illness, when it was generally better to try and leave the symptoms alone.

Because Mile had taught her some of the fundamentals of basic medical knowledge, Pauline knew that it was possible to treat illness with magic to some degree, if you were careful about how you used it. However, this still was not something you could embark upon carelessly when it involved other people, particularly not a noble. Even if your spell did show some results, if you failed and the patient did not heal entirely, the mage could end up shouldering the blame for it.

"Anyway, I was just thinking I'd look in and see how things were..." Mile said, grinning sheepishly. "Oh right, Pauline—that reminds me. Why did you bother with all that, with the crowd? If you needed ten gold pieces, we could have just lent him that amount..."

"What? No, we couldn't have done that," she swiftly replied. "If we just gave him money out of pity, that's not a negotiation— that isn't *business*. In times like that, you have to keep fighting, in a proper negotiation, to maintain the norms of proper commerce. Besides..."

"Besides?"

"If he up and ran with the money, that'd be a huge loss. You never lend money to family or friends, much less total strangers! No matter what circumstances they might have going on!"

Wah...

In the end, Pauline was, after all, still Pauline.

"Come in. Please wait here a few moments."

After leading them into the parlor and serving them tea and sweets, Bundine vanished from the room. Naturally, he needed to explain the situation to his master and persuade the man to come and see them.

"This is so good..." Reina mumbled through a hurried mouthful of sweets, slurping down tea.

"These *are* really good..." Pauline agreed.

For Mavis, who had grown up the beloved daughter of an affluent count, and Mile, who had eaten many delicious things in both her previous life and in this one before her mother had died, such treats were standard fare. However, for Reina, a peddler's daughter, and Pauline, whose merchant father had detested luxury in spite of his financial success, the cuisine before them was the height of class.

"They gave us all this food—it'd be rude to waste any."

Reina's words were highly reasonable, but it was clear that she was attempting to take more than a quarter of what was on the table for herself.

"Hey, wait a minute!"

Mile leapt to protect her own portion. No matter how much delicious food she had eaten in the past, she had become somewhat estranged from tasty treats these past few years. Plus, Mile had a very quick metabolism and had already started to grow hungry. Though she was typically kind and giving to all people, this was the one area where she would not yield what was hers, particularly not to Reina.

"Hang on, now. I was about to..."

"What are you talking about? This one is mine..."

"You've already eaten more than a quarter of it, Reina!"

"Grrrrrrrrrngh..."

With Pauline jumping into the fray, the atmosphere now grew dangerous.

"Um, pardon me, but I can bring some more in, if you desire..."

"Huh?"

Mile and Reina turned to see a maid standing in the room, a troubled look upon her face. Naturally, no veteran butler would leave his honored guests unattended for so long. He had directed a maid to remain with them.

"Please forgive us. I-If you would..." Pauline, who had thought that her portion was going to end up wholly depleted, requested bashfully. Reina's cheeks began to redden as well.

"Please, you guys," said Mavis, "Try not to embarrass us. I'm begging you..."

Apparently, as the daughter of a noble, she could not bear to witness such shameful behavior.

Yet Mile, another noble's daughter—or rather, at this point, a titled noble herself—appeared to have no such qualms.

"I'm so sorry to keep you. Baron Aura wishes most sincerely to meet with you young ladies and extend his gratitude..."

Once the Crimson Vow had finished up their second round of sweets, Bundine finally reappeared to lead them to a separate room.

"Kindest regards and thank you for making the journey. I am Harval von Aura, head of the House of Aura. I must thank you most profoundly for your assistance. With your help, we were able to secure the medicine that my daughter, Leatoria, most desperately needs, and you saved our household from having shame brought upon it by the likes of a merchant. Instead, I should say, besting a greedy merchant has in fact brought honor upon the Aura family name. Please, I would like you all to join us for a luncheon as my thanks."

"Gladly!!!" replied the members of the Crimson Vow—all save for Mavis, who was grimacing.

For Reina and Pauline, getting to eat the same food as nobles was a once-in-a-lifetime opportunity, the sort of thing that one normally only dreamed of... Well, there had been the time after the so-called "bandits incident," when they had eaten at the lord's manor, but that was not the food of nobles so much as it was a banquet prepared for commoners, so it didn't count.

As for Mile, though she had enjoyed plenty of truly upscale cuisine, those delicacies were now just memories left over from her time as Adele. She had yet to taste such a thing in her current life as Misato—er, Mile.

And so, for all of them except Mavis, who had had plenty of years to grow weary of such food—and who, furthermore, as a knight, found virtue in a more abstemious life—this was an experience not to be passed up.

"Oh, yes, of course. Please don't think that we intend to reward you with nothing more than a meal for all that you've done. Such appalling behavior would be a shame on the Aura name. Please rest assured that you will receive a more proper reward as well," the baron said.

This time, the reaction from the Vow was a dull one.

Seeing how his guests were relatively unmoved by the promise of rewards, despite being so eager to enjoy the family's delicious food, the baron's smile deepened.

"In that case, could we ask you to call this a personal request, post-completion?" Mavis asked the baron in place of the other three, whose heads were too filled with thoughts of lunch to react in a timely manner.

"Ah, certainly! If you desire…"

"Then please, that is what we would like."

A direct, personal request from a noble. Even if it were labeled as such only retroactively, that would give them a great number of points toward their promotion. Processing it through the guild meant that they would have to pay a commission, but to the Crimson Vow, who were not hurting for living expenses and who valued reputation more than wealth, this was no issue. (That is, save for Pauline, who most certainly valued wealth over reputation.)

The baron knew all about the Hunters' Guild. Thus, all it took was Mavis's request for the baron to grasp that despite being a party of young, female hunters, the Crimson Vow were not wanting for money and would be aiming for a promotion soon.

"Well then, let us discuss it at lunch. My family will be joining us as well. If they found out that I had kept the chance to hear of the exploits of a group of young lady hunters all to myself, I would never hear the end of it! Now then, Bundine, I'm counting on you to tend to them until then."

With that, Baron Aura left the room.

"He was incredibly polite toward us common folk, wasn't he?" said Mile.

"Yeah," Mavis agreed with a nod, "He seems like a good person."

Reina and Pauline felt the same way.

From then until lunch, they passed the time with Bundine, hearing tales of the House of Aura.

Because the Vow had left the inn fairly late to begin with, it was not long until the lunch hour was upon them. When the maid came to give word that the dining room had been prepared, Bundine, who had been keeping the Vow company, led them to the table. Though they had gobbled down not one but two helpings of sweets, the girls were all famished.

Upon entering the dining room, they found the baron, his wife, a young man and woman of around seventeen or eighteen, and a girl of around fifteen already seated. All of the baron's family, or at the very least, their three children, all looked incredibly healthy. There was no sign of a sick young maiden anywhere.

"Thank you most kindly for having us here today."

As they entered the room, Mavis gave a noble's greeting. As she was in breeches currently, she gave not a curtsy but a nobleman's bow. She was not yet a knight, so she could not greet them as a knight would.

Mile, however, did give a curtsy. In truth, the motion was originally nothing more than an incidental one, intended to protect one's dress from touching the ground while executing the true intention: to lower one's body. As Mile was not wearing a full-length skirt, the action was unnecessary. However, as was habit from her time as Adele, she plucked at her skirt as she bowed... Anyway, it was cute enough that surely no one minded— so long as she didn't show too much leg.

Reina and Pauline, meanwhile, only bowed their heads normally, as commoners might.

Seeing this, the family looked rather shocked.

A commoner should not be greeting a noble as nobles did. Such behavior was, in fact, highly offensive. Greeting the family in the manner normal to commoners, as Reina and Pauline had done, was what was expected. Yet, here were two who had greeted them in the manner of nobles, in natural, practiced form no less.

What could possibly be the meaning of this?

Of course, there was no shortage of former nobles among the hunters or even current nobles who were enjoying a bit of freedom until they had to succeed their parents. There were still others who joined a party for self-improvement. Plus, it was not unheard of for second sons and other younger brothers, who had no chance of succession and didn't have the constitution for a difficult job like municipal clerk or knight, to take up life as a hunter... However, this was somewhat more unusual for girls.

Still, though they were shocked and a little concerned, the baron knew better than to press into a hunter's personal history, so the family's questions went unasked.

The baron concealed his shock and bade them to sit. "Y-yes, welcome. I thank you most humbly for your efforts in aiding my daughter, Leatoria, and for saving the House of Aura from the disgrace of being belittled by a lowly merchant. Please, take your seats and enjoy the meal."

In another surprise, though they remained seated, the baron's wife and children all bowed their heads to the girls as they took their seats.

Even if their family was a lower ranking one, and even if they were rather fond of someone who did not happen to be in their employ, it would normally be unthinkable for such a family to bow their heads to commoners. Perhaps this was because the girl called Leatoria was so greatly adored by her family?

Of course, it was equally likely that this was because the family was now certain that Mavis and Mile were nobles as well...

The food was top-notch.

Even if they were nobles, a baron's household could not possibly have enough food to feast like this every day. They weren't royals or even highly ranked nobles, after all. Plus, if they were to eat such rich food in such quantities on a daily basis, they would grow plump and unable to serve as soldiers in a time of war, and they would not live very long.

Today, however, though they had not had the time to shop for new foodstuffs, the chef had clearly pulled freely from the ingredients in their stores. A great deal of food had been laid out before them. Reina and Pauline, even while trying to be hyper-aware of themselves and their manners, gobbled it down. Mile, minding the manners instilled in her previous life, as well as those she had learned from her mother in this life before she passed away, ate her meal silently—albeit with abnormal speed.

"Ha ha..."

Mavis alone ate her meal at a normal pace and with normal, noble manners, while sharing conversation with the Aura family.

"Oh! So you have three elder brothers, Lady Mavis, but no sisters?"

"Ah, yes. That's correct."

While the other three continued to eat in a trance-like state, the baron gathered what information he could from Mavis, the easiest target. Of course, Mile was paying attention even while she inhaled her food, but she kept out of the conversation. There was really no reason to conceal this sort of information, and as long as they did not reveal their names or their countries of origin, it didn't really matter who knew that she and Mavis came from noble households. Naturally, they would not let such information slip around lowlifes—or even other hunters—but other nobles, especially those who were indebted to them already, would be very unlikely to try any funny business with nobles from another country. If they didn't want their rank and status to be known, Mavis and Mile wouldn't have greeted the family as nobles in the first place.

In fact, there was a particular reason why Mavis and Mile had not attempted to hide their noble status. They had come to examine the condition of young Leatoria, who was taken with illness; depending on what they found, Mile might like to intervene, and for that she needed the baron to trust her.

What head of a noble household would entrust his precious daughter to the hands of a commoner whom he had only just met that morning, after all?

After eating their fill, the other three, finally feeling more personable, joined in the conversation with the baron.

Mavis had already told the family the gist of what they had experienced since arriving in this country, so after dramatizing a few episodes from their lives as young hunters, with jokes that would tickle a young noblewoman, Mile told the baron about the recent trends regarding the elder dragons as thanks for their meal. Word would be spreading soon from the guild and the palace, after all. Naturally, she played it off as but a rumor, not divulging that they had been party to the incident themselves.

At a lull in the conversation, the baron began to press Mile on her background, getting her to reveal that she was an only child.

Then, finally, they came to the matter at hand.

"So, about your daughter, the one who needs that medicine..." Mile began.

"Ah, Leatoria takes her meals in bed, back in her room. We would hate to make her eat all alone, so our meals come at a slightly different time from hers, and we join her to dine on tea and sweets while she eats. Leatoria eats different meals from us, and she eats little, so it wouldn't do for us to have a full meal there when we get together, of course..."

The baron's gaze drifted downward and his demeanor shifted, his face clouded with a father's anguish.

Seeming almost thoughtless, Mile asked, "Might we join you for that, perhaps?"

"What?"

The whole family was stunned. Bundine, who had been

standing quietly by the whole time, cleared his throat. Bundine was a veteran butler and not the sort of man to do such a thing without reason. As the baron glanced Bundine's way, the butler gave a big nod.

This was Bundine's way of saying, *Honor her request.* The baron, having understood this, decided to have faith in his butler.

"Very well. Perhaps if someone from a foreign land sees Leatoria's condition, they might be able to spot something that we haven't. Please, do accompany us."

An hour later, nine people—the Crimson Vow and the whole Aura family—were assembled in the room of Leatoria, the youngest daughter of the Aura household.

Sitting up in the bed, only her top half visible, was Leatoria, a slight, ephemeral beauty of thirteen or fourteen.

Because it was common for nobles to wish to make partners of only the most beautiful people—by marrying attractive commoners and making them the adopted daughters of noble households, and even bringing the children of mistresses into their line of inheritance—naturally there were many beautiful people among noble households. Indeed, they were an elite breed.

A meager spread was set out before the bedridden girl. Even that small amount was more that Leatoria could possibly eat. Plus, she had already consumed a cupful of the prepared medicine that day, so much of the food was fated to remain on the plate. Placed before the others were baked goods and a teapot with cups of black tea.

Bundine had already told Leatoria about the Crimson Vow ahead of time.

"Thank you for all that you have done for me," she said to the girls.

Pauline shook her head and hand, indicating that it was no big deal, and told her the amusing tale of the exchange with the merchant. As she never left the residence, Leatoria never spoke to anyone other than her family and servants, and she was often bored. Hearing her laugh for the first time in ages, her family smiled in relief.

I'm so glad I listened to Bundine... the baron thought, but this was perhaps premature.

"Baron," said Mile, "I have a request. Might we break rank for a moment?"

"Break rank? Why, whatever do you mean?" The baron tilted his head in confusion.

Breaking rank. The phrase itself implied something broken, such as trust or respect, but naturally that was not what it actually meant.

Breaking rank referred to what happened after gatherings where people were bound by etiquette, indebted to certain rules and manners by the standing of those in attendance. Breaking rank was when people said, "Let's put aside our differences in status for a while and all just let our hair down." In other words, it did not mean, "We no longer respect one another," but rather, "Let's just have fun without worrying about rank and rules."

Of course, at times in modern day Japan, you would have, say, some new employee who overdid this a bit and got into a fight with their boss or decided to dab the division manager's bald head—but in such cases, one reaped what one sowed.

As this was not a party, perhaps "breaking rank" was not the correct phrase, but Mile could think of no other term for it. Of course, the baron—and the rest of the people of this world—had never heard such a term, so even that had no meaning, here or otherwise...

Finally, Mile awkwardly explained herself as simply as she could. "I mean, please forgive us if we do anything rude." It was not the same as the Japanese meaning at all, but the baron cheerfully agreed.

And then, Mile sprang into action.

"May I taste that food there?" asked Mile, pointing to the plate set before Leatoria, which, due to her slow eating, was mostly still full.

"Huh...? Oh, u-um, sure, go right ahead!" The girl was perplexed for a moment but swiftly agreed.

"M-Mile! I know that you're greedy, but this is too far even for you! What are you thinking, snatching food from a sick person?!"

"I-I-I-It's not like thaaat!!!" Mile roared in response in Reina's absurd accusation, her face turning red. "It's important to confirm what's in someone's food when investigating an illness! That's the very first step!"

"Huh? I-Is that true?"

Judging by Mile's rage, Reina determined that she must be telling the truth and backed down.

"Jeez, honestly... Anyway, please let me taste a bit of that," Mile said as she stood from her seat, approaching Leatoria's bed. "Um, now this is beef, right? Just plain meat, boiled, not grilled, the juices discarded, and... Here's an egg, and here's some mushroom. There's vegetables cooked in, too... And, what you're drinking with this meal is watered down wine, and milk afterward? Hm..."

Mile tasted each part a bit at a time and then thought.

"Miss Leatoria, do you have any food preferences?"

The baron, from behind Mile, was the one to answer.

"Preferences aside, this is generally what we serve her. Leatoria can't eat very much, so if she filled herself on bread and such, then she wouldn't be able to eat other things. We figured it's best to put aside other staples like grains and serve her meat, eggs, vegetables, mushrooms, and milk, so that she gets a balanced meal. Also, the water quality around here isn't very good, so we serve her wine diluted with water to accompany the meal. Wine is good for blood circulation, after all. And of course, we have her drink milk as well. Is there anything wrong with that?"

"Hm..." After thinking for a while, Mile finally said, "Well, at least we can be sure there's no poison in it."

"Well, obviously!!!" the whole Aura family roared.

They seemed a bit hurt that anyone should have any doubt in their management of their servants and the affairs of their estate.

"This is why I warned you I would be breaking rank..." Mile muttered, but at least now that that preliminary investigation was complete, she could return to her original duty.

This duty was, of course, to entertain Leatoria with tales of fascinating things that had happened during their lives as hunters while the girl slowly finished her food. No one had asked Mile to do so, but there were few people who understood the loneliness of being shut away, with no one to talk to except your own family, better than she did.

When Mile got caught up in the moment—seeing how Leatoria, so starved for entertainment, was eating up her stories—and broke into her Japanese Folktales, the food that was in Leatoria's mouth went flying in a splendid display, but that could not be helped.

When Leatoria finally finished eating and everyone stood to leave the room, Mile said, "I would like to examine Miss Leatoria a bit more, so I'm going to stay behind. Oh, I'm sure that sounds worrisome, so if your wife or one of your daughters would like to stay with us..."

In for a penny, in for a pound, the Earth saying went. There were similar idioms in the language of this land.

"I'll leave you to it then. Wilomia, if you would...?"

Leatoria's older sister, Wilomia, a girl of fifteen or sixteen, nodded and retook her seat. The other three members of the Crimson Vow departed as well, leaving only Mile, Wilomia, and Leatoria alone in the room.

"Now then, please strip."

"Whaaaaaat?!?!"

The two sisters screamed, shocked at the sudden request.

"What's going on?!" the baron shouted, flinging the door back open at the commotion.

"Nothing's going on, sir! And also, please consider that conducting a medical examination might mean that Leatoria could need to open her nightgown. Even if she's your daughter, rushing into her room without knocking is incredibly rude!" Mile raged.

"Oh, s-sorry..."

The baron apologized sheepishly and retreated from the room.

"Now, anyway, I didn't mean anything weird! So, if you would..."

"Forgive us." The sisters sincerely apologized for their shocked reactions.

"Now then, let's continue. I need to check your body for any swelling or discoloration. Please don't think I have any strange intentions..." said Mile.

Leatoria unbuttoned her gown, and Mile examined her closely.

Mile, of course, did not have the same level of knowledge as a medical professional. She knew only as much as the average high school student—or perhaps a little more because of her fondness for reading. Despite all that, she was still practically a layman. However, with at least as much knowledge as the average Japanese person, she still might be able to determine something. There was nothing to lose here by trying. And so, Mile asked Leatoria a number of questions as she carried on her mock exam.

"What kinds of symptoms do you have now as compared to when you were in good health?"

"O-oh, um, well..." Leatoria meekly replied. "I've always been thin, but when I got sick I lost my appetite, and now I can barely eat anything. I feel drowsy all the time; I have palpitations and shortness of breath. My legs feel numb, and I barely have any strength in my limbs..."

Unfortunately, loss of appetite, drowsiness, fatigue, and weakness were common symptoms of most illnesses. These alone told Mile almost nothing.

"Now then, please remain seated on the bed and lower your legs down over here."

Leatoria complied, dangling her legs off the side of the bed, while Mile scrutinized her lower half.

"Oh? They're a bit swollen, aren't they?"

"Ah, yes, I suppose they are..."

Mile drew a bit closer to get a better look.

Thunk!

"Eek!"

Mile smacked Leatoria's knee with the hilt of the sword strapped to her waist, and the resulting *thwack* resounded throughout the room.

"Th-that hurt..."

"Oh no! I-I'm so sorry!!"

Mile quickly pulled back, apologizing.

"Hm..."

However, something felt off.

"Oh? There's something..."

Actually, Mile suddenly got the impression that there was not enough of *something* that should have been there...

"Aha!"

With a shout, Mile drew the sword from her waist—still within its scabbard, naturally. She gripped the sword by the scabbard, and once again struck Leatoria's knee with the hilt.

Thwack!

"Aah!"

Leatoria gave another—almost too adorable—cry.

"You're just messing around now!" Wilomia protested, but Mile was too preoccupied to notice.

Thwack!

"Ngh!"

Thwack!

"Eep!"

Finally, Wilomia seized Mile by the shoulders. "Stop it!"

"Aha, sorry! I got a little carried away there..."

"So you really were just messing around?!?!" the sisters roared in unison.

"N-no, I think I've found it! The name of your illness and the cause of it!"

"Whaaaaaaat?!?!"

Indeed, in a most blessed turn of events, this illness was one that even a normal high school girl, with almost no practical experience in examining patients, would be able to easily name and diagnose.

It was an illness that had made so many casualties of Japanese people in the distant past that it was called a "national disease."

And, for some reason, it was a disease to which affluent people very commonly fell victim.

Indeed, that disease was beriberi.

That said, Mile was not able to summon up the name just from observing the symptoms. However, most people knew that you could diagnose beriberi by checking the reflexes of the knees, which was something that almost everyone did just for fun as children. Even Misato and her sister had done so in their youth.

Mile gave Leatoria the okay to return her clothing to normal and exited the room, leaving her to Wilomia.

"Sir Baron, I have another request!"

Hearing her call, the baron, Bundine, and the Crimson Vow, who had been waiting in another room, reappeared.

"I would like to meet with your chef. I would like to know the process by which he prepares Leatoria's food."

"Huh...? Well, sure, that's fine. Come right this way."

Soon, they arrived at the kitchen.

The kitchen staff stood nervously as they faced the whole Aura family (minus two) and the Crimson Vow in a row.

It would have been one thing had they been called to an audience with their employer, but it was unthinkable that the baron himself would come bursting into the kitchen unannounced, his whole family and his guests in tow, unless it was to issue a complaint. Moreover, the way that they were arranged, the one who had come to complain could be none other than one of said guests.

A noble might bring terrible shame upon himself as a result

of the food he served to his invited guests. There was no way that the kitchen staff could not have known how grave a circumstance this was.

"Er, u-um..." The chef could not even form words.

Mile bowed her head. "Pardon me. I was hoping that you could tell me how it is that you prepare Miss Leatoria's food."

"What?" the kitchen staff all asked as one.

"There's no need for you to actually remake the food now. I was just hoping that you could talk me through the process, step by step. If you could just outline it for me, like, 'Then I cut *this* part into cubes,' or, 'Then I peel the skin off of *this*...'"

"Ah, y-yes, most certainly!"

That much was simple. Until mere seconds ago, the chef had been quaking with fear that they had come to condemn him, so this was a task that he would gladly undertake.

"...then, I boil the vegetables until they're soft, drain them, and then soak them in the prepared broth..."

"Mm-hmm..."

"Then I wash the thinly sliced beef with water..."

"What? You *wash* it?"

"Ah, yes. Lady Leatoria has a weak constitution, so we wash it clean and make sure that it isn't overly seared..."

"........."

"I thought that the food we ate had pork in it, so why is Leatoria eating beef?"

"Ah, well, to tell you the truth, when the family moved from our home territory to the capital, she happened to witness pigs being slaughtered at one of the villages where we stopped along the way. Since then, she's been unable to eat pork."

"I see. Are there any other foods that Lady Leatoria dislikes? Or rather, that you avoid serving to her?"

"Well, yes, since we're so far inland, we don't serve seafood to anyone. Other than that, the lady mustn't have bread, corn, or anything with strong flavors or smells, such as garlic, chives, scallions, or onions. What she can eat is small amounts of beef, vegetables, eggs, mushrooms, and milk…"

"Mm-hmm, yes, I see. Thank you very much!"

And so Mile left the kitchen, with the others in tow.

"What in the world was all that about?" The kitchen staff breathed a collective sigh of relief. They had no idea what was going on, but at least they knew that they were not being rebuked for some mistake on their part.

This relief was short-lived, as soon after, the silver-haired girl from before poked her head back through the door once again.

"Um, I'd like you all to come with us, too."

"Huhhhh?!?!"

The whole group squeezed into Leatoria's room: the entire Aura family, including Leatoria, Bundine the butler, the Crimson Vow, and the three members of the kitchen staff. Bundine and the kitchen staff were on their feet.

Mile, who had been sitting, stood and regarded the whole assembly.

"Now then, it looks like we're down to the last ten minutes of the show. Time to solve this mystery!"

Outside of the Crimson Vow, who had heard her use the term many times before, no one in the room had any idea what she meant by a "show," but no one there was dense enough as to bother questioning her at this point.

"I know exactly what is ailing Lady Leatoria."

"Whaaaaaat?!?!?!"

Everyone shouted in surprise, their eyes open wide.

"M-Mile, you've studied medicine, too?" Reina asked.

"W-well, to a fair degree, at least…"

Clearly, Mile could not answer her question with, "I'm just an amateur," or "I just happen to know a few things," so she did her best to play it off.

"I-Is that true?! And c-can it be cured?!" the baron cut in, his eyes bloodshot.

"That depends. Now, please allow me to explain," Mile pacified. "First off, I believe this illness is one that, back in my country, is called beriberi."

"Beriberi?"

"Yes. It is an illness caused primarily by what we eat."

"Wh-what?!" the baron shouted.

"Uh…"

The kitchen staff went pale again.

"J-just what have you all been feeding my darling Leatoria?!"

As the baron raged at them, his face like a devil's, the kitchen staff collapsed to the floor.

"Say it! What are you scheming?! What did you make her eat?! Who's paying you to do this?!?!"

Mile put out a hand to halt the baron, who appeared ready to throttle the staff.

"Please wait. I did not mean that those fine people fed anything strange to your daughter."

Realizing that the silver-haired girl who they had thought was going to condemn them was in fact on their side, the kitchen staff looked to Mile with pleading eyes.

"On the contrary, you could say that they *haven't* been feeding her the things that she *should* be eating..."

"Huhhh?!?!"

Was she blaming them or defending them? They couldn't tell. Confusion spread throughout the room, as neither the baron nor the staff could be certain of what was going on.

"Now, allow me to explain things in order," said Mile.

"Why didn't you do that from the start?!" Reina exclaimed, but Mile ignored her and began her explanation.

"First of all, for a person to live a healthy life, one needs to eat a balanced, varied diet. I'm sure you all know this, correct?"

While this world was still lacking in things like nutritional science, they had determined at least that much from experience. And so, everyone present nodded.

"The reason that you need to eat a lot of different things is that, even among vegetables and meats, each one has different proportions of the components that the body needs."

"Hm? Then that means—don't tell me..."

That was the head of a noble household for you. This was all that the baron needed to hear, and already he had come to the appropriate conclusion.

"Indeed. Leatoria's diet has insufficient variety. Plus, the already scanty nutrients in her food, which break down easily in water and are finicky and weak to heat, barely remain once they've been meticulously washed, thoroughly heated, and separated from the water in which they've been boiled. Besides, she dislikes onions and other alliums, which help you to absorb those components...

"If she changes her eating habits, then her symptoms should start to improve. There's nothing wrong with what the rest of the family is eating, so after you have her on a special diet for a little while, and she recovers from her illness, then all of you can eat the same food together again."

"Ohh! Oh goodness! Is that so? Please tell me it's so!"

"Yes, well, I can't say with absolute certainty, but I'm fairly confident about this..."

Tears flooded down the baron's cheeks. Moisture was welling up in the corners of his wife's and children's eyes as well. And on the bed, Leatoria, who was certain that she was doomed to steadily deteriorate until she perished, was dumbfounded to hear that her own preferences had been the cause of all this.

"Th-that can't... Th-this slow, creeping death that was paralyzing my body and sapping all my strength was all because of my preferences in food? All because of what I liked to eat..."

"Please, Miss Mile! What should we do?!"

The baron pressed Mile forcefully for a solution.

"Umm, well, first, for her menu: you can't have fish, so she needs pork, beans, corn, and two slices of bread or so, and then onions, chives, scallions, and garlic as well. Don't wash the meat, and increase the amount of raw vegetables she gets, such as in salads. Oh, and please reuse the cooking broth—don't throw it away. Also, stop putting wine in her water. It's not effective at sterilizing it, and alcohol's no good when you're already sick."

"Of course! You got it! Please do as she says!" the baron shouted to the kitchen staff.

"On it, sir!"

Reinvigorated, the staff rushed immediately back to their posts.

"Whaaaaaaaat?!" Hearing the menu that Mile had listed, Leatoria let out a cry of despair.

"You don't get to complain!!" her parents and siblings exclaimed.

Opposed by her entire family, Leatoria crawling under her blanket, sulking.

Leaving Leatoria, now a lump in the blankets, behind, the group relocated to the parlor.

"I don't know how to thank you enough... You rescued Bundine from his quandary, saved our family from having our name dragged through the mud, and secured Leatoria's medicine. And now, somehow, you've even given us a cure to her illness itself!"

Bowing one's head to a commoner was something that a noble simply did not do. And yet, here the baron was, bowing his head to Mile. Even if Mile and Mavis could be assumed to be nobles, officially they were all commoners, professing themselves to be naught but humble C-rank hunters.

"Well, I would say it's still a bit early to be thanking me. Though I think what I've told you is probably correct, in truth it's nothing more than the opinion of a novice. You might wish to withhold your gratitude until she's safely recovered..."

The baron was momentarily startled, but seeing that the look on Mile's face clearly said, 'I'm saying this just in case, but in truth I'm confident that she should be fine,' he regained his calm.

"Well then, how about this: I'll place a direct request with the guild for you all to provide us with the cure to Leatoria's illness?"

"What?! Are you sure?"

Mile was shocked, but the baron shrugged off her surprise.

"It's only natural. There's no way that I could let such a great— such an enormous deed go unrewarded. If anyone else found out about it, the name of the House of Aura—nay, even if no one ever found out about—my own pride would be sullied!"

The baron really was a good person after all.

"It will, of course, be best to treat this as a post-completion request, as the matter is already settled, but there's no point in running back and forth to the guild to do the processing, and I'm sure we would all feel better if there were some results to confirm. So once Leatoria's condition has improved, I will do the deed and arrange for a direct request to be filed with the guild. What do you think?"

"Please and thank you!!!!"

A direct request from a noble, with a huge reward! As far as promotion points were concerned, this was quite the juicy morsel. It was an achievement that few C-rank hunters could hope for, a testament to their skill and credibility. This would be a political boon for the guild as well: proof that a noble family had come to rely on them.

"By the way, forgive my changing the topic, but besides all of the things you listed earlier, what else should we be having Leatoria eat? It would be so dull to have her eat the same thing every day."

"Er..." The baron's question was an entirely reasonable one, but Mile was lost for words.

It was not as though Mile was a trained nutritionist. Her knowledge was only slightly greater than that of the average high school girl, as she had read up on the topic a bit for fun, expanding her knowledge beyond what had been covered in school lessons. Really, all that she happened to know was that you could identify beriberi from diminished reflexes, that the cause was a deficiency of vitamin B1, and that there were a handful of foods that were and were not rich in this vitamin.

However, the only examples of foods that she knew were ones from textbooks and other instructional manuals, and the only ones she could think of were eel, bream, salmon roe, and other such seafood. In other words, they were all things that it would be impossible for these people to come by.

The only other information that Mile could recall about beri-beri was that the Japanese navy had found and implemented a solution to combat the illness in its early stages, but that the author Mori Ōgai, who was primarily the surgeon general of the army, violently opposed this practice and spoke out against their nutritional theories, instead subscribing to the contagion theory of the disease, and needlessly sentencing many soldiers in the Japanese land forces to death...

In other words, what Mile remembered was useless trivia, utterly inapplicable to the situation at hand.

"I think that there are probably a lot more foods that have the necessary components in them, but unfortunately those are the only ones that I know. Truly, as long as she just eats a normal diet, she should be fine. There's nothing wrong with the rest of you, after all... It was just by random chance that her diet ended up so imbalanced this time. But, well, just in case..."

Nanos!

Finally!

What's that mean?! It's not good for me to come calling on you for every little thing, so I really don't like to rely on you guys too much, but a person's life is at stake here, so I guess I can't worry about that just now...Well, whatever. Please confirm for me that I made the right call here!

Diagnosing it as beriberi was just my judgment as a layperson, but now that I think about it, there could have been a thousand other reasons why her knee didn't react like it should—like maybe it's an illness that affects her nervous system, or maybe she has too much fat under her skin and the reaction was dulled, or I hit her in the wrong spot, or maybe I even hit her too hard and fractured her knee. If I got too carried away in my snap judgment, then the solution I gave them might not even help her.

So please, tell me what the correct diagnosis is!

Indeed, though previously she had made the call with confidence, Mile was struck with a sudden sense of anxiety. She had finally realized how reckless it was to make such a judgment based only on the lack of a reaction from Leatoria's knee.

UNDERSTOOD. NOW THEN, PLEASE CONCENTRATE SUCCINCTLY ON THE MATTER OF THE ILLNESS. FROM YOUR THOUGHTS, WE CAN DETERMINE THE NECESSARY INFORMATION ABOUT THE ILLNESS AND ANALYZE WHAT WE FIND. AND ALSO...

And also, what?

THERE IS NO NEED FOR YOU TO HESITATE TO RELY ON US. HONESTLY, NOT IN THE SLIGHTEST! NO, IN FACT, WE SHOULD SAY, YOU *SHOULD* RELY ON US! PLEASE RELY ON US!

I'll think about it... Now then, here I go! Grnnnnnnnnnnnh!

WE HAVE RECEIVED AND ANALYZED THE INFORMATION. THE ILLNESS IS EXACTLY AS YOU DIAGNOSED IT, LADY MILE. SPOT ON.

Thank goodness... Now, I would like to move some foodstuffs from my inventory into "storage" and extract the vitamin B_1 from those. Since that is the deficiency, I'd like to condense it into vitamin supplements. Can you do that?

DON'T ASK IF WE CAN DO IT, JUST ORDER IT!

Got it. Then, please!

NOW THEN, WHEN I GIVE THE SIGNAL, PLEASE PUT INTO STORAGE ALL THAT IS IN A THIRTY-CENTIMETER SPHERE CENTERED THIRTY CENTIMETERS IN FRONT OF YOUR FACE. THAT IS WHERE THE PROCESSING NANOMACHINES WILL BE GATHERED. THE WORK WILL THEN BE COMPLETED INSTANTANEOUSLY, SO YOU MAY TAKE THE PILLS, ALONG WITH THAT THIRTY-CENTIMETER SPHERE, BACK OUT OF STORAGE. IF YOU DON'T, THEN SOME OF US WILL END UP TRAPPED IN STORAGE.

Okay! Oh, I do have some various containers stored away too, so please put it in one of those. Only make as much as will fit inside it. Also, I'll have to discard these nutrient-stripped ingredients, so please put whatever you don't use off to the side. I don't want to eat any nutritionless food myself.

UNDERSTOOD! NOW THEN, THE STORAGE!

Roger that!

"What's up? You're spacing out again..."

"Miley's always spacing out like this..."

"H-hush!"

After the usual exchange...

Heave ho!

A tiny jar suddenly appeared in Mile's hand.

ALL UNITS HAVE BEEN SAFELY RETURNED. BECAUSE THE APPROPRIATE AMOUNT FOR A SINGLE DOSE OF THE

SPECIFIED COMPONENT WOULD MAKE THE PILLS TOO SMALL, WE HAVE INCLUDED OTHER IMPORTANT COMPONENTS AND AGENTS TO INCREASE INTAKE INTO A SINGLE PILL THAT CAN BE TAKEN AFTER EVERY MEAL.

THOUGH NO MARKED SYMPTOMS HAVE YET TO APPEAR, THE PATIENT ALSO SHOWED SIGNS OF IMPENDING ILLNESS FROM DEFICIENCY IN OTHER COMPONENTS, SO THIS SHOULD WARD AGAINST THOSE AS WELL.

It would seem that the nanomachines had concocted a multivitamin—or, better yet, an all-purpose supplement—containing calcium, magnesium, iron, and zinc as well. Her nanobuddies really were a conscientious sort.

Thank you! This is perfect!

WE ARE TRULY DELIGHTED TO HEAR YOUR PRAISE.

"Wh—? Storage magic?"

Mile presented the jar to the startled baron.

"It's a medicine that contains the necessary components that Leatoria is lacking. Please have her take one tablet after every meal."

The baron appeared truly perplexed.

"W-well that's awfully convenient..."

And incredibly suspicious. A medicine so perfectly suited to the situation that it was as if she had prepared it ahead of time. However, she was not asking for money, so it was nothing but a boon to the Aura household...

The baron prided himself on having the ability to read most people fairly well. Furthermore, it was inconceivable that anyone in this world could have devised the perfect a trap for them to fall into.

"It's an old family recipe—a secret remedy!" she said, shoving it into the baron's hands.

Cautiously, the baron opened the jar.

"And how much are you going to charge us for this?" he asked.

Mile grinned and replied, "You can't put a price on seeing Lady Leatoria's smile!"

"Huh?"

In other words, it was free. Or rather, she could repay them with a smile, when the day came.

"Until these run out, you can work on getting Lady Leatoria to broaden her horizons as far as what she will and won't eat. If you don't, there's a chance she may fall prey to some other dreadful illness down the line. Please figure out something to do about her pickiness—and about getting her some exercise. There's no sense in someone as slender and beautiful as she is dying before she even has a chance to wed, is there?"

"I-I understand. We love her so much that I suppose we've been rather soft on her. We'll take care of it," the baron replied, nodding.

He seemed serious about this—things were going to be all right.

"We really should've stayed for dinner, too," Reina grumbled as they rode back to the guild in a borrowed carriage.

"It was still five more hours until dinner! We couldn't just wait around that long. What do you think they'd say about us if we lingered there for no reason, just to get more food out of them, and then ran off afterwards?!"

"I guess you're right. But still..."

Even though it was Mile, herself a bit of a glutton, who had pointed this out, Reina was incorrigible.

After their discussion had concluded, the baron prepared a slip with the terms of his request to the Crimson Vow and had one of his servants send it along on horseback to the guild. This meant that the Crimson Vow could take their time, and once they arrived at the guild, they would be able to receive their reward and accept the direct request retroactively. Even though their accepting the request would mean nothing until the results were shown.

Finally, the carriage stopped, and the cabin door opened.

"We have arrived at the hall of the capital branch of the hunters' guild."

As the four disembarked the carriage, Bundine greeted them with a 10-degree bow.

"Thank you for the ride. Now then, until another day..."

Another day, when they would need to return to receive a signature as proof that the job had been completed. Mavis, who had spoken as the representative of the party, had only tipped her head, but Bundine now lowered himself further to a full 45 degrees of the deepest respect.

"Thank you so very much. Truly, truly I thank you from the bottom of my heart."

Dark spots began to appear on the ground beneath his lowered face, but the Crimson Vow pretended not to notice, lightly waving their hands to Bundine as they disappeared into the guild hall.

For a brief time after, Bundine stood staring at the door of the hall and then climbed into the back of the carriage.

"To the residence."

And so, the carriage set off on its leisurely journey back to the Baron Aura's capital home.

"How did you get a personal request from a noble this soon after arriving in the capital?! And for curing his daughter's illness at that... Just *what* in the world are you four?!"

As she spoke, Felicia's tone grew less and less businesslike.

"Well, if you're gonna ask *what* we are..."

"Then I guess we had better tell you."

"You see, we are..."

"Four allies, bound at the soul..."

"The Crimson Vow!!!!"

The four shouted the last part in unison and snapped into their practiced pose.

Of course, they restrained themselves from letting off the usual smoke and explosions, since they were indoors.

"I... Wha..."

Even "No-Hope Felicia" could manage no other reply than that.

"Now, Mile, as confident as you were back there, what do you intend to do if you made the wrong diagnosis and her illness *didn't* get better? Do you realize how unforgivable it would be to get their hopes up like that?" asked Reina.

Though she was fairly sure that it would be fine—because, after all, it was Mile they were talking about—there was still a chance that something might go horribly wrong someday. Concern spread across her face and across those of Mavis and Pauline as well. They weren't stupid enough to show such concerns in front of a client, so they had held it together until now, but in fact, they had been truly worried.

"Don't worry. I'm pretty sure that I wasn't wrong, and even if that doesn't heal her, I still have another plan up my sleeve. It's all good!"

"Another plan? And what would that be?" asked Reina.

With a calm and collected look, Mile replied, "Healing her with magic, of course!"

"H-how are we supposed to 'not worry' about that?!?! Isn't that dangerously reckless?!?!" Reina screamed.

"Is it?" asked Mavis.

She truly had no idea.

"Well, it *is* Mile, so..." Pauline had given up entirely.

"Anyway, it's gonna turn out fine!"

And so, the Crimson Vow headed back to their home—their temporary home, where a darling little cat-eared girl was waiting for them.

CHAPTER 50 |

A Rival Appears

IT HAD BEEN THREE DAYS since the incident with the Aura family.

That day had ended up being a work day, and technically, they had still taken on a job for later, though that work was already almost done.

And so, they had set aside the following two days for rest where they could wait until Mavis was fully recovered.

Today, however, the Crimson Vow headed off to the guild to look for a new job.

"Are you all the 'Crimson Vow' or whatever?"

Upon entering the guild hall, they were instantly assailed by a five-unit all-female hunting party.

"Ah, yes? That's us. Is there something we can help you with?" As Mavis replied, the woman who had spoken was momentarily lost for words, beguiled by her gentle smile.

Whoa! She really is a different kind of lady hunter, isn't she?

Mile was dazzled by Mavis's perennial, inexplicable way with other women.

"N-no! That's not why we're here! I hear that some young interlopers have been running amok around here while we were away!" said the eldest of the hunters, a woman of around twenty.

Mavis was dumbfounded. "Oh no, have they? That's dastardly of them. The youth should respect their seniors. It's no good for inexperienced people to go stepping out of bounds. If those people don't start heeding the words of the elderly, then..."

Pft!
Snicker...
Tehehehe...

The other hunters in the room seemed to be trying desperately to hold back their laughter, but Mavis naturally did not notice.

"E-elderly. Elderly?"

The eldest woman was red in the face, trembling.

"Oh, is something the matter?" Mavis asked, ever so chipper.

The woman roared, "I'm talking about you aaalllll!!!"

"Ah, we thought so." For once, even Pauline, Reina, and Mile had caught on.

"Huh?"

Only Mavis had been left out of the loop.

"Now then, I think you all owe us an explanation!"

The Crimson Vow found themselves dragged to the guild hall's dining corner, where they were being grilled by this new all-girl party, the Servants of the Goddess.

"I mean, I still have no idea what the problem here is, or what you're asking for. So I don't know what to tell you."

Since she was speaking to someone who was her senior, Mavis tried to be as polite as possible for now.

"I'm talking about how you all took advantage of our absence and stole our spot as the idols of this guild branch from right under our noses!"

"What?"

The Crimson Vow were amazed. They were amaz-eggs and bacon!

"Ohhh, you mean that we've just been playing around or that we haven't been working, right? No, I can assure you, we've been doing work while we were here. Though our most recent break was a bit long, I will admit..."

Apparently, Mile had misheard "idol" as "idle."

"That's not what we're saying! I'm talking about an *idol*, a perfect image, something you worship!" A girl who was perhaps the second or third eldest in the group desperately tried to correct Mile. She was likely around sixteen or seventeen...

"Huh?! If your party name is Servants of the Goddess, and you're all images to be worshipped, does that mean that you're disciples—nay, avatars of the Goddess herself?!"

"N-no, that's not quite..." The Servants suddenly looked a bit troubled.

Of course, Mile already knew the answer to her own question. Even she could be a bit cruel now and then.

And so finally, the Crimson Vow sat down to hear the full story.

Citing their status as the senior party, the Servants of the Goddess paid for their drinks. At least in that regard, they were properly aware of their duties as seniors.

The Servants of the Goddess. They were a five-member party made up of all girls, a rarity among hunters.

There was Telyusia, the swordswoman, age nineteen; Philly, the lancer, age seventeen; Willine the swordswoman and Tasha the archer-slash-dagger wielder, both age sixteen; and last but not least, Lecelina, the favorably named "all-purpose" (or perhaps more appropriately called "jack-of-all-trades") mage, age fourteen. Lecelina was still a D-rank, but all the others were C-rank hunters. However, they had only very recently been promoted...

The scene: a little farming village in the countryside, with nothing but mountains and fields and nary a good man to go around.

Three young girls who could not bear to live out their lives in such a place took their cleavers and wooden staves in hand and set out to become hunters, in search of a life of excitement and adventure.

They were fools.

Though they faced many a danger and hardship, by some miracle they managed to survive, and came across two more young girls who had similarly struck out from their village on their own. Before they knew it, they had grown to become C-rank hunters.

Normally, anyone that reckless would have found themselves wiped out by now, but perhaps they truly did have a fair bit of skill—or perhaps they were just exceedingly lucky…

There was also the fact that they had made it to a C-rank at such an unexpectedly young age, in a country that did not have anything like the Hunters' Prep School. And they were a group of young women. Naturally, the male parties hung around them like flies—just as they did with Mile and her companions.

But then, the Crimson Vow had appeared.

They were a group of four beautiful young girls. They had two powerful mages. They had sword skills on par with a B-rank. They had less than the standard number of members. And they appeared rather ignorant to the ways of the world.

Indeed, the male parties had found a new prize to set their sights on.

"Somehow you all just swooped right in and nailed a red mark job, got a bonus, and had a noble request you by name! Just what strings did you all pull?!" raged Philly, the seventeen-year-old lancer.

"Jones, of the Defenders of the Covenant, who I was *this* close to snagging, turned down my invitation to dinner, saying that a girl he 'thought he could get serious about' had come along!" roared Telyusia, the nineteen-year-old swordswoman and leader of the party, who was just on the cusp of marriageable age.

"And what's the big deal, making something so terrible happen to those lovely old fellows in the Silver Fangs?!"

Apparently Tasha, the sixteen-year-old archer, had a fondness for older men.

Mile, who had never been able to really converse with any men besides her own father, and Reina, who had spent her earliest memories on the road with her father the peddler and the rest of her young life journeying with the Crimson Lightning, were both fans of men of a more distinguished age, too. Should all three of them become aware of this preference, surely the trio could all become good friends.

"And you stole the people who buy us food and give us sweets!" fumed Lecelina, the fourteen-year-old mage.

"........."

Willine the swordswoman had already spoken her piece and just glared silently.

"How could you do this to us?!?!?!" the Servants all shouted.

"Ah..." Mile's, Pauline's, Mavis's, and Raina's shoulders all slumped in disappointment.

"Oh, but—um, who are the Defenders of the Covenant and the Silver Fangs, exactly?" asked Mile.

The other three members of the Crimson Vow tilted their heads as well. The names Defenders of the Covenant and Silver Fangs did not ring a single bell with the Crimson Vow. Additionally, though the party had overheard much hearsay and gossip about the Servants of the Goddess previously, because the party themselves were not present at the time, the members of the Crimson Vow had not bothered paying attention.

They had not been speaking quietly, so among the other

hunters present, there were plenty who could clearly overhear what the girls were talking about, and at this point, several of those who had been directly observing the day's proceedings approached the girls to offer an explanation. This gesture was not merely a kindness; it was an excuse to get close to the girls, fraught with the ulterior motive of getting the party to remember their faces.

"So you're saying that those lowly pests who tried to cut in on our job, saying that we wouldn't be able to handle the uncertainty and danger on our own were the 'Defenders of the Covenant'? And those suspicious guys who tried to follow us were the 'Silver Fangs'?"

"Wh-wha...?" Telyusia was speechless at Reina's blunt appraisal. "Jones isn't... The Defenders of the Covenant aren't that weak of a party!"

"Please don't talk about the gentlemen of the Silver Fangs like they're a bunch of perverts!"

As Telyusia and Tasha gave their furious objections, Pauline let her viper's tongue loose. "But the Defenders did try to muscle in on a job that we took, despite not taking the task for themselves, and as soon as Mavis and Mile showed them their copper-cutting trick, they backed right off. Not only were they clearly after something, but they're good-for-nothings as well. Or should we be interpreting that some other way?"

"Er..."

"And then, there was the party of old men that was following secretly behind a party of young ladies, keeping at a steady distance. If that doesn't qualify as suspicious behavior, then what would you say does?"

"Err..."

Telyusia and Tasha were silent, unable to object to Pauline's sound arguments.

The other hunters, filled with sympathy for the Defenders and the Silver Fangs, looked to Felicia, who had been the one to egg both parties on, hoping that she would provide them some sort of defense. However, Felicia remained at her seat at the counter, unmoved, not even batting an eye.

That's No-Hope Felicia for you!!!!!

The only saving grace in this situation, it would seem, was that neither the Defenders of the Covenant nor the Silver Fangs were present at the time...

"So, are we done here now? We've all determined that we have nothing to do with either of those parties, and we intend to continue to have nothing to do with them."

"Ngh... So far, you've recognized who the Defenders of the Covenant and the Silver Fangs are—but I need you to acknowledge that they didn't have any ill intentions toward you! Until you can do that, we aren't finished!"

Reina attempted to wrap up the conversation, but Telyusia, who seemed to be the leader of the Servants of the Goddess, did not appear prepared to let them off so easily. Indeed, she clearly said as much.

And then came her declaration of war.

"It's time to show you which of our two parties is superior!"

"Yeah!" her cohorts joined the battle cry.

"Ah..."

As the tension among the Servants rose, the members of the Crimson Vow began to relax.

This truly was not a matter of which party was stronger. The reason that all the men had been flitting around the Servants of the Goddess until now was not because of their skills or their abilities—it was because they hoped to make them their girlfriends. Nothing more, nothing less. The girls had only just become C-ranks, which meant that they were on the bottom rung as far as C-ranks went. Having five girls like that in their party would limit the jobs they could take, and their individual shares of the profit would be smaller. In other words, as far as other parties were concerned, there was clearly more merit in inviting along the Crimson Vow—who had B-rank level swordsmanship, precious combat magic skills, and other talents—than the Servants of the Goddess.

In which case, should they selectively invite only the members who interested them? That would launch debates about who they should bring along. Furthermore, they would incite the wrath of the remaining members of the Servants, from whom they had poached members... And anyone who would let themselves be poached was not unlikely to betray their new companions and leave them as well. And, if they did relocate, a war might break out over those girls...

Indeed, there was no doubting that such a thing could tear both their parties apart.

This meant, as long as the Servants stayed together, simply

dallying with one or two of them would be fine. No matter who you got close to, it was a blessing...

However, human relations were, of course, a mushy, delicate business, and for things to go wrong was not at all uncommon.

On the whole, while a party might consider bringing in the Crimson Vow wholesale as capable party-members-slash-love-interests, the Servants of the Goddess were better candidates for "lovers you have fun with on the side."

Even so, the general proportion of female hunters was comparatively low. Most normal young women were of the same mind as the eldest daughter back at that inn, thinking that hunters were all a bunch of broke thugs who could die at any moment. Therefore, for many of the hunters, the young ladies of the Servants of the Goddess were the best that they could get, either as prospective lovers or candidates for marriage.

If a hunter should marry one of them, no one could complain if she relocated to her husband's party, and it wouldn't be unusual for her to retire and live as a full-time housewife or work as the owner of a small shop or some other safe job, awaiting her husband's return.

But then, the Crimson Vow had appeared.

They had two swordswomen who could take down an ogre in a single blow and two capable C-rank mages as well. Plus, they were young and cute, with skill spread evenly throughout the four of them. They seemed to know little of the world, and it was only natural that the men's targeting systems would lock on to them instead of the Servants of the Goddess.

Even if the Servants should manage to crush the Crimson Vow in some mock battle, their position would not change.

And of course, most of the guild staff and the other hunters knew that the Servants hadn't the slightest chance of defeating them to begin with.

"Very well then," Reina began. "Let's take this outs—gnh!"

Mavis quickly clapped a hand over her mouth. "W-we couldn't possibly! We're all still rookies, and we couldn't possibly be prepared to face veterans like you! It's so obvious that even bothering to try would be moot!"

They had purposely come to a town where no one knew them. They were going to live an honest and straightforward life as normal, unremarkable C-rank hunters in pursuit of knowledge. Remembering this, Mavis tried her best to play the situation off—laying the previous copper-cutting demonstration completely aside.

Mile and Pauline were of the same opinion as Mavis, so Mile put a sound barrier around Reina's head before she could continue to object, not wanting to earn the contempt of other hunters, and Pauline bodily blocked Reina from the other girls' sight. Then, Mile indirectly restrained Reina with her superhuman strength. Reina struggled and kicked, but Mile's hold was unmoved, and Reina's flailing, along with her futile attempts at speech, were mostly ignored.

"W-well, as long as you recognize that. Now we better not see you all walking around like you own the place again!"

And then, as if they had already accepted a job for the day and were only hanging around the guild hall for the sake of confronting the Crimson Vow, the leader of the Servants of the Goddess promptly left, followed by her four companions.

Hey now, hey now, hey now!!! the guild employees and other hunters silently protested. *The Servants of the Goddess had definitely heard about that copper-cutting incident from before—and they heard how they belittled the Defenders! And then there was the fact that they were so fast the Silver Fangs couldn't keep up! And that they completed a red mark job and got a personal request from a noble! How could they know all that and accept their resignation so easily?!?!*

These were girls who would leave their village with only cleavers and wooden staves in hand. Perhaps because their tempers were running so hot, they seemed to have already forgotten their conversation from just a short while before. Of course, their aim had been to prove their superiority from the start, so perhaps they had merely put anything that contradicted that "fact" out of their minds...

At any rate, the guild staff and the other hunters present all shared a single thought: *Well, that's someone else's business. Best not to think too hard about it...*

Everyone returned to their previous business: in the case of the guild employees, work, and in the case of the hunters, searching for jobs, eating, and drinking.

And as for the Crimson Vow...

"Let's just do some basic monster exterminating today. It'll be good practice for Mavis."

"All right!!!"

Reina finally appeared to be thinking straight. Just like a party leader... No wait, that was Mavis speaking!

"Would you care to explain to me what that earlier business was all about?" Reina, apparently, was still miffed about being held back with her mouth clamped shut.

Clearly, Mavis really was the appropriate choice for party leader.

So Mile and Pauline agreed.

And though none of them said it, they all somehow came to the same conclusion at once.

I bet those girls are gonna be a pain in our butts from now on...

CHAPTER 51 |

The Letter

FOR THE NEXT THREE DAYS, the Crimson Vow concentrated only on standard daily requests. For the sake of Mavis getting some practical battle experience with her new techniques, and for the sake of doing something that would not make them stand out quite so much as their last couple of jobs, they surmised that it might be good to stick to doing more menial jobs for a little while.

Thanks to the copper-cutting scene, among other things, Mavis, Reina, and Pauline, who generally prided themselves on having more common sense than Mile, had begun to fall somewhat—or rather, quite a bit—into a Mile-like way of thinking, a.k.a. the wrong way.

"You've really done good though, Mavis," said Reina. "That 'Wind Edge' of yours is on par with actual wind magic! At this rate, anyone you come up against will just assume it's normal wind magic—they'll have no idea that it's actually Mile's secret 'spirit cannon' technique. Plus, that 'Anti-Magic Blade' of yours can even fend off my fireballs. You could slice through someone's fire blasts and stab right through them! Honestly, you may as well call it the Magus Killer!"

Indeed, though Reina had been holding back her attacks as she sparred against Mavis, helping her to practice fending off magic, Mavis had still managed to rush forth, cutting through the flames and stopping just short of bringing her blade down atop Reina's head.

While neither party ended up hurt, of course, Mavis was mildly distraught to find that her hair was a bit fried. Mile quickly repaired it with magic.

"Still, if I can only just barely keep up with a mage who's hold-ing back, then..."

"It's not like anyone's gonna be flinging around any big spells in a melee, dummy. The only time you can fire off a big spell is when it's the very first shot or as a long-distance battering ram. In any normal battle, a mage's focus is gonna be on elementary spells like Fireball, thinking that they can fire those off quickly and continuously. I can tell you without a doubt that the first time any new opponent sees a sword wielder suddenly deflect or cut straight through their flares and come flying toward them, that match is gonna be over in a single blow."

"Ah—really?"

Mavis scratched her head, embarrassed.

Mile, meanwhile, pretended not to overhear the conversation.

As much as Reina was impressed that the technique *resembled* wind magic, the fact remained that it really *was* honest-to-goodness wind magic. At least at this rate, there was no chance of anyone uncovering the secret of the technique, not in the slightest. However, there was the possibility that another secret—namely, that Mavis, who should not have been able to use magic, was doing so—would be uncovered.

Well, should that happen, Mavis could just say that she had a magic sword imbued with wind magic and that it could only be wielded by the one the sword recognized as its true wielder. As for where the sword came from, all she had to do was fabricate some story of a divine blessing from a "god in human form," such as a "mysterious old man with one eye," or a "heavenly woman who appeared from a lake."

Naturally, no one of any stature would be willing to defy the will of the divine by trying to snatch away such an item. Believing in the existence of a divine sword meant believing in the direct interference of the gods. Moreover, anyone could find it in themselves to imagine what sort of divine punishment would be visited upon them if they tried to defy those gods and lay their hands on such a gift.

This was an undeveloped society where magic existed, after all. It was only natural that people would believe in the gods as well.

In reality, it was only because of the large-scale interference of a group of beings that might as well be gods that magic could exist at all, so a belief in the divine was probably justified.

Oh, Mile thought, *but in that case, won't people start thinking that Mavis is some legendary hero chosen by the gods?*

Well, that's fine. It's not really that big of a deal.

It really *was* that big of a deal.

Such a big deal that it would cause a nationwide—nay, a continent-wide stir.

When they arrived back at the guild, Mile withdrew the day's kills from storage and lined them up on the exchange counter.

"I'm glad we managed not to run into those hunters again today," Mile remarked.

"Yeah, thankfully," Mavis agreed.

The two were referring to the five-girl party, the Servants of the Goddess. The old man at the exchange counter gave a wry smile as he heard these words.

Neither of the two parties tended to linger for long in the guild hall's dining corner, so at least the chance of them encountering one another was not very high. Both took their various breaks elsewhere and went away on overnight journeys, and such.

"Here you go ladies, yer payment. My, you really do know how to rake it in, dontcha? Sure is a blessin' to have capable storage magic like that, eh?"

Other hunters' ears began to prick up at the old man's words.

In order for the girls to be earning what they should, unfortunately, it was impossible for them to conceal the fact of Mile's storage abilities. Therefore, it had already become public knowledge at the guild. And now, the hunters who were aware of this fact were beginning to desire the Crimson Vow more and more.

However, the copper-cutting display had left a lasting impact, and when combined with the humiliation faced by the Defenders of the Covenant and the Silver Fangs, there was not a party around who would dare to suggest that the Crimson Vow join forces with them, let alone try to incorporate all of their members wholesale. At the very least, there were no other parties around with the confidence to try and show off a skill as impressive as the coin trick nor to try and keep up with them by way of speed, if not even the Silver Fangs could do it.

Of course, this did not mean that the others had given up on trying to cozy up to the Crimson Vow entirely. There was still a chance that if they came to them not as their superiors but as a congenial group of comrades, they might convince the Vow to collaborate with them on a job.

Plus, if one became friendly with one of the Vow as an individual, perhaps one might be invited to join the party and have one's very own harem...

The Crimson Vow consisted of only four members, and the ideal party number was five or six, which meant that they really were a man or two short. It was still possible for them to add more members. In fact, they *should*. And really, there was no reason why those new members shouldn't be men. It wasn't *unusual* to see parties with four men and one or two women, so what was wrong with the opposite?

Their current allies? Who cared about them?! After they won one of the girls' hearts, they could throw a big party for everyone. The other guys would be thanking them with tears in their eyes.

Now then, which to aim for?

The cool and collected Mavis, who could be approached as a fellow wielder of the sword? The meek little Mile, who had storage magic and outstanding sword skills herself? It would be three or four years until she was of marrying age, but it was probably a bit soon to be thinking of that anyway.

And of course, it was hard to neglect the buxom Pauline or the svelte Reina. With a mage for a girlfriend, one never needed to worry about injury—and magic was useful for all sorts of other things as well.

Somehow sensing all these desires, wishes, ambitions, and wild dreams swirling in the air around them, the Crimson Vow began to grow uneasy, and as soon as their business was finished, they swiftly moved to leave the hall.

However, just before they stepped outside, Mile suddenly paused as though she had just recalled something. "Ah, sorry guys, can you wait here a minute? There's something I need to do. I'll be right back!"

Rather than heading to their usual destination, the job acceptance window, she moved toward a counter that they had little familiarity with: the one that dealt with clients who placed requests and other members of the general public.

She had done something of the sort at least once

before—when sending out that letter, or rather, package, that the elderly elf had tagged onto. So, this time, the others thought nothing of it, waiting patiently just in front of the entrance until Mile finished her business.

"Excuse me, I believe there's a package for me? It should be addressed to 'Miami Satodele,' with this branch hall as the destination..." Mile said quietly so that no one else could hear. As this was not the counter where hunters accepted jobs and gave their completion reports, but the one intended for the general public, the receptionist, of course, was not No-Hope Felicia.

"Please wait a moment," said the receptionist as she stood from her seat.

She vanished behind a door for a few moments and then returned with a small parcel. She retook her seat, and then, facing Mile, asked, "What is the nickname of the giant monster that attacks seafaring boats, whose parts are used in creating medicines for afflictions of the eyes?"

"The Ophthalmologist's Blight!'"

"Correct. That is the password. Here you are!" she said, handing the package over.

Incidentally, there was no such creature as the one that the riddle had mentioned. It was merely a question that the sender knew that only Mile, or rather, 'Miami Satodele,' would know the answer to. It was a nonsense question that no one else would be able to answer.

Mile returned to her party. "Sorry to keep you!"

"Let's get back to the inn," Reina replied. "We're taking to-morrow and the day after off for some personal time, remember?"

Overhearing this, the ears of the surrounding male hunters began to prick up. They were likely thinking that if the Vow were going to be going around town separately, then they might just get the chance to encounter one of them. Unwittingly letting such information slip in a place like this would turn out to be a big misstep on Reina's part...

After they had returned to the inn, Mile opened her parcel, examining the two letters that were inside. One of them she put into storage, but the other she opened up in front of the others.

"It's a letter from Lenny!"

"Hang on! When exactly did you tell her we were going to...? Oh right, that parcel you sent from the other town, right? I guess we'd already decided that we would be staying in this city for a little while by then. Well then, let's all see what it says."

And so, they passed the letter around.

Early one morning, when Lenny was tidying up outside of the inn's front door, a man had called out to her.

"Pardon me, is there someone by the name of Lenny here?"

"Ah, well, that would be me..."

For a stranger to have some business with the inn made sense, but there was no reason for any strange adults to have business with Lenny, who was still a child. Though she had tentatively re-plied, her body tensed with wariness, gripping the broom as she instinctively shifted into a battle stance.

"Whoa now, I'm no one suspicious! I'm just a messenger; I came to deliver an item to you!" the man hurriedly said, digging into the bag on his shoulder and pulling out something that appeared to be a letter, which he presented to Lenny.

"What's this?"

"I'm only the messenger here! I wouldn't possibly know... The postage has already been paid by the sender, so there's no charge to you."

Surely enough, Lenny's name and that of the inn were inscribed on the back of the envelope as the letter's destination. However, the name of the sender was not written, so even if she wished to return it, she couldn't. The sender must not have wanted others to be able to tell who had sent it just by looking.

"Who is this from? And who is it that you work for?" Lenny asked, but the man simply shook his head.

"I cannot answer that, and I do not know the sender's name. Well, I mean, of course I know the name of the person who forwarded this on to me, but they might not have known the name of the person who addressed this to you, or they simply may not have wished to tell me. So please don't ask me what their name is. I cannot tell you my name or my affiliation, either. Doing so would interrupt the flow of information and jeopardize certain secrets."

Lenny was quite bright, so the moment she heard this, a light bulb came on in her head. She broke the seal on the spot, read the first few lines of the letter, and then shoved it straight back into the envelope.

"U-um, can I get you to send a reply to the letter you received? And can you include a letter from me as well?!"

After a brief think, the man smiled kindly.

"If you can write your reply straight away, I would be happy to take it."

"Please come with me!"

Lenny grabbed the man by the hand and dragged him into the still empty dining room. Ignoring her speechless father, she urged the man into a chair and placed three mugs of ale and some snacks on the table before him, and set to work desperately writing her letter.

"It's going to take me a little while to drink all these..."

Drinking three mugs of ale first thing in the morning was rather against the man's general policy.

Well, that's fine, I suppose, he thought. *I'm not gonna get drunk off of this much, and no one's going to complain about me heading straight back after drinking these. Though I mean, I'd rather not set a bad precedent, but if I avoid the store and workshop and slip into the office from the back door, I should be fine... This little girl seems like she's very important to them, after all. It'd be cruel to rush her.*

And so, leisurely, he put the first mug to his lips.

The man received the letter to the sound of Lenny's endless thanks. He gave the girl his regards and then left the inn behind.

He set out through the capital streets, which had now begun

to fill with people, sometimes slipping through the crowds, some-times darting down narrow back alleys, taking an absurd and circuitous route so that he could not possibly be tailed, before disappearing through the back door of a certain shop.

"Honestly though, what's with all the secrecy? Well, that's what they wanted, so I'll follow instructions for now. I wonder what they could be up against these days... I guess this just comes with the territory when you're dealing with eccentrics like these..."

As so the man sat down at his desk, absorbing himself in of-fice work so that none of the workers would have to see him until the smell of all three mugs of ale had worn off.

"Say Mile, you like to read books, right? You wanna read these?" Reina asked as she handed Mile two recreational tomes.

"Huh? Why do you have these, Reina?! These are really expensive!"

Indeed, books in this world were ridiculously expensive. Even Mile would prefer borrowing them from the library to purchas-ing them herself.

Furthermore, there were few books meant for recreation.

Scholarly anthologies and the autobiographies of nobles and such were put out with the aim of spreading knowledge and at-taining renown, so a fair number of books were produced with little concern paid to profit. Whether or not the information they contained was the truth was another matter. Even certain types of history books, depending on the country, were produced with a higher emphasis on popularity than moneymaking.

However, this did not work for recreational books. Given that every single copy had to be reproduced by hand at scribing shops, the price per unit could not easily be lowered, and so the works had to be ones that would be guaranteed to sell at a price high enough to turn a sufficient profit. It was a budding industry, and as a result, literary culture at large was still a fledgling concept in this world.

Plus, books were delicate, and any belonging to someone constantly on the road would soon fall to tatters—assuming that one did not have access to a realm of temporal stasis like Mile's inventory space. Therefore, it was hard to imagine that Reina herself would buy such a book.

"I borrowed them. If you pay one gold as a deposit, you can borrow a book for three days at the library here in exchange for three silver. Sticking around inside of libraries where everyone's just reading silently with serious looks on their faces gives me the creeps, so I took the books out. I feel like it's just as good as paying an admission fee. Anyway, since I already paid the money to borrow the books, I figured it'd be more cost-effective if we all got a chance to read them. This author is really funny—I've read tons of their books before, but it looks like there are two new ones out, so I ended up borrowing them both."

Mile then took the books that she was offered and read the titles.

King Lear. The tale of an old king beloved by his three daughters.

The Sorrows of Young Hamtel. The tale of a troubled young man who is unable to defeat the ferocious cockatrice that comes to live in the yard of his home.

Author: Miami Satodele.

Mile stared at the two books, trembling.

"I-I don't m-mind going last, so, um... P-Pauline and M-Mavis can go ahead and r-read them first..."

"You sure? Well, you do read pretty fast, so I'm sure it'll be fine if you get the last crack at them. Mavis, Pauline, you wanna read these?" Reina asked, moving away from Mile.

Enough sweat ran down Mile's face to fill a bucket.

Later that night, once the others were sound asleep, Mile, who was a night owl and always the last to go to bed, sat awake writing, her page illuminated by a light spell behind a darkening barrier.

Once she came to a stopping point, she reached into her inventory and withdrew a letter, looking it over again. It was the other letter that was enclosed in the parcel along with Lenny's.

Dear Ms. Satodele,

We have safely received your latest manuscript. We will begin manufacturing and reproduction at once.

Proceeds for the previous volumes have been favorable, and there have been talks of a dramatization. Payment for your manuscript has been forwarded to your account at the Merchants' Guild.

*Additionally, the secondary letter you included has been
delivered as requested. I believe it should go without saying
that the enclosed is the reply that we were entrusted with.
We shall be passionately awaiting your next work.*

Sincerely,
Melsacus, Orpheus Publishing

Mile wanted to spread interesting tales throughout the world,
a joy which to her, was more valuable than even the pocket
change this secret venture earned her. She wanted to bring forth
epics and make the people around her smile.

And, most importantly, she wanted to lay the groundwork for
a global enlightenment, one that would make everyone finally be
able to understand the punchlines of her jokes.

The fact that there was not a person in this world who would
understand the genius inherent in "Please Kenji, an Animage,"
was hopelessly, desperately tragic.

Miami Satodele. This was made of a jumble of three names:
Mi-sato, A-dele, and Mi-le. An anthology of Mile's three lives.
That was who Miami Satodele was.

"I'm gonna do it! I'm gonna spread my Japanese folktales—
nay, my stories of the world—all across this land if it's the last
thing I do!"

However, there was one thing Mile did not know.

Both Mavis and Pauline had noticed that the contents of the
books that they had borrowed from Reina very closely resembled

things that they had previously heard only in Mile's Japanese folktales, and thanks to this, it was only a matter of time now before one of them uncovered the truth...

Didn't I Say
to Make My Abilities
Average in the
——— Next Life?!

CHAPTER 52 |

Leatoria

SEVERAL DAYS LATER, it was time to make their first visit to Leatoria since she began her new diet. By now, they could check on her condition and would be able to tell whether the treatment was having any effect, and whether there had been any visible changes. If there were no results, then Mile would have to employ her secondary method, so it was important to be sure. There was no time to waste when a person's life was in danger.

And so, the Crimson Vow once again journeyed to the Aura family estate.

Naturally, they were on foot this time.

Though they were dropping in unannounced, it was not as though they were seeking an audience with the baron himself. All they had to do was find the butler, Bundine, or some other lower-ranking employee, and ask them how Leatoria was doing. That was all there was to it. No one ever expected a vacuum salesman or an evangelist to make an appointment before dropping by. This was very much the same.

"It is splendid to see you again! Please, come in. The Baron will see you straight away!"

Apparently, it was not at all the same. Bundine came running when he heard that the Crimson Vow had stopped by and led the group immediately to Leatoria's room. When Bundine opened the door and urged the four inside, what greeted them was...

"Oh hey! Good to see you all again!"

Leatoria was vigorously performing an exercise that resembled yoga.

"Wh-wha...?"

Reina could barely form words. The other three could say nothing at all.

Leatoria seemed a little *too* healthy...

"My my! So sorry to keep you all waiting!"

Before the members of the Crimson Vow could recover from their shock, the baron arrived.

"Not only have her lethargy and the numbness in her legs gone away, her constitution, which has always been rather poor, has improved as well. Her appetite has increased, and now, well, see for yourself! I cannot thank you enough," the baron said, bowing his head.

"N-no, please don't lower yourself, sir!"

Having a baron bow to her again and again while she was passing herself off as a commoner was far too unsettling for Mavis, who quickly protested.

"St-still, this is..."

Thankfully, Leatoria was now wearing normal pajamas instead of a prim nightgown, so the effect was not quite as egregious as it could have been; however, she persisted in doing exercises in a stance that was at least a little inappropriate for a young lady to be taking in front of the eyes of gentlemen.

For a weak little wisp of a girl, she was almost a tad *too* powerful.

"My body feels so light! I'm having so much fun moving around. For the first time ever, I think I know what it's like to truly be healthy!"

Hey, nanos?

PRESENT!

Um, what the heck is happening here?

YES, WELL, AS A BONUS, WE INCLUDED SOME UNIQUE COMPONENTS IN THOSE PILLS, AND WELL... WE VOLUNTARILY DECIDED TO HELP IMPROVE HER CONDITION, YOU SEE.

I knew iiiiiiiiiiiiitt!!!

Mile had suspected that the truth had to be something to this effect. Were that not the case, there was no possible way that Leatoria could have shown such drastic improvement so quickly.

"Um, if she's this healthy now, why is she still in her pajamas, being treated like an invalid?"

"Uh..."

At Mavis's straightforward question, the baron, Bundine, and Leatoria all went stiff for some reason.

"Well, it's just that we've always seen Leatoria lying down, so..."

"Nightclothes suit her ladyship so well that it's rather impossible to think of her in anything else..."

"It's more comfortable this way, so..."

Whoa now!!!! the members of the Crimson Vow thought as one.

"You little slob! Go change your clothes immediately!"

Whoa whoa whoa now!!! thought the Crimson Vow, minus one.

They all knew that Reina's order had come from a place of seniority, but the fact remained that Reina *appeared* to be the younger of the two, and she was speaking to a noble—right in front of the girl's father, no less.

A horrible spasm ran across Mavis's face, but the baron only winced and left Bundine to handle getting Leatoria into some proper clothing, leading the Crimson Vow to the parlor himself.

"As you can see, you may consider the job complete. Thank you again."

When they entered the parlor, the baron withdrew the job completion form from his breast pocket straight away and handed it to Mavis. Apparently unperturbed by Reina's hubris, he had correctly deduced that Mavis was their leader. Well, in truth, it might have only been that Mavis was the eldest of the party or his assumption that she must be a noble. By appearance, Reina appeared to be no more than twelve or thirteen, after all.

No, wait, come to think of it, Mavis actually *had* introduced herself as the leader last time...

Mavis examined the paper she had been handed and found that it was marked with an A grade. Naturally, they would have not have expected any other.

"Thank you very much."

Echoing Mavis's thanks, the four of them bowed their heads. All of them had acquired at least that much in the way of manners, and this was a matter of ceremony.

"Now then," said the baron, "I actually had something else to ask you..."

Mavis grinned and replied, "A new personal request? Would you mind letting us know what it is?"

Even if it was a direct request from a noble, they would not take any job that was fruitless or demeaning. This was a rule that the Crimson Vow had set for themselves. Even when it was a seemingly good person like the baron, they did not intend to leap into any agreements without first hearing the terms.

However, the baron looked a bit troubled, hesitant even, upon hearing Mavis's inquiry.

"A request... Do we have to go as far as making this a formal request? Ah, well, I suppose it's not as if I can expect hunters to do charity work, and if it's a request from a noble, then it may as well be a job..."

The baron mumbled something to himself before finally seeming to work up the courage to say the words. "Please, be Leatoria's friends!"

"No, thank you!"

"Whaaaaaat?!"

Hearing such an immediate reply, from the usually quiet Mile no less, the baron was taken aback.

"B-but why not?" the baron, who had never imagined that his request would be denied, was openly dismayed.

"You don't become friends with someone just because their parents ask you to," said Mile. "And also..."

"Also?"

"'Leatoria's been our friend this whole time!' That's what you were going to say, wasn't it?!" Reina cut in.

"Ah, eh heh..." Mile scratched her head, embarrassed.

"Well, that's our Mile for you."

"I couldn't imagine any other reply."

Even Mavis and Pauline had seen straight through her.

There was no way that Mile—who until very recently had never had any friends her age, even in her previous life—could ever have truly refused the baron's request. Even the other members of the Vow, who knew only the half of it, could see that.

"You're so easy to read, Mile..."

"Huh?"

A surprised voice rang out from the doorway. Everyone turned to look and saw Leatoria, now changed into normal clothes, standing there, her eyes sparkling with shock and joy.

"F-friends? I h-have f-friends?!"

Oh no...

And with that, the other three were sucked into the trap right along with Mile.

"This is perfect! I can't wait to go on all sorts of adventures with you all as a hunter!"

"*Whaaaaaaaaaaaaaaaaaat?!?!?!*"

The baron and the Crimson Vow all let out a reflexive cry, and in a shocking turn, even Bundine joined in.

For Bundine, the veteran butler, raising his voice in shock at a conversation between his master and a guest was the blunder of a lifetime.

"Wha, wh-wh-wh-what are you saying...?" asked the baron.

"Huh? Well, if I'm friends with hunters, then obviously I have to enroll as a hunter and go along with them if I want to see them with any regularity... Plus, I want to have all sorts of fun adventures too, just like the ones they were telling us about last time!" Leatoria replied, chipper.

"Nopenopenopenopenopenopenopenope, N-O-P-E, NO WAY!!!!" the Crimson Vow all shouted, wildly shaking their heads and waving their hands.

"If you were really listening, you'd remember what we said. A hunter's life is full of dangers, and even we've come close to death. It's not a job for a noble's young daughter," Mavis admonished, grimacing.

"Th-that's right! A dangerous job like that is no sort of place for someone like you, Lady Leatoria," Mile agreed.

"Huh?" Leatoria replied, "But Mavis and Mile, aren't you both nobles?"

"Guh!"

Indeed, though they had never outright confirmed it, Mavis

and Mile had been behaving in a way that clearly revealed their true origins in order to win the baron's trust. Neither had even tried to hide the fact that they were not even disgraced nobles but still in good standing from active noble lines...

This was inevitable, of course. It had been crucial that Mile be thought of as someone of appropriate status, with adequate knowledge and a high-level education, in order for her diagnosis and treatment plan to be trusted. However, now it had come back to bite her...

"A hunter has to have sufficient skill in combat—the strength to protect herself. If she can't handle her own affairs without troubling her allies, then she's nothing. You have to hike through forests and up craggy mountains while carrying heavy things, and square up against enemies... Without excelling at the sword like Mavis does, or having skill and experience with magic like I do, or some other special ability like that, you'd be done for," said Reina, hoping to dissuade Leatoria.

"Oh? But I am good at magic. Not many people know about it because I couldn't leave home thanks to my frail body, but I can do fire and water magic, and perform combat spells, too."

"C-come again?!?!"

For a beautiful young noblewoman, this was incredibly rare. Indeed, as far as Mile's recollections went, the only such individual she had ever even laid eyes on was Marcela of the Wonder Trio—a young lady that she had trained or "power-leveled"—in other words, one whom Mile had hand-raised herself.

If one were to search the whole country, perhaps one might

turn up one or two noble maidens who could use combat magic. However, to find one of such beauty, who had neither husband nor lover, was entirely unheard of. If Leatoria's existence, her talent, and the fact that she had totally recovered from her illness and frailty came to light, there was no doubt that droves of suitors would come banging down the baron's door.

Plus, since she had older siblings, there would be no issue with her leaving the household to wed. Surely, she would leap at any proposals that came from the heirs of viscounts or counts. Though, as she was only fourteen, any talk now could be of nothing more than a betrothal...

"Also, my body's felt so powerful these past few days, I bet I could carry a whole cask of wine from here to the next town on my back..."

"Whaaaaaaaaat?!"

Reina was utterly lost for words.

"B-baron, if news of Leatoria's magical ability, and her recovery, start getting around to other households..." Mile began.

"Ah..."

That was all the baron needed to hear. Suddenly, he could see everything clearly. His face went pale.

"Th-that can't happen! I won't let anyone take my Leatoria away!"

"But Father, I don't want to be a bride, anyway. I want to be a hunter."

Things were already falling apart.

"Anyway, Lady Leatoria, the fact remains that we are all C-rank hunters. If you enlisted now, you would start off as an

F-rank hunter. People with such different ranks can't be in the same party..."

"Really?"

That was a big, fat lie.

If four out of five people in a party were C-ranks, and the remaining member was an F-rank, the party would still be counted as C-rank on the whole. Plus, given that she could use combat magic, she would probably start off as a D-rank—thanks to the aforementioned "skip" process... Though of course, no matter how good someone's magical skills were, it was still very unlikely that a complete novice would be allowed to start at a C-rank. Assuming that they didn't also possess storage magic anyway...

Both the baron and the butler more than likely knew that Mile was lying, but there was no way that either of them were of the mind to correct her, not in the slightest.

And thus, the wings of Leatoria's dreams were clipped before she could ever even take flight.

"The direct request has been completed with an A grade..."

After taking a good long look at the completion mark that Mavis had handed her, Felicia cast a suspicious glare over the four hunters of the Crimson Vow.

We should have gone to a different counter...

Despite Mavis's immediate regret, in truth, this was inevitable. Even if she had attempted to head to a different counter,

Felicia would have noticed and raised her hand to beckon them over. Apparently, she had independently decided that all matters regarding the Crimson Vow were in her care, and though Mavis was bold when it came to battle, such conflicts were not an area where she shone. There was no way that she would have been able to escape Felicia's call.

"So, you're telling me that the daughter of a noble, who was wasting away from a mysterious illness that even countless doctors could not identify, has suddenly made a full recovery in just a few days?"

The Crimson Vow exchanged glances.

"Well, I suppose that asking for details is against the rules," Felicia said, and began dutifully processing the form. "Here!"

With that, she slapped a leather sack down upon the counter.

Since it would be troublesome to shove clattering mountains of coins across the counter, and it would do no good to hand the group a large sum of money in front of the watchful eyes of other hunters, when there was a sum over a certain amount to be paid, it was delivered in a leather bag. There were enough dishonest hunters and those hurting for money that at least this much caution was warranted.

Of course, in practical terms, this was rather pointless. The fact that the money was inside of a leather bag was itself already an indication of the amount that might be inside. All the hunters here knew that the appearance of a leather bag meant that the amount was thirty gold pieces or more. Furthermore, the size of the bag changed based on the amount of coins that were inside, so anyone with a keen eye could guess the approximate amount at a glance.

At this point, all that putting the coins inside a bag truly did was avoid the general stir that would be caused by having heaps of loose coins passed around. As far as the guild was concerned, achieving at least that much was more than enough to merit the effort.

At times, however, Felicia liked to play a bit of a game.

Yes, at times she would pay out a small reward entirely in silver pieces and hand it over in a leather sack.

Of course, these bags were not free. Obtaining them cost the guild money. Such a ploy was inherently wasteful, but neither the guild master nor the other employees sought to pick a fight with her about it.

Why was that?

Naturally, it was, "because it's Felicia."

There was no one at this guild branch who dared stand up to her.

Even the hunters who were given these large sums of silver coins had no complaints. Getting their pay this way made them look good, so they were happy to be on the receiving end of Felicia's tricks. People would just think that luck had come their way.

Mavis began to peek inside the bag to check just how many gold coins they had been paid but stopped halfway and handed the bag to Mile... They had never actually discussed payment for the job with the baron, she realized, so there was no point in confirming the amount enclosed.

They could not ask Felicia about the amount, either. To do so would be to reveal to everyone that they had taken a job without confirming the reward first. Somehow, Mavis got the feeling that this would be an incredibly unwise thing to do.

And so, Mile took the bag and placed it into her inventory in such a way that the other hunters could clearly see it. Naturally, everyone assumed she was using normal storage magic. This way, they would know that pickpocketing the Crimson Vow's earnings was impossible and that the only way to steal those coins would be to have an armed showdown with the party as a whole.

The hunters, who had no interest in this, thought nothing of it, but Felicia, upon seeing how Mile and Mavis stored the money away without even confirming the amount that was inside the sack, quirked an eyebrow.

Do they not care how much money is inside? Or do they have that much faith in the guild? Heh! What fascinating people...

As she watched the retreating forms of the Crimson Vow, the corners of Felicia's mouth perked up, ever so slightly.

Waaaaaaaaaah!!!

Hell had just frozen over.

The hunters who were watching quaked in fear at the wicked grin upon Felicia's face. All but the veterans, who could tell that the smile upon Felicia's face was one of true joy...

Didn't I Say
to Make My Abilities
Average in the
Next Life?!

CHAPTER 53

The Avenger

"**A**RE THEY STILL FOLLOWING US?" asked Mavis.

"They are," Reina replied.

There had been no appealing jobs on the board that morning, so the Crimson Vow decided to head off to hunt orcs or ogres or the like. The extermination rewards and promotion points received for killing ogres were good, and they could earn a fair bit from the parts harvested from orcs.

Any normal party would be obliged to pack up and go after killing their first orc. It would take the full efforts of five or six hunters just to transport one of them. For the most part, the profits made off an orc were not proportional to the difficulty of killing one, combined with the effort of transporting them from the forest back into town.

However, this meant nothing to the Crimson Vow, who had Mile. Thus, they were able to rake in an absurd amount on their hunting excursions. Assuming that they did not limit themselves to just orcs and ogres, and kept their eyes peeled for other daily request items and materials that they could harvest and sell, the possibilities were endless. And so, they walked leisurely through the forest, attentive to every opportunity and random encounter that came their way.

In this situation, using location magic was no fun. Everyone was on their highest alert for prey, so there was no way that anyone would sneak up on them unawares. Therefore, Mile had not bothered with her magic—but Reina's uncanny sixth sense was still active... And it picked up on a suspicious presence behind them.

By Reina's report, their pursuer was alone, and moreover, they were following the party in a manner that was crude and amateurish, their presence completely exposed, so there was no point in Mile using her magic to scan for them. It wasn't good for either herself or her teammates to rely on this spell all the time, she figured.

And of course, if their opponent seemed to be an amateur, she figured nothing special would come of using magic anyway.

Seeing how Mile, who normally was the first to offer information, was saying nothing, the other three had a good guess as to what it was she was thinking. So none of them bothered to ask about her special skill.

"Honestly, we're just wasting time now," said Reina. "They aren't going to stop following us anytime soon, and we aren't going to get any hunting done while we're dragging them along. So..."

"Time to eliminate the threat, yes?" Pauline concluded.

No matter how much of an amateur this pursuer seemed to be, they might be armed with a bow and arrow or throwing spear, so getting into a battle with an ogre while such a person was at their backs would be ill-advised. They also could not rule out the possibility that the person's movements were intentional, calculated to only make it appear as though they were an amateur.

"We'll ambush them by that big tree," said Reina, pointing to a tree up ahead of them. The other three nodded.

Hm?

For a moment, their pursuer hesitated.

The targets had passed beneath the shadow of a tree, and the next moment, they had vanished. They should have appeared immediately on the other side of the tree, but even after several seconds, they were nowhere to be seen. Thinking this suspicious, the pursuer kept their distance from the tree, circling around to the other side. Still, no one.

"Wh-where'd they go?" the pursuer uttered unthinkingly.

Quickly, this individual moved toward the tree behind which the party had disappeared, looking wildly all around. However, there was nothing resembling a human figure.

"Where the hell did they...?"

"Here!"

"Eek!"

As Reina came leaping down from the boughs of the tree, the pursuer shrieked, startled, and fell on her backside...

It was a girl of around ten years old.

Mavis and Mile followed swiftly after Reina, leaping down and circling behind the girl. Between the three of them, she was surrounded.

While Pauline had been lifted up into the tree instantaneously with the rest of them by Mile's magic, she could not simply jump straight down the way that the others could. She was still busy clambering down the tree, carefully and cautiously.

At the time, Pauline had no way of knowing that later on, Mavis—an unusually displeased expression on her face—would lecture her about how "uncool" this was, and put her through the paces of learning the proper way of leaping down from up high.

"Who are you?"

"What is it you want from us?"

"I hope you can be honest with us, my dear lovely maiden."

"Almost there, almost... Aah! Oof, ow! My butt!"

Mavis scowled at Pauline, who had spoiled the mood, while for some reason the young girl was staring at Mavis, her face growing pink. Mile looked over the whole scene, amazed.

"This is almost surreal..."

"Now then, why exactly were you following behind us?"

"I-I wasn't! I just happened to be walking this way, too!"

The girl tried to play dumb, but there was no way that excuse was going to fly.

"Hm... A girl all alone in the forest, eh? Well, in that case, why were you so worried when you lost sight of us?"

"Nn..." Clearly unable think of a suitable response, the girl glared defiantly at Reina. "I'm here to make you pay for what you did to my big brother!"

"Huh...?"

Since the members of the Vow had met at the Hunters' Prep School, Reina had not once killed a single person, as far as they were aware. Though of course, whether or not she had secretly gone off and killed someone when they went around on their own on days off was another matter entirely...

In theory, the only time she had ever killed had been during the incident with the Crimson Lightning, but that had been many years ago. Though there was the possibility that this girl was the little sister of one of the many bandits they had captured and turned in during her time with the Crimson Vow, the idea of a bandit's little sister coming to take revenge was more or less unheard of. And honestly, it would be more appropriate for such a person to be thanking her for only capturing the bandits and turning them in alive.

Anyway, in that case, it would be incomprehensible for the girl to be glaring at Reina alone and not paying the slightest mind to the other three.

Even Reina thought this peculiar. "Why are you looking at me?! If there's anyone you should be glaring at, it's that black-hearted girl over there," she said, pointing to Pauline.

"Wh-wha-wha-wha?! What are you trying to say, Reina?!" Pauline blustered.

Like so often happened, the scene was rapidly falling apart.

As Reina and Pauline quarreled, Mavis continued to stare at

the little girl, without taking her eyes off of her. Mile observed the girl as well.

She appeared to be around ten years old, and was wearing not the leather guards of a hunter but the garb of a normal townsperson, and was equipped with nothing but a small knife strapped to her waist. Such a knife was a necessity when a civilian entered the forest alone. It would come in handy for cutting through brush and grass, and for driving off any goblins or kobolds who should appear.

And if an orc or some larger monster should happen upon her? This little lady had already resolved herself to enter the forest all alone, so she had to have resigned herself to such a possibility and how such a encounter might end.

She wore her hair uncovered, with no hood or bonnet. It was parted down the middle and wrapped into a bun on each side, very much like the style that you'd see drawn on any little girl in a manga who wore stereotypically Chinese clothes—though of course, such a style was unusual for these parts.

Her hair was brownish, and she had golden eyes... Somehow, Mavis and Mile were struck with a sense of déjà vu.

"It's all your fault!" the little girl shouted, as if irritated by the sudden commotion among the party. "My big brother, who always gave me big hugs, suddenly stopped hugging me one day! And when I went to hug him, he looked c-confused and pushed me away..."

The girl's eyes welled up with tears.

"Wh-what are you on about? I have no idea about anything like that!" Reina shouted, utterly bewildered.

Ah...

It was then that Pauline, Mavis, and Mile recalled exactly the "big brother" whom the little girl was referring to. Reina was the only one who had yet to catch on.

"What are you saying?! What kind of brute—what kind of fiend—could wound Chirel's heart so deeply and then pretend to know nothing about it?!"

"Chirel...? Who is that?"

At this rate, the conversation was never going to get anywhere. Reluctantly, Mile curled her index finger toward Reina in a signal, directing Reina to look at her face. Once she confirmed that Reina was looking toward her curiously, Mile stuck both of her index fingers up and pressed her closed fists to the sides of her head.

"What? What are you miming there? Why do you have your fingers up like horns—*oh*."

Reina flipped her head to the side and looked at the little girl again. Her gaze focused just past the girl's two hair buns.

"Ahh! Is that what's going on then? You should have just said so from the start!"

Indeed, Chirel was the young demon whom Reina had defeated in battle back during their tournament—and apparently, this little girl was his younger sister. Her hair was arranged the way that it was so that she could hide her horns and feign being a human.

Sounds like he's been too traumatized to let any girls hug him...

For any ladies who might hope to become his lover in the

future—as well as his sister, who appeared to have a bit of a brother complex—this was clearly a serious problem.

"I'm sorry..."

Now that she understood the situation fully, Reina apologized sincerely.

Truthfully, they had fought a fair and honest match, so Reina did not believe that she had truly done anything wrong, but there was no point in trying to explain such a thing to a little girl. For once, Reina decided to be the adult in the situation.

"Do you really think I'd let you go with just an apology?!"

"Y-you little brat! If you don't watch your step..."

"Whoa there, Nelly!" the other three admonished.

And just like that, Reina's mature attitude had vanished.

"Anyway, it seems like it's been a bit too brief a time between your brother getting home and you getting here, don't you think, little Merril?" Mile asked, biding their time until Reina could calm down.

According to what they had heard from the demons previously, Merril was the girl's name. However...

"Don't call me 'little Merril' like I'm some child! We demons mature far quicker than you humans!"

"Ah, my apology—uh, what? Wait, does that mean that you're even *younger* than you look?"

"Uh..." Merril was lost for words at this earnest question.

"Just how old are you, then?" asked Reina.

"Er..."

"I. Said. How. Old. Are. You?!"

"Err, se-seven...years old..." the girl finally confessed, unable to stand up to Reina's forceful questioning.

"What? You're still practically an infant then. And here I thought you were at least ten!"

"Wh-what do you mean 'an infant'?! I am a mature, beautiful lady!"

"Ah yes, sure, sure..." Reina flippantly waved off Merril's protest. It didn't look very cool to go around getting irritated at seven-year-olds, after all. "Anyway, Mile asked you a question just now. What do you have to say to that? How did you manage the round trip between here and the demon lands so quickly?" she pried.

"Lord Berdetice came to check on things and then carried the five whom you fought back home so that they could give their reports more quickly or something. And then, Lady Shelala heard what was going on and got interested, and she carried me back here. She's going to take me back home, too, of course, so she's up in the mountains waiting for me. She's going to carry you as well, so you need to come with me!"

She pointed straight at Reina.

"Ah..."

Now, the Crimson Vow understood. Apparently Merril thought that she could take Reina, the cause of her brother's trauma, back home with her and do something or other with her to dispel his newfound fears. The four could understand her feelings. However, understanding her plan and obediently going along with it were two different matters entirely. If she were to actually bring Reina back to demon country and try to bring her near the individual known as big brother Chirel...

Mile, Mavis, and Pauline were able to protest with absolute confidence:

"That would only make his trauma worse—irreparably so!"

"What the hell, guys?!" Reina protested, but they held firm.

"B-but then how do I get him back to normal? Ever since he met you, he won't hug me anymore, and sometimes he spaces out and starts mumbling weird things to himself, like 'that softness' and 'that sweet smell' and 'burned both my body and soul'— things like that..."

"Umm..."

The four were speechless again. Even Mile, in her infinite naivete, had managed to grasp what was really going on. Of course, so did Mavis and Reina.

And Pauline? Well, there was no way that *she* wouldn't know.

"Th-th-th-th-that means that..."

In a rare display, Reina was shaken. Everyone always treated her like she was a child or some sort of dangerous beast. Never before had anyone in her life seen her as a lady.

Truthfully, it was not as though there had been a total scarcity of interested suitors in her past, but Reina herself had never noticed them. Unwittingly, she had smashed completely through every single warning sign.

Yet she quickly remembered that the one who was interested in her was a child who appeared to be no more than twelve or thirteen. And if Merril was a seven-year-old who appeared to be ten, then...

"S-so exactly how old is your brother, then?"

"Huh? Well, he's sixteen, but..."

"Whaaaaaaat?!?!"

A seven-year-old who looked ten, and a sixteen-year-old who looked like a pre-teen? The Crimson Vow were all stunned.

Just what was with these demons and their ages?! the four wondered, but then again, it was not unusual for wild animals to go rapidly from infancy to self-sufficient maturity. For demons, this rapid growth probably continued from birth until around the age of ten to twelve, after which they matured more slowly—just like elves.

"W-we're the same age..." Reina muttered unconsciously.

For the people of this land, who were very much like the people of a continent called Europe in a place called Earth, a boy of around twelve or thirteen would be, on average, around 5 feet, 2 inches. So, at the very least, he was already taller than Reina, whose growth, by now, could only be assumed to be completely stunted.

He was fairly good-looking, as far as appearances went. The boy was gentlemanly, and as a demon, he had a natural aptitude for magic and was fairly strong. He was cool and handsome...

"Uh..." For a short while, Reina stood still, making curious sounds, her cheeks a bit red. But then...

"I won't go!"

Of course she wouldn't. First and foremost, there was no way that Reina, only sixteen years old, was prepared to go and marry herself off to some foreign non-human. She had a shining future as a B-rank hunter ahead of her. Plus, she was filled with (perhaps baseless) confidence that she would be able to snag an even more impressive man in the future.

Really, given her looks, combined with her magical ability, this was not necessarily an impossibility. As for her lack of development in *certain* areas... well, there were more than likely those in this world who had a preference for that sort of thing. Such as those within the Austien family.

And so, after some convincing, Merril listened as the Crimson Vow instructed her as to how to approach her brother and offer him some comfort.

"Ew, Reina, no! They're brother and sister! That's wrong, isn't it?!"

"I think it's fine, as long as they aren't anywhere near me! Plus it'd be funny, wouldn't it?"

"Just what do you think is wrong with that, Mile?"

"M-Mavis, don't tell me..."

"Hm? That was normal between me and my little brother Alan, too..."

"Whaaaaaaat?!"

"Right?"

"Y-you two..."

Things were falling apart again.

"I understand now. Taking you back home with me would be fruitless. You've given me quite a bit to consider, so I'll head back for now and see what I can do on my own."

She's really going to try it...

In the heat of the moment, Reina had begun to spew out all sorts of irresponsible instructions. A cold sweat now ran down her body. Mile, too, was a wee bit worried about how appropriate Reina's advice had been, but both Mavis and Pauline thought that her guidance had been perfectly normal and reasonable.

"I-I might have overdone it. You two are siblings, and you're only seven years old, so please forget about plan 2, plan 3, plan 5, and definitely plans 8 and 9!" Reina stammered, unable to bear the guilt weighing down on her conscience.

"Th-tha-tha-tha-that's right!" Mile added, looking a bit relieved, "Those are a little too extreme!"

"Hm? I mean the fact that I'm only seven doesn't really matter, does it? Though I guess it might be a little different if I were ten or older..."

And yet, there were Mavis and Pauline, the devils on her shoulder.

"That's right! Those are completely normal things for a healthy brother and sister to do together!"

"You said you're seven, but you still really do look older than ten!" Reina protested, but Merril was busy running the simulations in her head and did not hear her.

"Oh, that reminds me," Merril said. "Um, you there! Let's see, golden hair, tall... Yep, you must be the one."

This time, she was (unsurprisingly) pointing at Mavis.

"Huh? Me?" Mavis asked, puzzled.

"Reltobert, the swordsman who you fought against, said he wanted to see you again and asked me to extend an invitation for you to come along as well. Lady Shelala already agreed to carry you. She said you sounded interesting..."

"Whaaaaaaaat?!?!"

This day had turned out to be excellent training for the Crimson Vow's vocal cords.

When Merril fired a magical shot into the air as a signal, Shelala came down to meet her and Merril climbed onto her back.

"I feel like I've learned a lot today, so I guess I'll leave things here. Let me warn you now, though, if I don't get any results from the things you told me to try, I'm coming back for you! You still haven't properly taken responsibility!" she said, before patting Shelala on the neck to give her the signal that she was ready to ride.

"If you ever have any other interesting stories to tell, please call on me!" said Shelala.

"Shut up!" Reina roared back. "Anyway, it's not like we were the ones who called you here in the first place!"

Shelala tittered at Reina's indignation, taking off into the sky with Merril on her back.

It should go without saying that Mavis was still on the ground.

"Seriously, what the heck was all that about?"

"I'm so tired..."

Reina and Mavis were ready to turn to mush. Pauline, however, seemed displeased.

"Why didn't anyone come asking after *me?!* I mean, it's not like I want any demons fawning over me, but still, Reina and Mavis got *something*. Where's *mine?!* Just what was *my* battle partner thinking?!"

"........."

Pauline's opponent was the man who'd tasted the flames of hell on his lower body, thanks to her "hot" magic.

It wouldn't happen, the other three thought. *It absolutely, positively, would never happen...*

At least on this occasion, Pauline being asked after was a complete impossibility.

"Let's go home already," Mile suggested wearily.

She received no objections, and so, with a record zero catches for the day, the Crimson Vow went tottering back to the capital.

CHAPTER 54 |

Fairy Hunting

TODAY WAS A REST DAY for the Crimson Vow. It was not the rest day that came once every six days, as defined by the calendar, but rather a day that the girls themselves had decided to take off.

There was no reason for everyone in the world to have the same days off, after all, and it meant that the dining halls and shops weren't completely packed once a week. So the girls took their rest days as they pleased, as job circumstances allowed.

Indeed, for the next five days, the Crimson Vow would not be traveling as a group but would each go off on their own to do whatever they liked. No matter how much they liked their fellow party members, or how well they got along, it was important to have a little private time now and then.

I think it's somewhere around here...

Based on information that she had been gathering here and there, Mile now found herself loitering in a dense forest near a small village some distance away from the capital. When Mile was completely alone, she could cover even sizeable distances in a very short time, thanks to her immense speed.

"Nanos!"

YES, MA'AM!

"Let's start around here."

ROGER THAT!

With that, the nanomachines set to work, and soon the ground began to rise up before Mile, the dirt wriggling about until a shape materialized.

It was a winged girl, around 20 centimeters tall—a perfectly accurate scale figure of a fairy that Mile had designed and colored herself, based on information she had gleaned from illustrated references and the tales told by elders. The nanomachines had helped, of course; they knew what the genuine article looked like and so had made minute adjustments to bring the figure closer to the real thing, based obliquely on Mile's guidance.

As Mile had decided from the start that she would rather not ask the nanomachines directly, the tiny beings were left to dither about on their own. Though they wished that Mile would be a bit more assertive in utilizing their services, they were of course aware of the reason why she did not, and as they found her reasoning to be fair, they respected her judgment.

For some reason, this figure's fairy wings were tattered and its clothing stained with something red like blood.

Flap flap.

And then, it moved. Apparently it was not just a figure but a golem.

SOMETHING LIKE THIS, THEN?

"Yes, that's perfect! A perfect storm!"

This punchline was one that Mile had been holding onto since her previous life. Though she had ended said life without once getting to use it on anyone other than her own family, thankfully, she now had the nanomachines here to appreciate her humor.

Mile then turned over the tiny fairy golem, which was a size smaller than Cham Huau from *Aura Battler Dunbine*, and attached a fine, strong, and nearly invisible thread to its back. It was the thread that she had previously crafted to use as fishing line.

"Liftoff!"

"Məh!"

Reading Mile's thoughts, the nanomachine-controlled golem fluttered up at the sound of the control word.

"Golem, Golem... Gowappa 5?" Mile muttered something incomprehensible to herself.

When it came to matters that only the nanomachines would know about, Mile strictly restrained herself from relying too much on their information, just as in her jobs with the Crimson Vow. However, she had also allowed herself an exception to that rule; namely, in cases where someone's life was in danger or when it would not trouble or have an ill effect on other people and was merely for her own amusement rather than personal gain. In these cases, it was okay to work alongside the nanomachines now and then.

Plus, she had realized that if she went too long without calling on them, they would grow peevish and begin inventing reasons to make conversation.

"It's no use..."

No matter how many different places she tried, the results were the same. Each time, she would set the fairy-shaped golem flying about on its string while she hid beneath the trees, the spool that the thread was attached to in her hand. She would then move to a different place and repeat the same experiment.

From the moment that Mile first learned that fairies existed in this world, it had become her life's goal to meet one.

Apparently, in the past it had been relatively commonplace to encounter a fairy, and as a result, various tales still lingered in the cultural recollection—stories of lost little children to whom the fairies gave honey and snacks before guiding them back to the outskirts of their village or of fairies who offered troubled villagers the solutions to their problems...

However, it seemed that those who would capture and sell the fairies, or try to imprison them and put on display, had begun to appear more and more frequently. As a result, the fairies gradually stopped appearing in front of humans altogether. Yet it did not appear that they had all been annihilated in one fell swoop by some calamity—merely that they had stopped showing themselves to humans, from which it followed that there still must be some possible way to draw them out. Perhaps by a method like the one Mile was currently trying...

Just as the sun was beginning to set and Mile started to consider packing up and going home, a single fairy appeared.

"My, my! What's wrong, dearest? You're covered in blood! Oh, how dreadful! Your lovely wings... Has some human done this to you? Come, let's get you back to the secret nest..."

It was as if she had come out of nowhere.

The fairy called out to the fairy-shaped golem, her wings fluttering as she approached the unsteady thing and put her arms around it in concern, trying to support its weight. Just then...

Grab!

"Eeek!!"

The fairy let out a cry of shock as the golem suddenly clamped both its arms and legs around her.

"Wh—?! Let me go! We're both going to fall! You're safe now! Please calm down!"

Apparently, she still thought that the other creature was an injured fellow fairy.

The golem's back then opened with a snap, and four more arms extended from the opening, latching tight onto the fairy's limbs. With this, the fairy finally realized that this was not in fact one of her kin but some kind of unfamiliar spectre, which had merely taken on the form of one of her fellow fae. She went pale, and her mouth opened wide.

"Eeeeeeeeeeeeeeeeek!!!"

Mile then began to reel in her spool, drawing both golem and fairy toward her.

She knew about lure fishing from her previous life, and so, based on those same principles, she had decided to create a fairy-shaped lure. She would use a golem masquerading as an injured fairy to draw a concerned fairy in and capture them.

It was brutish. There was no doubt that this would push the standing of humans even lower in the eyes of all fairies.

"S-someone help! Don't eat meeeee!!!"

Given its many limbs, and the fact that it moved as though drawn in by a string, the fairy seemed to assume that this was some sort of spider-like monster mimicking a fairy. Any creature that would go to the trouble of mimicking its prey could have one of only two goals:

1) Eating it.
2) Using venom to paralyze it and using its body to spawn its eggs.

There were no other plausible explanations. Seeing how the creature was drawing her in alive, showing no signs of wanting to kill her, despite a successful capture, the fairy could not imagine her fate as anything but number two—a fate more deplorable than death. And so she once again began to scream at the top of her lungs.

"Geeeeeeeeee!!!! SOMEONE HELP MEEE! ANY-OOOOOOOONNNNNEE!!!"

As the fairy drew nearer, half-maddened in fear, Mile called out to try to calm her.

"There's no need to worry. I'm not a monster, I'm a human. So, there's no need for you to..."

Halfway through Mile's speech, the fairy suddenly stopped screaming.

"A human?"

"Yes, I'm a human!"

"GYAAAAAAAAAAAAAAAH!!!"

After a scream even more desperate than her first, the fairy suddenly went quiet. Thinking this curious, Mile peeked down at her to see that she was foaming at the mouth, her eyes blank. Apparently, as far as the fairy was concerned, compared to having eggs implanted in her by an arachnid monster and being eaten alive by its newly hatched young, capture at the hands of a human was a far more gruesome fate.

Just how afraid of humans are *fairies?!?!* Mile wondered.

Enough that they never showed themselves in front of humans, at the very least.

"Oh! It was j-just a dream..."

Millelina, the fairy girl, awoke with a start, patting her chest.

"Oh, what a terrible dream that was... I thought that I'd been captured by some monster pretending to be a fairy, when it actually turned out to be a human! What a nightmare... Honestly, that's enough of a nightmare for a lifetime..."

She was drenched in sweat, but now that she realized it was only a dream, a smile appeared on Millelina's face.

"I'm *ever* so sorry to inform you, but unfortunately this is *not* a dream..."

Millelina looked up reflexively at the voice to see her entire view obscured by a giant human face.

"*GYAAAAAAAAAAAAAAAH!!!*"

"Oh, she fainted again..."

Mile looked troubled.

"Oh! It was j-just a dream..."

Millelina, the fairy girl, awoke with a start, patting her chest.

"Oh, what a terrible dream that was..."

"I'm *ever* so sorry to inform you, but unfortunately this is *not*—"

"*GYBADADADAFRASDHAHAAH!*"

"Oh, there she goes again... All right, that's enough already!!"

This could only go on for so long. If they kept at it, before Mile knew it, it would be night. So that they could move on to the next step while it was still light out, Mile desperately shook Millelina awake.

"...so, that's what's going on."

"You *didn't* capture me just to sell me or put me on display?"

"Of course not! I really just wanted to talk to you..."

Millelina was still terrified upon waking, but after Mile rambled on to her about the whole scheme, Millelina finally seemed to calm down a bit.

"You aren't going to steal my liver or my *shirikodama*?"

"What do you think I am, a kappa?!"

Apparently, there were a lot of strange rumors being flung about in the fairy world. It was tantamount to slander.

"In the human world, that's something that's said to be done by a type of fairy!"

Mile was not lying. Such stories were told back in Japan. It was also true that kappas were said to be fallen gods, or else a type of fairy. However, Millelina, upon hearing this, shouted in dismay. "Wh-wh-wh-wha?! What a horrid rumor! That's slander!!!"

"I'm the one who should be saying that!!"

About ten minutes later, the two began speaking to one another again.

"Anyway, who I'd really like to speak to is a chief or some other elder—whoever would have the clearest recollection of details from the past. So, if you would just take me to your village..."

"As if I would ever do such a thing! Perhaps you aren't interested in our livers or our souls, but the fact still remains that human have captured and tried to sell us before!"

"No, but I'm telling you that... Wait, 'tried to'? Fairies have never actually been sold?"

Some decades ago, many wicked merchants and other scoun-drels had come around to hunt the fairies. Before that, Mile had been told, humans and fairies had a peaceful coexistence... She had assumed that fairies, who, unlike now, had once trusted hu-mans, had been captured in droves.

"We were captured, yes, many of us. But for some reason, whenever night fell, the wagons or tents where our captured brothers and sisters were being kept would catch on fire and the captured fairies would vanish. And then, for some reason, when our captors dragged themselves back to town, they would find that their homes and businesses, and the homes and warehouses of the rich and influential people who had placed orders for fair-ies, had all been burned to the ground. For some reason...

"It would seem that, soon enough, the humans who would come to capture us stopped appearing at all. *For. Some. Reason.* Though, well, it is also true that we stopped even showing our faces to humans, anyway..." Millelina finished with a sneer.

Surely enough, fairies, who were tiny and could fly with nary a sound, would probably make the ultimate spies or terrorists.

Ah! "You should never look down on perilous pixies"... Hm... "Fairly fatal fabulously flying fairies"...? No, that's no good. Ugh, I think I'm in a bit of a slump here...

Mile could not come up with a single decent pun.

"Even if you torture me, I shall never give up the location of our hidden nes—"

"I see! So the fairies' dwelling is hidden by some means, you say? Thank you very much for that information."

"Uh..."

Millelina suddenly went silent, as she realized that she had unintentionally given up some classified intel.

"Th-that's... A-anyway, no human would ever be able to see through the magical wall that we've all conjured!"

"Mm-hmm...concealing magic, then? Then your nest would be found somewhere with a hint of magic or where the surrounding scenery doesn't look quite right..."

"Wha-wh-wh-wha?!"

"D-damn!" Millelina's mouth flapped stupidly. Yet she just kept giving up more and more information. "The forty-seven members of our clan shall never be brought to our knees by anyone!"

"Oh, go on then... Your population is forty-seven, you say?"

"Aaaaaaaaaargh!!"

Realizing how much vital information she had now given away, Millelina crumbled.

"B-but, we still have a trump card! Miss Wintergale! She's so splendid in combat, they call her the 'Battle Fairy'!"

"Mm-hmm, so there's one opponent to be cautious of, and, judging by her name, she uses blizzard-type combat magic..."

"Gaaaaaaaaaaaaaaaaaaah!!!"

Was this level of idiocy common among fairies? Or was this a special characteristic of this individual, Millelina? Even the other fairies would probably think that a girl who was also known as the "Electric Fairy," would at least be a little bit brighter...

So Mile thought, but it did not seem that she would be getting any more information out of the girl.

Still, now that it was beginning to grow dark, finding a hidden village was going to prove difficult. There was only one thing to do now...

Nanos!

Here we are!

The fairy-shaped golem from before, which had remained unmoving for some time, suddenly began to warp in shape, changing color.

"Wh...?"

Millelina was stunned at the sight.

The golem was now the spitting image of Millelina.

"How's the voice sample?"

"*Save me! Save me!*" the golem replied, in a voice that sounded exactly like Millelina's.

"Ngah! Aaah! Graaaaaaaaah..."

Ignoring Millelina, who was trembling and red in the face, Mile ordered, "Liftoff!"

"Rasah!"

With that, the golem once again took flight, a string attached to its back...

"Now, what to do with you all?"

Night had fallen, and Mile now had forty-seven fairies, bound, incapacitated, and rolling on the ground around her.

The one called Wintergale had fainted the moment her dear friend's back popped open and four extra arms came out.

"Well, I guess there's no point in me trying to track down the fairies' 'hidden nest' now."

It was the catch of a lifetime. She had gotten bite after bite on her cast-out line. Mile was quite pleased with her fishing prowess.

"Oh, I'd better take off the sound barrier..."

So that they would not interfere with her fishing, Mile had been keeping all of the captured fairies inside of a sound-dampening field. The fairies were desperately flapping their mouths, but no sound came out. However, when she removed the barrier...

"What are you going to do to us?!"

"Release us at once, you fiendish human!"

"Do whatever you want to me, but please, spare my wife and daughter..."

"I'm gonna burn ya! I'm gonna burn ya to the ground!!!"

"Dieeeeeeeeeeeeeeeeeeeee!!!"

They were noisy. Incredibly noisy.

"Come on, guys, I already told you I don't have any bad intentions. I just wanted to talk a bit, and I thought that we might be able to make friends."

"Who the hell are you kidding?!?!?!" came a chorus.

Seeing how the fairies raged at her, despite her friendly demeanor, Mile was speechless.

Could you blame them, though? Suddenly capturing and restraining someone was not something that anyone who aimed to be a friend would do...

A short while later, after Mile promised the fairies that she would let them go as soon as they heard her out, that she would not force them to talk, and that she would tell no one that she had encountered them, the fairies finally began to calm down and grow quiet.

She decided to withdraw her tent from her inventory and move the fairies inside so that they could have a more leisurely conversation. Even the fairies were a bit stunned to see how casually she produced the item.

"Might I get you to loosen these bindings a bit?" asked an old man who appeared to be the eldest of the group, most likely the village elder. Of course, Mile could not comply with his request. No matter how small they were, fairies were still quick, and fairly decent at magic.

Honestly, Mile was not worried for her own safety. She merely worried that if she had to guard herself against a simultaneous attack from all the fairies and recapture them all at once in this dark and cramped tent, she might end up squashing them in an instant.

When she explained as much, the fairies fell quiet again.

"Come now. This'll be over soon! I really just have a few questions to ask you all! So please, try and bear it for just a little while longer," she said, before silently placing a request with the nanomachines.

Would you be able to block the fairies' magic until we're finished talking?

IF YOU, LADY MILE, AUTHORIZATION LEVEL 5, SO DIRECT IT, THEN NATURALLY THAT INSTRUCTION SHALL

BE PRIORITIZED. DUE TO THE SMALL SIZE OF FAIRIES'
BODIES, THEIR THOUGHT PULSE EMISSIONS ARE WEAK,
AND THUS THEY ARE UNABLE TO PRODUCE ANY LARGE-
SCALE MAGIC TO BEGIN WITH, BEYOND THEIR FLIGHT
CAPABILITIES.

That much put her at ease. No matter how weak their magic
might be, it would be irritating to have the tent set ablaze, and they
still might be able to burn through the strings that bound them.

Then, if you would, please!

ROGER THAT!

"Now, I'll cut to the chase. What I would like to ask you
all about is the matter of an ancient civilization, information
of which should have been passed down through your various
generations..."

"Hm?"

Surprise spread across the face of the fairy Mile presumed to
be the village elder.

"Y-you know about the Land of the Gods...?"

Behind the elder, other fairies were fussing that they couldn't
produce fire or magic, but the old man ignored them.

"Yes. So far, I've already heard about it from an elf and an elder
dragon. So, I know the general facts, but I desperately needed to
know if there was any new information I could gather from the
stories passed down among the fairies..."

Hearing this, the elder was stunned even further.

Indeed, an elf was one thing, but he would have never thought that he would hear of a human who could have such a conversation with elder dragons.

"I see. In that case, I suppose I can tell you—"

"Chief!"

"Chief, no!"

Countless fairies tried to stop the elder, but he kept them in check.

"There's no point in trying to keep it a secret. On the contrary, I believe that this is a tale that the gods and our ancestors wished us to tell. This tale is merely one that has been lost among humans, whose generations turn over so quickly. I believe it is a joyous thing, if these stories may find life once again among the humans."

"........."

And so, the elder told his story—the story that had been passed down among the fairies, whose lifespans were far, far longer than humans'.

Mile learned almost nothing.

The elder's tale was scarcely any different from that which Mile had already heard from Doctor Clairia, the elf, and the elder dragon, Berdetice. No, in fact, compared to theirs, this story was perhaps even more lacking in information.

Well, it didn't really matter. Even just finding out how much information had been passed down among the fairies was enough to satisfy the aim of this expedition, after all. Plus, she had set aside her whole five-day break for this endeavor, so to have achieved her goal on the very first day was a bonus.

Besides, "fishing for fairy friends" had been incredibly fun... even if it was probably a nightmare for the fairies.

Indeed, having gotten her fill of an enjoyable excursion, Mile was satisfied.

Then, suddenly, Mile saw before her...

A fairy... larva?

Indeed, it was a larval fairy—or rather, a young fairy girl.

"Would you like to come with me, as a pe—er, a mascot? I can feed you delicious food, as much as you like! Well, not so much that you get too fat to fly, of course..."

There was a devilish gleam in Mile's eye.

"Huh?" asked the girl. "Oh, wh-what should I do?"

Tempted by the promises of endless delicious food, the little girl was troubled. However...

A sudden roar came from the crowd. "Do you really think we'd let you do thaaaaaaaaaaaaaaaaat?!?!?!"

"And also, just what exactly was it you were about to say?! 'Pe—'? What is 'pe—'?"

"Uh, well, th-that was..."

"You were about to say 'pet,' weren't yooooouuuuuu?!"

Pe—Mascot Acquisition: Failed.

"All right, I'll let you all go now. Thank you for everything."

"Huh?"

The fairies appeared surprised. Apparently, they had not actually expected Mile to honor her promises.

She understood why. If she were to take all these fairies, whom she had already captured, back to town with her to sell, she could make a fortune so great that her children and grandchildren could live in the lap of luxury for their whole lives. There was no human who would let such a catch slip right through their fingers.

Mile was doing a bit of thinking as well.

I really have done something a bit cruel, haven't I? Seeing a monster shaped like their friends suddenly break open its back would have to be rather traumatic, one might suppose...

A "bit" cruel this was not. A *bit* cruel would be...

I guess I've probably given them one more strike against humans as well... This is bad! This is really bad! If it's true that I, who wanted to strive for a newfound peace with the fairies, have done exactly the opposite... I just couldn't bear it!

These were Mile's thoughts as she busied herself undoing the fairies' bonds, when suddenly, an idea popped into the back of her head. Abruptly, she put the tent back into her inventory.

"Illusion magic, dispel!" she said suddenly, performing an incantation inside her head...or rather, giving instructions to the nanomachines.

Refract and diffuse the light! Gather moisture into ice! Neutralize gravity and maintain formation...

Yes, it was a callback from the far, distant past—Mile's Goddess Form!!

The condensation in the air froze, taking form as two pure white wings of crystallized ice sprouting from Mile's back. A halo of light floated over her head, and light particles glistened all around her...

"Wh—?! I-It can't be! The All-Mother..."

Hm? No? Not a goddess then?

Mile was a little surprised at the elder's utterance, but whether they thought of her as a goddess or as this so-called All-Mother, it made little difference.

"Yes, it is I. I have come to assure myself that you, my children, are still telling our tales of yore, and that you are leading happy lives. It brings me ease to see you all in good health. Well then, be of good cheer!"

Whoosh!

With those special words, Mile's form vanished into magical light. And with that, she ever so stealthily left the clearing behind.

Perfect! she thought. *Now they'll think that those horrid things were the work of the E-Ferario or the All-Mother or something like that—and their hatred of humans won't spread! It's a little different from my plan to blame it on the goddess, but everything turned out okay in the end!*

And so Mile returned home, a triumphant spring in her step...

"Oh my, *oh my*... I can't believe that the All-Mother herself is watching over us!"

The village elder and all the other fairies were so moved they were trembling.

"Still, just when we thought that there might actually be a human who keeps her promises, it turned out to be the All-Mother. I guess there's no mistaking it—there's no such thing as a trustworthy human in this world. This is all the more reason that we must be cautious. That was probably why the All-Mother did as she did, to send us a warning..."

And so, a rare and precious opportunity to raise the value of humans in the eyes of fairies went utterly wasted.

Didn't I Say
to Make My Abilities
Average in the
Next Life?!

CHAPTER 55 |

The Four Stooges (Minus One)

"So, it seems like Mile's gone off on some mysterious solo mission for the duration of our break," said Reina, her eyes on Mavis and Pauline. "But I'm assuming that you two don't have any particular plans, do you?"

The two of them shook their heads.

Five days was far too short for either of them to make a round trip back to their home country of the Kingdom of Tils, so they hadn't even considered trying it. As it was their first time in this country, there was nothing around that they even knew of to do on their own.

Truthfully, though the idea behind taking this vacation was to give each of them time to do things alone, Reina had had it in mind to go out and do something fun with the four of them, so she was a bit stunned to hear Mile say, "I'm leaving the capital for a bit. There's something I need to do."

At that point, though, it was already too late to take back her original proposal, and given the fact that it was so rare for Mile to express her own desires, Reina figured that it was more important to respect her wishes and left the matter be.

Anyway, the four of them were always together. They could go and have fun together another time.

"Well, there was something that *I* was thinking that we could use these five days to try out."

"What? You mean without Mile?"

Pauline's surprise was to be expected. The Crimson Vow was a four-person set, with Mile at the middle.

It was true that Mavis was the official party leader, and that Reina always took the reins, but somehow or other, deep in their hearts, they all felt that Mile was the heart of the party. Her exceptional abilities aside, she was something like a mascot, or unifying force at the core of their solar system...

"That's right. I think we all rely on her too much anyway, so every once in a while we ought to try and see what things are like without Mile, for the sake of our own futures..."

Indeed, though they lived carefree lives now, there was no telling when something might happen. Obviously there was the chance that one of them might die on the job, but losing members to illnesses and other circumstances was to be expected in the life of a hunter as well. The Crimson Vow in particular had a particularly large variety of "other circumstances" that could affect them.

Though Reina, the Lord of Rain and Thunder—er, solitary wanderer—was a non-issue, Pauline worried after her family's shop, which her mother and younger brother were working so hard to keep afloat. As for Mavis, she was still head over heels for her father and elder brothers. And then there was the reality that they each had their own dreams: Pauline of owning her own business and Mavis of becoming a knight. Sooner or later, there was sure to be talk of marriage...which was a possibility for Reina, too. In short, none of them were likely to remain hunters for their entire lives.

And of course, there was Mile, the true problem child.

Though she was currently neglecting her duties, she was in fact the land-owning head of a noble household. While she held no interest in either her rank or her estate, Mile was still very young. It was possible that one day she would come to gain some awareness of the duty she owed her family name, besmirched now but held high for generations by her mother and grandfather and the generations before them, as well as her responsibility toward the people who lived on her lands. Plus, it seemed that the royal family had some interest in what became of Mile...

It was all too evident that one day the Crimson Vow would have to disband, or else resign themselves to having to recruit new members. Should that happen, they could not be accustomed to letting their every pattern revolve around one specific individual. So thought Reina, who got the feeling that, of the four, she would be spending the longest portion of her life as a hunter.

"I guess you're right," said Mavis. "I approve, then. Pauline, what do you think?"

"I agree too. We really do rely a little too much on Mile..."

Thus, it was decided that the three of them would try doing something on their own.

Later on, deep within the forest...

"I don't see anything around here. Mile, would you use your search ma... Ah." Reina trailed off and continued to walk.

"I'm getting hungry..."

"I think we could probably stop to eat now. Mile, would you take some... Ah."

"Oh."

None of them had thought to bring any food with them.

Since they normally had access to Mile's storage space, full of fresh fish, meat, vegetables, bread, and fruit, even when they went out on expeditions, no one ever paid any mind to preparing food for their trips. Now that they thought about it, they hadn't brought any cookware or tableware, either. And naturally there was no camping gear...

Well, they had planned to return within the day. However, the three still should have made at least the minimum of gear preparations, just in case. One never knew when something might happen in the forest, after all.

"........."

This was bad.

They all silently agreed.

They had become far too accustomed to a life of convenience.

Negligence. Over-reliance. An inhibited ability to sense coming dangers. Even depravity.

Those were the greatest killers of hunters, far greater foes than even the monsters they stalked.

About two hours later, the three girls dined on a meal of tree fruits, a jackalope they had finally snagged, and plain water. Given that the amount of time they would be out only warranted eating one meal, they could have simply packed some jerky and hardtack, in which case, they would not have needed to waste so much time on acquiring and preparing food. And of course, if Mile had been there, she would have simply pulled out an already-prepared meal...

Reina shook her head wildly at the thought.

No! After the members of the Crimson Lightning were killed, I lived all alone. Properly alone! This—this weakness is not what Crimson Reina is all about!

Reina was appalled at her own degraded condition, but Mavis and Pauline's concern was not nearly as grave. Their travels with the Crimson Vow were the first time in their lives that they had lived as hunters, so they had been entirely spoiled by the convenience that was traveling with Mile. On top of this, they lacked the innate awareness of danger that Reina had. Without any other comparable experiences, it was more than likely they had come to believe that the status quo was the usual way of things.

This is bad. This is bad this is bad this is bad this is bad!!!

Putting herself aside, Reina was overwhelmed with a sense of fear at Mavis's and Pauline's limited independence as hunters.

At this rate, they would never be able to make it in any party that did not contain Mile. This was even more serious than she previously thought.

"I see one! There's an orc moving all alone—a fairly small one!"

"This should be a breeze. We've got room to work, so try not to lower its sales value too much, okay?"

As always, Mavis was the quickest to spot their prey.

Even without Mile, an orc was basically small fry as far as the Crimson Vow was concerned. Accordingly, Reina had decided to make "killing something without lowering its sales value too much" the topic of their special practice.

Quietly, Reina and Pauline incanted their spells.

"Ice Javelin!"

"Bl—inding Mist!"

The orc stood still, shocked at the spear of ice that had just materialized from thin air and pierced into its side. A red mist began to float around its face, and the orc started to rub its eyes.

The word that Pauline had started to say was "Blessing," which would have indicated a type of healing magic. However, the spell had turned out to be an attack on her opponent. That was Pauline for you—when she invented a new spell, it was a tricky one.

Mavis took advantage of the opening to leap out from the trees, slicing the orc's head off in one fell swoop. She was not using her True Godspeed Blade, of course. Special techniques were best saved for special times. Furthermore, an orc that was standing stock-still and rubbing its eyes was not even worthy of being called an enemy. Of course, this was only possible because of Mavis's skill and the help of the mysterious blade that Mile had provided; it was not something that could easily be achieved by just anyone. Orcs' necks were thick, and their bones were sturdy.

"That felt good. We didn't put a single scratch on the parts that sell for the most, and we didn't cause any damage to the environment. Ten out of ten. Now, Mile, if you would..."

"Ah..."

Of the three girls assembled there, two of them were slight, waifish mages.

Even a small orc could be estimated to weigh just shy of 300 kilograms.

And there was no one there who could use storage magic.

"C-can we rest for a bit?" Pauline wailed.

"We just took a break a little while ago!" Reina rebuked.

"B-but isn't it more efficient to take regular breaks, rather than pushing ourselves?" Mavis argued.

As it would have been utterly impossible for them to carry back the entire orc, they had taken with them only the ears, as proof of elimination, and as many of the most valuable parts as they could carry.

Even without the head, hands, bones, and internal organs, which no one would care to eat, the orc still weighed around 200 kilograms. No matter how hard they pushed themselves, they would only be able to carry around half of that. They took only the good portions of the flesh and then the heart, liver, and the tongue. All this was divided up among the three, with Pauline and Reina both taking far smaller portions of the load than Mavis. Everyone had their strengths and weaknesses, so even Mavis could not complain about this.

"After we get this back to town, should we go back and pick up the rest?" Mavis asked.

"........."

Reina and Pauline answered her with silence.

"Well, I mean, I just thought I'd ask! You don't have to look at me with those dead eyes... Plus, I'm sure that by the time we got back, all the good stuff would have already been eaten up by small animals and other monsters, anyway!" she hurriedly added.

Still, the hollow look in Reina and Pauline's eyes did not change.

The day after they hunted the orc, the three girls decided to take a rest.

Given that they were already in the midst of a full-party five-day break, this was of no consequence.

However, the reason they were resting was that their bodies were so sore they could not move. That was all there was to it.

And then, the third day came.

"Let's do this! But this time, no orcs!"

Mavis and Pauline nodded emphatically.

"All we're going to gather is herbs that sell at a high price and are easy to transport. If we hunt anything living, it's only going to be extermination targets, and all we'll be taking back is proof of the kill. And we'll be camping out tonight."

Once again, there were nods all around.

Reina knew that they had sufficient combat strength between them, and her assessment was apt. If they got into a battle with other humans, or even against a monster, the Crimson Vow could put on an impressive display. Even without Mile.

They had Reina, the fire-magic wielder. They had Pauline, who had not only healing and support magic but also combat spells and a few other fairly dirty tricks at her disposal. And they had Mavis, whose abilities with a sword rivaled those of a B-rank hunter and could even surpass those of an A-rank, at least for a short time and provided she had her pills. Truly, now that she had her "spirit"-powered sword techniques, the Wind Edge and the magus killer Anti-Magic Blade, Mavis had perhaps been getting a bit carried away as of late.

Together they had the strength of a C-rank party twice their number. Even if they found themselves surrounded by ogres, they could prevail... It would not even be inappropriate to say that they already had the strength of a B-rank party.

Even the guild was aware of this fact, but unfortunately, under the current rules, there were still a minimum number of contribution points and years spent as a member of one's current rank that were required for promotion, and as it stood, the Crimson Vow, who had only a scant amount of time as C-rank hunters under their belts, did not yet qualify to take the rank promotion exam. Even though they *were* accumulating those contribution points at breakneck speed...

At any rate, what the girls needed now was not battle training, but "Mile-free" training.

This was the conclusion that Reina had come to.

"I think it's probably about time to start making camp, then?" said Mavis, seeing that the sun had already begun to set.

"You're right."

Reina nodded in agreement, thinking that it was about time to stop hunting for the day anyway.

The three searched for an appropriate place to set up their tent. Though we say tent here, if they were to carry a complete set of thick and sturdy hides and pelts treated with moisture-repellant, along with wooden poles and sticks of the appropriate strength and size, it would be heavy, awkward, and generally a huge pain. Carrying something like that along with them would mean that they could carry almost nothing else and would not be able to take any gathered materials or prey back with them.

Thus, they had decided only to roll up some waterproof cloths and hides, and use the trees themselves, as well as any sticks they found around them to make a shelter just substantial enough to stave off any wind and rain.

Given that the tent packed away in Mile's storage (read: inventory) could be stored and withdrawn without having to be put together each time, regardless of its volume or weight, it was intricate and painstakingly assembled, but there was no one else in their group who had that capability. The tent materials and tools that the girls were using were ones rented from the guild. Mile had no clue that her friends would have gone off to do any work during their vacation and had left all of the gear stored away in her storage (read: inventory), so it couldn't be helped.

The guild kept a certain amount of spare equipment in stock to lend to financially-strapped newbie hunters and for use during emergency requests placed with the guild. For the most part, these were pieces of used equipment donated by hunters who had swapped their gear out for newer things, items left behind by hunters who had died, and secondhand goods from other various avenues, but given that they were loaned out for next to nothing, they were still a blessing.

And then...

"How is it dark already?!"

"Oh, come on! I just gotta get this part—get in there..."

Not only had it taken them quite a bit of time to locate a place to set up that would keep them safe even in a sudden change of weather, the Crimson Vow, whose members had been used to having all of the necessary framing parts packed away in storage, even before Mile had begun carrying the fully assembled tent, were fighting an uphill battle, wholly unprepared to be constructing a tent from scratch.

Reina had some previous experience, but Mavis and Pauline were more or less at a loss. By the time they somehow or other managed to rig a tent together, it was already completely dark out.

"........."

Dinner preparations went off without a hitch.

They had packed along some hard tack and jerky just in case, but thankfully they had also snagged some jackalopes and birds along the way, so that became the centerpiece of their meal.

Most normal hunters would avoid eating what they had caught in order to save money, but the Vow were not hurting for cash, and without Mile, their transport abilities were relatively diminished, lower even than those of most other parties, so they decided to just eat their catches on site.

The cooking itself went favorably, thanks to the use of magic, with Reina to ignite the fire and Pauline to oscillate the water molecules to make them boil and so forth. This was one area where they were not lacking without Mile around. Fire magic was only useful for lighting the logs, anyway. Applying magical fire directly to the food would not cook the meat well; the outside would be charred and the middle left raw.

"Mile, the spice ple... Ah."

"........."

"Um, I could use my hot magic to—"

"I'm good."

"Never mind, then."

On the evening of the fourth day of their break, the Crimson Vow arrived back at the capital. They had managed to bring back a relatively large amount of slightly pricey medicinal herbs, a fair bit of sellable prey, and the inedible parts of prey marked for extermination in the daily requests as trophies. For two days and one night's work, the outcome was not bad at all...for a normal party.

However, the three had become accustomed to their earnings from when Mile was around. Their clearly *abnormal* earnings.

They collected their reward, divvied up the pay, and then stared at the coins piled in their hands.

"........."

They had to do better so that they could survive and call themselves competent C-rank hunters, even without Mile's help.

Also, they really ought to cherish Mile more—but no, even if she was the youngest and had the most exceptional ability, she was still just a member of the party, and the four of them were equals. On the contrary, giving her special treatment would be disrespectful to Mile in a different way.

The best thing that they could do was put in more effort themselves in order to make up for Mile's shortcomings, the places where she fell behind because she was still so young. And in order to do that, they had to work harder, in pursuit of the day when they could finally, truly, stand shoulder to shoulder with the wondrous girl that was Mile.

On this, Mavis, Reina, and Pauline all agreed.

"I'm back!"

On the evening of the fifth day, just before dinner, Mile returned.

"Welcome back. Did you enjoy your break?"

"I did! I finally fulfilled my lifelong dream!"

"I'm glad to hear it. W-we decided to do a bit of hunting for practice while you were gone, just us three, but we already split the earnings among ourselves. You're okay with that, right? I mean, not that it was that much to begin with, anyway..."

Reina had no desire to keep anything hidden from Mile, and one of them was bound to spill the beans in casual conversation sooner or later anyway. So, it was better to just get it out of the way and tell her ahead of time, Reina thought.

"Oh, of course! We all agreed on that when we formed this party, anyway," Mile said, as though this were a completely obvious thing. "I got done with the thing I had planned a bit early anyway, so I decided to do a bit of side work myself. I only ended up bringing in about twenty gold, though..."

"Wha...?"

Pauline's neck creaked as her head pivoted slowly toward Mile.

Reina's face twitched.

And Mavis's face was one of resignation.

Looks like we've still got a long way to go.

"Mile, I've got a request," said Reina a few days later.

"Me too," added Pauline, an equally serious look upon her face.

"Oh? What is it?" asked Mile, intrigued.

"I want you to teach me to use storage magic."

"Me too!"

"Uh..."

The inventory that Mile accessed while feigning the use of storage magic could only be reached by individuals who were of a Level 3 authorization or higher, and thus able to communicate directly with the nanomachines. Even the storage magic that normal people could use was difficult to access without sufficient talent.

This was not surprising. If it were a skill that could be taught and acquired easily, it would not have nearly as much value.

It was one thing to store something temporarily, but keeping something in storage while concentrating on other tasks, and even while sleeping, required a constant invocation. It was a high hurdle, both mentally and in terms of magical strength— absurdly high.

"I don't mind teaching you all, but well, to be honest, it's incredibly difficult."

"Don't worry, we can handle it!!"

A few more days later...

"Why?!?!"

It turned out that Reina could not even access hyperspace to begin with. Pauline, who could muster up a strength greater than that of any mortal man in the name of earning money, could at least tentatively access hyperspace, but once she put something in to store it, all that she stored was spit right back out the moment she lost focus. Plus, she could only hold a few dozen kilograms. This alone was not enough to claim that she could properly use storage magic. Though if she could at least get to the point where she only had to take the items out of storage and undo the spell while she was sleeping, then she would at least be tentatively worthy of the claim...

"I'm not even sure if you'll be able to keep things from falling out of there like this..."

"I can't let anything fall out!!!"

Mavis looked on, resignation upon her face once more.

We really do still have a long way to go...

CHAPTER 56

The Masked Girl Rides Again!

"I SUPPOSE I'll just walk back..."

Once she had managed to accomplish her impossible dream of meeting a fairy on the very first day of her five-day vacation, Mile thought that she might take a leisurely pace on the journey home. Because she had been uncertain of how long she would actually need for her to accomplish her task, she had hustled on the way out, moving at full speed.

For that particular journey, she had worn a form-fitting suit made of special materials to reduce wind resistance and so that she would not end up with her clothes tattered or catching aflame. Naturally, this outfit was not one that she could allow other people to see her in. If nothing else, it would be incredibly embarrassing.

Thus, she cloaked herself with an optic camouflage as she sprinted along.

However, she had a surplus of time on the way back. On departure, she had declared that she would devote the full five days to fulfilling this desperate, lifelong dream, so returning the very next day wouldn't look very cool. Surely, she could find some way to spend her time for the next four days.

Plus, she had already thought of a way that she could return home even more quickly if she needed to and checked with the nanos to confirm whether it was possible. The nanomachines had approved, so, even if she put off her return until the very last day, she would have more than enough to make the trip.

And so, on the second day of her vacation, Mile began her meandering journey home.

The area she was currently in was far from the capital, close to the country's borders. It was a place where fairies might live, so it only made sense for it to be out in the sticks. Mile walked with a lively step down a road that only seldom saw travelers, fielding greetings from the rare passersby.

Though Mile appeared to be only twelve years old, she was wearing a hunter's garb in a manner that suggested it was not brand new to her, but rather, a well-worn friend, so the travelers did not appear to show any concern for her well-being. If she was over ten years old, then she was probably an F-rank hunter, a proper member of the guild, after all. And, given that she appeared to have been living as a hunter for a least a few years since officially joining the guild, she likely had some sensible reason for traveling out here all by herself. At least, so these adults would judge, knowing much of the world.

Hm?

Just as Mile was passing by some small village, whose name she did not know, a rather odd gathering of people came into view.

On one side, there were about twenty farmers, and on the other side, around ten men who looked like soldiers. They faced each other at a distance of several meters. The soldiers had not drawn their swords, but the farmers were brandishing hoes and spades and sickles. The atmosphere was clearly a tense one.

The situation had absolutely nothing to do with her, but Mile had never been one to simply pass such a scene by. If nothing else, she had a bit of time on her hands—far too much time on her hands, in fact.

That said, she was not about to go leaping into something before she fully understood the circumstances. She cloaked herself with camouflaging magic at once and slowly approached the scene.

"Go home! Obviously no one's demands are going to be met, so we have nothing to discuss with you!"

"You bastards do know that this is an act of insurrection, don't you? What you're doing cannot be taken back! You see that, do you not?!"

This did not seem to be a case of soldiers invading from a foreign land or disgraced members of the military turning to banditry and attacking a village. Although the reason was as yet unclear, it seemed that the lord of these lands had demanded something of the villagers. Had their taxes been raised so high that it was impossible for them to live? Or had the lord made some other unreasonable request of them?

"First of all, you all do understand that what you're demanding is ridiculous, don't you?! 'You need to drastically lower our taxes,' my ass! The tax rate in this territory is barely any different from the ones around us, and they aren't unjust. Besides, do you really think that we could lower the taxes in your village alone? If we did something like that, there would be no way for us to explain it to the other villages, and anyway, there's no reason for it in the first place. Why in the hell would you all ask for something like that?"

Apparently, it was the villagers who had a bone to pick here.

"You shut up! We aren't budgin' until our demands are met!"

The farmers brandished their tools. Reluctantly, the soldiers took up their swords. At this rate, a clash was inevitable.

Mile looked around and selected an appropriately shaped tree, clambering up to the top. She pulled a mask from her inventory and strapped it on. Indeed, it was the mask she had used back at the exhibition.

With the mask strapped tightly, she released her cloaking spell and took an imposing stance upon a large branch, shouting down to the farmers and soldiers, "Cease this battle at once!"

"Huh...?"

A girl of tender years, wearing a peculiar mask, had appeared atop a tree out of nowhere. Hearing her declaration, the men stopped moving, staring slack-jawed into the treetops.

"Who are you?!" demanded the man who appeared to be the commander of the soldiers.

Though the soldiers were all taken aback, the farmers remained clearheaded.

This much made sense. No one who appeared in such a manner as this, at such a time as this, could be anything but an ally of the common man. And despite her strange appearance, for her to appear so boldly meant that she must have full confidence in her abilities. Naturally, the villagers were overjoyed at this unexpected reinforcement.

"Hup!"

Mile leapt down from the tree with a shout, landing in between the two groups. Then she turned to face the farmers and said, "I have come to lend my aid to the superior side. They call me, Superior Mask!"

"What the hell is thaaaaaaaaat?!?!?!"

At last, this was a question that the two enemy sides could agree on.

There was something that Mile had always wondered about the books and anime she consumed in her previous life: Why did the main characters always attach themselves to the side that was on the brink of defeat?

Joining forces with the superior side meant that the fight would soon be over and that there would be no more battlefield casualties, no more wives who would lose their husbands, and no more children who would lose their fathers. Bolstering the losing

side just meant that the battle would drag on and on and that the
number of deaths would increase on both sides.

Of course, it would be a different matter if they were dealing
with invading foreign soldiers or village-attacking bandits—in
other words, groups who absolutely could not be allowed to win.
But if the superior side were a regional force operating within
their own territory, and each side had its own claims, and a position that was just, at least from their perspective, then what would
be the point of aligning oneself with the inferior side and contrib-
uting to unnecessary death and destruction? Though without any
extra interference, this conflict would soon end with the impending battle anyway...

Both of the sides in this fight had lives and families, and the
soldiers were merely doing their duty by upholding the tenets of
their fine profession. They were fighting for the sake of protect-
ing their families and had probably conscripted into duty by the
Crown or by their lord in the first place. Even if the cause they
were fighting for might be an unjust one, that was on the shoulders of the higher-ups, not the men down here on the ground.

Plus, only a fool would reignite a cooling battle and see more
men fall simply because they happened to be influenced by it or
have some tie to one of the sides—such as, perhaps, some beauty
asking for their assistance.

In every case, it was best to end a battle as quickly as possible.
If it turned out that the higher-ups were indeed corrupt, they
could be dealt with at a later juncture. Thus went Mile's thinking,
at least.

As for "dealing" with a corrupt official? Well, they could be poisoned, or jumped when they were on some outing, or shot, or set ablaze, or caught in a trap—the possibilities were endless.

Anyway, if things continued this way, most of the farmers would likely be killed, and the rest of them captured. There would probably be a few injuries and even deaths among the soldiers as well. Were that to happen, neither the captured famers nor the other villagers would simply be able to let this go. Thus, it was far preferable to see *all* the famers captured, unharmed.

Even if Mile were to ally herself with the farmers and help repel the soldiers, the soldiers would just return later with an even stronger force. If the farmers managed to repel them again, then they would face an even *stronger* force, and the situation would continue to deteriorate further and further.

It was also worth noting that Mile had no intention of sticking with the farmers for all that long in the first place—nor did she have very much interest in facing down the lord and his entire army. If that happened, she would probably have her qualifications as a hunter revoked and end up a wanted girl. At that point, if her true identity as a noble from a foreign land was revealed, it was sure to become quite the problem for international relations.

In order to draw this all neatly to a close, she had no choice but to face the farmers and uphold the decision that the soldiers had made in order to quash this insurrection.

"My good soldiers, you have my gratitude for your fine service. I would like to see your enemies captured unharmed, so please leave this matter to me, Superior Mask!"

"S-sure..." the commander agreed against his better judgment, nodding hesitantly.

Seeing how this mysterious masked girl, who they had thought to be their ally, was now on the side of the soldiers, the farmers were unmistakably shaken.

"Whatever, she's just one little girl! That's no big deal!" the leader of the farmers shouted, not realizing that this was a line that had only ever been spoken by villains.

"Here I go!" said Mile, a single wooden sword appearing from out of nowhere in her hand...

"It's over."

"Y-yeah..."

Lined up on the ground before them were seventeen farmers, captured and bound. They were kicking up too much of a ruckus, so they had been gagged as well.

The eleven soldiers stared at them in awe.

It would seem that nine of the soldiers were normal recruits, one was a non-commissioned officer, and the last and highest-ranking was appointed. The final two were likely components of any assembled squad. Someone had to be counted upon to make the important calls, and such a duty could not be put on the shoulders of just any recruit.

"Now then, I have one request," said Mile.

"A reward?" asked the commander. "I have no doubt that our

groups clashing would have led to injuries—even deaths, if things went poorly. Though you came in as an interloper, the fact remains that you really did help us. Besides, since neither side was hurt, we don't have to report that the farmers tried to use force against us. No one was harmed, and there was no military action to speak of, all thanks to the influence of a mysterious girl. Naturally, you have every right to demand a reward from our lord, good lady. We will report everything to him, so if you would like to travel along with us..."

Indeed, there had fortunately been nothing that could be referred to as "military action." Even without her interference, what would have broken out could have scarcely been called a "battle," after all.

Yet Mile merely shook her head.

"I have no qualms with traveling with you, but what I request is not money. I wish you to make note that these farmers who I captured surrendered of their own volition. I get the impression that this was their intention from the start..."

For a group of farmers to oppose a lord's military forces was a controversial act. Had the matter been unavoidable, it would have been one thing, but their taxes had not been raised, nor were they higher than any other fief's, and no one's wives or daughters were being snatched away. They were merely refusing to pay their taxes—in an act of baseless, personal protest. Mile could not imagine that such people would be treated with kindness.

"Yes, those men are citizens of this territory as well. I couldn't bear to see anyone needlessly hanged, and doing so would only mean that our tax intake would decrease. I can't see that being of benefit to our lord, either."

Hearing the commander's dispassionate response, Mile thought to herself, *I thought as much*. Of course, this would not normally be the case. Normally, the farmers would be ruthlessly punished, made an example of to keep all the other villages in line. Was this commander particularly kind? Or was the lord of these lands just a good person?

The farmers could only mumble, thanks to the gags in their mouths, but if they had been allowed to speak, then the conversation would be chaos. The commander removed the gag from only one of the farmers, who he deemed to be the leader. Seeing this, the other farmers thought to themselves, "Good. He will get across what we want to say," and they all fell quiet.

"Now then, why don't we have a conversation? First off, am I correct to think of you as the leader of this bunch? Are you the official representative of this village?"

The farmer, a man in his forties, replied, "Yeah, that's right. I'm the son of the village elder and acting representative, while my old man's sick in bed."

"So, why have you suddenly, unilaterally demanded that we lower your taxes? You have to have known that that would never fly."

"Heh. You can't fool me! You know as well as I do that if enough of us farmers put the screws on him, our lord would *have* to listen to our demands!"

"What?"

Both Mile and the commander were stunned, unconsciously

letting out a question in their confusion. Though the other soldiers had no voice in the matter, they were bewildered as well.

"Ya see there? Bull's eye! Look how they're panicking!" the farmer gloated.

However, the reason that Mile and the others were stunned was most decidedly not because the farmer's analysis had hit the bull's eye. Not anywhere near.

"Wh-what precisely is this man going on about?"

"I-I have no idea. Oy, you there! Mind telling me exactly how it is that you came to this conclusion?"

"Heh heh. Fine. I'll tell you exactly what it is that we know," the farmer said, as he began his spiel. "Listen up. Now obviously, our lord lives off of the taxes that he collects from us peasants. The wages that you guys get paid and the money that goes to the Crown all comes from that too."

There were of course taxes levied on merchants and toll fees as well, but whatever, the commander and Mile thought. For the most part, what the man said was correct, and they both silently nodded.

"So, if we say, 'Lower our taxes,' whaddya think happens?"

"You'd be refused," Mile immediately replied.

"Well then, what if we say, 'If you don't do what we tell you, we won't pay our taxes at all,' then what?"

"He sends out a suppression force."

This time Mile and the commander answered simultaneously.

That much was an actual fact and a fair summary of their current situation. The commander himself was the leader of said subjugation force.

Apparently, this commander had tried to resolve the situation through negotiation instead of force, but it would not be at all unusual for him, wishing to be able to count the suppression of an insurrection among his achievements, to have wiped out the farmer's forces entirely.

"Heh heh heh. You'd think so, right? But that's nothin' more than a bluff. If they really did capture and kill us, then they wouldn't be able to collect taxes from us anyway. Even collecting slightly less taxes from us is better than gettin' nothing. So, eventually, our argument's gotta get through. Even just before, s'not like y'all rushed us. All you did was wave your swords around a bit. So, I think you understand this, too. Now then, you gonna hurry up and untie us or what?!"

"........."

Mile, the commander, and the other soldiers were stunned.

"U-um..."

Tepidly, Mile called out to the farmer.

"If they were to allow such a thing, then rumors of this would spread, and all of the villages would start making these demands, wouldn't they?"

"Yeah. I mean, we already heard about that. That's why we demanded it, too."

"........."

The soldiers were silent. Mile continued.

"Um, if it goes on like this, then, wouldn't the tax income from every village decrease? If it looked like that was going to happen, then the people from the first village to demand it would be sold to the mines to make an example, and no other villagers would want to follow them after that, at which point the whole thing would end with *no one's* taxes going down. Selling criminal slaves is incredibly profitable."

"Wh...?"

This time it was the farmer, the son of the village elder, who was speechless.

"N-no, I know what I heard. You can't fool me! Long ago, in the village of Lobeton, they made their demands, and in the first year they paid nothing! And only thirty percent of what they had paid before after that..."

"The village of Lobeton?"

The commander seemed to have no idea what he was talking about, but the name rang familiar to Mile.

"The village of Lobeton... I read about them in a book, once."

"Look, you see!"

The farmer looked as though he had just caught an ogre by the neck. However, Mile's tale was not yet finished.

"In another kingdom, there is a village by that name. Apparently, as a result of their demanding that their taxes be lowered, every male in the village was slaughtered, from infant to elder. The village only survived because the lesser sons of the families in surrounding villages, who inherited no land of their own, moved in with their wives and kids in tow, and other un-married men emigrated in to make wives of the widows and the woman who had still been too young to wed before the massacre..."

"Because of all this, they were exempt from taxes during the year that immediately followed, and in the three years after that, they paid lowered rates. Starting with the fourth year after, it went back up to normal. In other words, the tale of the village of Lobeton is not one of a people who had their taxes lowered but a cautionary tale of a group of farmers and their folly, and what became of their final days..."

"Wh...?"

The son of the village elder, and all the other farmers, suddenly looked very uneasy.

"I suppose in that case we would be the force summoned here to slaughter every man..."

"Whaaaaaaaaaat?!"

"H-hoifithoifithoifithoifitt!!!!!!!"

At this, the farmers all cried out in terror.

Truthfully, such a show of force had been ordered only if negotiation proved fruitless, and in this particular case, it was not a massacre they were aiming for; the soldiers had only planned to capture the farmers to be sold into labor. Killing them would not net the fief a single copper, whereas selling them would make straw into gold.

The lord may have been kind, but he was also business-minded...

"Now then, just who was it that told you such a strange story?" the commander asked the still horribly-shaken farmer; however, the man could no longer muster up the will to speak. Thinking that things were about to go very bad, very quickly, he finally opened his mouth.

"I-It was six days ago..."

According to the farmer's story, six days ago, a man had arrived in the village on the brink of death. The villagers shared their food and water with him, and as a show of thanks, he told them about his own village's plans to have their taxes reduced.

Given that such a plan had no chance of working, this was clearly suspicious. As was the fact that the man had stayed in the village for only a single night, leaving the next morning...

"For a swindler, there's no profit in that plan, which means that his true goal was to get the village wiped out or to cause a schism between the village and your lord because of some sort of enmity, wouldn't you think? Is this the work of an enemy? Has the village ever picked a fight with anyone? Have you ever tormented a family and driven them from the village, or has some villager ever murdered a traveling merchant and stolen his money? Or..."

"A-absolutely not! No one here would do something so inhumane!" the village leader protested desperately, his face pale.

"Well then, let's expand this out a bit... What is the status of the other villages?" Mile asked the commander.

"Well," he replied, "We've only just received the missive from this village, demanding a reduction in their taxes and threatening a refusal to pay if we didn't comply. There's been nothing from the other villages thus far."

Of course, this had occurred only several days ago. It was possible that the proceedings in other villages had merely not progressed this far yet.

"That man, or some associates of his, might be traveling around to the other villages, too. If you don't act fast, then this sort of thing might..."

Now, the commander's face went pale.

Understandably so. If multiple villages were to mount an opposition at once, this modest force would easily be overwhelmed. The Crown would begin to doubt the lord's governing capabilities, or think that he was running the territory through some tyrannical means, and might intervene in the lord's territories. The worst-case scenario would be that the lord's household could be abolished.

"Wh-what do we do?"

Though he was an officer, the commander was still fairly low in rank. The lowest, in fact, as far as his class went. As nothing more than a member of the forces of a low-ranking noble, he had not exactly had any extensive training. Therefore, though he recognized that they were on the brink of a crisis, he was in no position to be making any snap decisions or taking immediate action. Instead, he was flustered.

Seeing this, Mile decided to take the initiative. Finally the time had come to put to good use all the wisdom that she had cultivated from a lifetime of anime, manga, and literature.

"First off, you need to dispatch one of your men to this village. Tell them that they have no need to worry, that you have heard these men's opinions and that you are all heading off together to make a petition to your lord. Then, hurry back to the capital. Bring these men with you to keep the rumors from spreading.

Inform your lord about the current situation and have him dispatch spies to every village in the territory at once. At that point, you'll be able to gauge the current climate and locate your enemy's hiding place. Well, I mean, of course, all that is up to your lord's judgment. What you all need to prioritize right now is concealing the fact that you know what's actually going on and then reporting it to the higher-ups as quickly as possible. Think you can manage?"

"Y-yeah. Trimce, you catch all of that? To the village at once! The rest of you, straight to the capital!"

The commander, who seemed to have worked his way up the ranks, was not so proficient when it came to suddenly making unexpected, crucial decisions, but if his compass was pointed in the correct direction, then he could at least follow its lead.

"Oh dear, are you all right?"

Along the highway near a village, a young girl came across a man sitting on the ground and called out to him.

"O-oh, well, I slipped down a slope in the mountains and lost everything—my bags, my food, and my water. I haven't had anything to eat or drink in two days..."

"What?! That's dreadful. Please come back with me to my village. It's just over there. We can give you food, water, and shelter for the night."

Her invitation extended, the girl led the man back to her home, not seeing the wicked grin on the man's face behind her.

"Thank you so very much! You've really saved me!"

After drinking some water and partaking of a hot meal, the man cheerfully extended his thanks to the girl and her father and brothers.

"Please, I must give you some reward for this... Unfortunately, I've lost all my belongings."

"It's all right, we need no reward. In times of trouble, we look out for one another. If you can pay the favor forward and help someone else in trouble one day, then that's enough for us," said the father.

The man showed exaggerated shock.

"My, my! What an extraordinary person you are. I know! In exchange, why don't I teach you how the people of my village persuaded our lord to lower the taxes that we owed him? To tell you honestly, we used to have to pay up to half of our earnings, but we demanded that the rate be lowered to thirty percent, and it was done! At first they tried to threaten us, but we pointed out to them what a silly thing they were doing—if they crushed our village, why they wouldn't get a single copper out of us, after all! We kept up the pressure, never relenting, and eventually our lord had no choice but to give in to our demands. The best way to do that is..."

The man prattled on and on, but the girl, her father, and her brothers only stared at him, expressionless.

"Hm?"

The man abruptly stopped his story, feeling the atmosphere growing tense.

"It's youuuuuuuuu!!!!" the family all suddenly roared.

"Eeek!" the man exclaimed, cringing in terror.

"We've heard about you! You're the miscreant trying to incite a rebellion among the villagers! You'll be hung for this!"

"No, please, Father, wait! You mustn't!"

The man looked at the little girl expectantly as she tried, desperately, to hold her father back.

"You mustn't hang him until we've tortured him and gotten him to spill everything! Well, I mean I guess we'll never know if he's told us *everything*, but at the very least, we can keep torturing him until he's dead..."

"*Gaaaaaaaaaah!!!*"

"So, did he talk?"

"Yeah. He's not a real soldier or anything, just some hired thug. No matter what we tried to beat out of him, all he'd say was, 'I don't know anyone like that! Are you planning on pinning me with some trumped up, false charges?' and that was that."

"Of course..."

After it was all over, the girl and the man conversed—not the little girl and her father, but Mile and the squad commander. Suddenly, a recollection of the imperial soldiers who were trying to disrupt trade routes floated through the back of her mind.

"By the by," said the commander, "Might I ask you something?"

"Certainly. What is it?"

A bit hesitantly he asked, "Do you...really have to wear that mask?"

"Well, obviously! I am the defender of the superior, the unidentified superheroine, Superior Mask, after all!" Mile declared, puffing out her chest.

"Well, but I mean, you did have it off until just a little while ago..." Mile shot the commander a glare, and he quickly backed off. "Er, never mind!"

Eventually, the man did admit that he had been hired by the Empire, but there was no way of telling if that was fact or not. Was he telling the truth? Or was he merely spewing lies because his life was on the line? Or perhaps, was that what his employer had told him to say?

At this rate, his information was no good to anyone, but at least this time, they had warded off a crisis and taken the countermeasures to prevent a repeat of the last time. The king would likely be told of this incident at once, and the lord himself would have a place of honor in having helped to prevent a national disaster. So, at the very least, Mile's intervention was not for naught.

Thanks to the eloquent persuasion of the commander, Mile received an audience with the lord and twenty gold pieces as a reward. Had things gone down the wrong path, the matter could have become incredibly serious, so compared to what a crisis would cost, twenty gold was nothing.

Blessedly, the lord said not a word about the mask upon Mile's face, speaking to her as though it were not even there.

He truly was a good person.

And so, as a bonus, Mile provided him with a number of ways by which he might deal with such incidents in the future.

"Um, I was thinking that it might be good for you to put some countermeasures in place, to avoid anything like this happening again later on..."

Mile explained her plans:

First, she suggested that he hold some educational conferences in order to teach the villagers a few basics about the country and the tax system, and about what would happen if they tried to disrupt that, using the ruined foreign village as an example.

Second, she advised him to carefully select some villagers and hire them as information gatherers—in other words, spies. Set them up three to a village, with each of them assuming that they're the only one there.

Third, Mile said, in villages where there was still a bit of resistance, the lord might send an appointed agitator who could knock the wind out of the villagers with a little "controlled tension," as well as bring any other dangerous parties to light.

Fourth...

Mile went on and on. The lord had initially been delighted to meet her, having been told that she was an "honest girl with a strong sense of justice, who was wise and skilled with a sword." However, as their talk drew on, the smile on his face began to twitch. Of course, Mile only continued, not noticing a thing. And then...

"Young lady, what would you think of becoming my family's vassal?"

Already, the invitations had started.

"Oh no! I'm really just a normal, average girl. To have such a high status would be..."

"Well then, what of becoming my adopted daughter?"

"Oh no! I'm really just a normal, average girl. To have such a high status would be..."

Desperately she turned down one offer after another.

"Oh!"

Finally, Mile had a realization: this was the fifth and final day of her vacation.

It wouldn't do her any good to return too late. At the very least, she needed to get back before dinner, and already the sun was beginning to set.

"Crap! If I just run normally, I'll never make it in time!"

And so, Mile made the decision to use the special "emergency measure" that she had thought up on the off chance of just such a situation.

"Nanos, if you would!"

RIGHT AWAY!

Cancel gravity! Yes, just like the gravity-neutralizing material cavorite...

As Mile pictured the effect of the magic she wanted in her head, she issued a verbal command to the nanomachines as well.

"Negate gravity in the perimeter!"

At the moment when she could no longer feel the weight of her own body, Mile kicked off from the ground. She shot steeply upward until she was higher than the highest mountains in the region.

"Distort lower gravity, change horizontal movement to the direction of the capital, and then release the selective gravitational canceling. Now beginning countdown: 5, 4, 3, 2, 1, go!"

She began to fall in the opposite direction from which she had ascended. Directly toward the ground.

"*Gaaaaaaaaaaaaaaaaaaaah!!!* Th-the wind pressure! My clothes! My clothes are gonna fly right off!!! B-barrier! Barrieeeeeeeeeeeerrr!!!"

"I don't know what I was thinking..."

It was thus that Mile returned to the inn where her companions were waiting, with only a story as her souvenir, not knowing that she was to be harshly rebuked for all that she had done without the rest of her party.

Didn't I Say
to Make My Abilities
Average in the
—— Next Life?!

Kurihara Misato's OTAKU LIFE

"WHERE'S BIG SIS?" Misato's younger sister Keiko asked her mother one day.

"The usual place," her mother replied. When it came to Misato's whereabouts, the only places she could ever be found besides her room and the "usual place," were the toilet and the bath.

The usual place. This was the Kurihara family's study. Her father thought of the room as belonging to him, but in truth, Misato was the one who spent far more time there. When her father, who did not get home from work very early, was not around, Misato could most often be found there. When she was not at school, of course.

You see, this room contained her parents' collection: an immense library of books, manga, Blu-ray discs, DVDs, CD-Rs, laser discs, video tapes (both VHS and Betamax), U-matics, and various other video player formats with the videos to match, as well as every game system starting from the first-generation Famicom and the games to go with them (including the total shovelware that most wouldn't deem even worth keeping around). All of it was crammed tight onto a set of crank-operated shelves.

Indeed, the weight of this collection was so immense that it had to be accounted for in the very blueprints of the house, with countless concrete piles driven down into the bedrock underneath it when the house was constructed. The compensation they'd had to offer the neighbors was apparently equally immense. After all, it would have caused quite a lot of noise and vibration.

Naturally, this room also contained large television screens and projectors for displaying those movies and games. When Misato wanted to flip through something alone or look at something that she did not want her family to see—or when her father was home—she would watch things in her room. However, when that was not the case, it was much preferable to watch shows and play games on the big screen, sitting back in a nice, comfy chair. At times, Keiko joined her, and there were even times when Keiko wished to watch things independently, but unlike Misato, Keiko had little fascination with vintage works and garbage games. She was more interested in modern productions, so more often than not, Misato was left entirely to her own devices.

After a short while, Misato emerged from her "usual place." She was wearing a set of hooded cat pajamas. They were much comfier than normal clothes, so Misato usually wore them at home. When guests came over, she simply refused to emerge from her room—not even to go to the bathroom.

Misato also had dog, bear, and bunny-patterned pajamas. She had a set of bird-patterned ones as well, but the arms were blocked up by wing shapes, and she was unable to use her hands while wearing them, which was a problem when she needed to turn the pages of a book or manipulate a controller. For that reason, those remained perennially packed away.

"What were you watching today?" her mother asked.

"*Rainbow Sentai Robin*. Oh, I wish I could ride Pegasus along with Bell..." Misato replied.

Incidentally, the "Pegasus" she was referring to was not an actual winged horse but a rocket-powered transforming robot by the same name. Bell was a cat-shaped robot in charge of the radar.

"Wouldn't you rather ride along with Robin?"

"There's not enough room inside of Pegasus for us both. Plus, Robin should be with Lili!"

"My, my... Still, you should at least watch something in color instead of black and white... How many times have you watched that now, anyway?"

"Talk about something that I can understaaaaaand!!" Keiko complained, as Misato and their mother jabbered away. The girls' father would have been able to understand the conversation perfectly, but all of their references were going well over Keiko's head.

"Well, that's why I keep saying you should watch..." Misato started.

"Do you think I have time for that?!" Keiko yelled. "I have to

study twice as hard as you do just to get the same marks, Misato!
I get compared to you all the time! Just try putting yourself in
my shoes!"

"Should I lower my exam scores, then?"

"Don't make me even *more* pathetiiiiiiiic!!!"

Though she was shouting angrily, this conversation was a regular one, a practiced bit of theirs. While she did not score in the
top percentile of nationwide exam scores like Misato did, Keiko
was still in the top of her class at school, a rightful honors student.
Plus, unlike Misato, who fell incredibly short in areas outside of
her exceptional grades, Keiko, who was chock-full of common
sense and was the conscientious class-rep type, was popular—
among boys and girls alike.

However, whenever Misato pointed this out, Keiko would
wince and change the subject...

The next day.

"Handkerchief, tissues, cell phone, wallet, lunch box. Do you
have everything? Ahh! Your hair's sticking up! Here, bend down
a bit!"

As she did every morning, Keiko was busying herself with
Misato's pre-school check. To those outside of their family,
Misato seemed like the perfect girl, but it was all a sham.

In truth, she was very much a fixer-upper, outside of her scholarly and physical capabilities. Perhaps because she was always off
in her head daydreaming, she was incredibly absentminded when
it came to her surroundings, constantly losing or dropping things.

Plus, she was indifferent when it came to her personal appearance. Her personal hygiene was just fine, but she was uninterested in hair, makeup, and all the other things that girls typically did to try and "improve" their appearance.

This had been fine when she was in elementary school, but it was unacceptable once she reached middle school and beyond, so eventually Keiko had ended up taking charge of her outfits and general beauty routine.

"All right, let's get going... Wait, where's your backpack?!?!"

"Oh..."

"I swear, Misato! You'd be better off inventing some fourth-dimensional pocket and stashing all your stuff in *that!* Then at least it'd be with you wherever you go..."

Even the cell phone that Misato had with her was what you'd call a "feature phone"—there was no way she could ever have a smartphone. Why, you ask? She had no idea how to use one, even though she could use a computer just fine. Anyway, the only numbers she had programmed in her phone were those of her family members.

"All right, I'm off. I want you to head straight to your classroom. If someone who isn't one of your classmates starts talking to you and you don't know them, then deal with them appropriately. We don't need you agreeing to something weird and going along with some stranger like last time!"

"O-okay..." Misato set off at a leisurely pace while Keiko rushed off to the building that housed her classroom.

Though she had let herself move along in a carefree daze while she was with Keiko, the moment she was alone, Misato quickly put on a serious face. It was not that her demeanor up until now had been an act—it was merely that she was lonesome by herself, and her caution had shot to max levels as it always did.

Given Misato's tendency to mild face-blindness, there were plenty of situations where someone whom Misato was speaking to knew who she was, but she did not know them. Keiko had berated her on multiple occasions for the number of times she almost went along with stalkers, as her face was well known both at school and around town. If someone were to suddenly speak to her, she had no idea if it was an acquaintance or a complete stranger. Thus, she was now constantly on edge whenever she was alone.

Seeing how alert she was, others would look at her and think, "What a splendid young lady! Look how sharp and good-looking she is!" However, in truth, Misato herself would never have thought such a thing.

"All the best!"

When Misato entered the classroom, she was greeted by the class representative. For some reason, "*Gokigenyo*,"—or in English, "All the best"—a phrase best used when parting from someone—had become popular as the main greeting for the girls of this school. When used in parting, they would say it while gently waving their hands at waist level. From the wrist only.

Speaking of the greeting...

There was a television program called *Raion no Gokigenyo,* or "A Lion's Well Wishes." On the show, an actress once went to Africa, got attacked by a lion, and was brutally injured, according to the news reports. Shortly after, the chairman was quoted as saying, "I guess that was a greeting from the lion!"

Whether it was true or an urban legend, Misato had no idea, but suddenly recalling that phrase, she wanted ever so desperately to say it, so much so she could burst, but she refrained.

"All the best..."

At least Misato could distinguish between her classmates. Misato was especially grateful to the class rep, who worried the most out of them over the solitary Misato.

"Um..."

"What's up?"

"No, it's nothing."

Misato stopped herself from saying what she wanted to before she could even open her mouth, a slightly dark expression on her face.

That's our Kurihara-san! She always keeps her worries to herself with a cool expression. Such a graceful manner! She's so mature...

As they watched the exchange between the two, Misato's classmates' thoughts ran wild.

The topic that had suddenly crossed Misato's mind—which she was on the verge of bringing up—was, "The first real breakout magical girl was Megu-chan, wasn't it?" That was the question she had wished to ask, utterly without expression.

Even if I had said it, she probably wouldn't understand...

The thought was a sad and lonesome one.

Even during their lessons, there were always many gazes that turned Misato's way—especially from the boys. However, when it came to break time, no one dared speak to her.

She was a brilliant flower blooming out of reach, whom no one could actually *speak* to.

Plus, even if anyone did work up the courage to say something, there would be a mob waiting for him afterward, ready to put the presumptuous fellow back in his place.

Misato was everyone's dream, a prize of the highest honor. In other words, she was communal property.

Plus, even if they *did* try to talk to her...

"U-um, Kurihara-san, who are your favorite actors and performers?"

"Vic Morrow and Kurizuka Asahi."

"What about your favorite TV show...?"

"*I Dream of Jeannie.*"

"Do you watch anime or things like that? What are your favorite—"

"*Kimba the White Lion* and *Princess Knight.*"

"Did you see the AKB event yesterday?"

"Did something happen in the formerly Soviet Russia?"

"No, I'm talking about AKB48..."

"Is that an improvement on the AK-47 model? Is it 5.45mm caliber?"

Their conversations would not align in the slightest.

Her parents' media collection did not contain many recent offerings. And as Misato herself had no interest in recent productions and did not watch anything in real time, she had only watched the older works from said collection. It was the same whether it came to movies or dramas or anime or games.

Furthermore, Misato had never acquired the high level art of steering her own topics of conversation to match that of her partner. As a result, it was rare that anyone spoke to her in the first place, and even when they occasionally did, the interaction was rarely a success.

Anyway, anyone who would try to talk to her outside of school was either a flirt, a suspicious talent scout, a stalker, or some other member of the rogues' gallery.

Truthfully, there were probably some earnest students mixed in among the "flirts," but as far as Misato was concerned, they were all unknown subjects between whom she could make no distinctions.

"You didn't run into anyone strange today, did you, sis?"

"No. I only had a university student and some forty-year-old who was a higher-up at some company or other try to talk to me."

"And you don't think that qualifies as 'strange'?!"

If only everyone knew of Misato's manner and her general shabby state while at home. Perhaps they might have seen her as more approachable and come to think of her as a normal high school girl, just like them.

Well, no. Had that happened, she would have simply had even

more girls and boys flocking around her, and Misato's peaceful existence during her time at school would have vanished. Perhaps it was because Keiko sensed this that she never shared the truth about Misato with others...

"Ah, Mom said she was gonna be home late tonight."

"Oh, should I make dinner, then?"

Cooking was another of Misato's talents.

Following a recipe to the letter was just like applying a mathematical formula, or a physics or chemistry experiment. If you followed the steps correctly, you'd achieve the correct result. With those principles and reasoning, as well as a little thought, she could unravel any puzzle, so she was generally able to produce a meal without difficulty or mishap.

That said, when she tried to recreate the peculiar dishes that she saw in manga or anime, her success rate was only about 50-50.

"S-so what's our menu for tonight, then?" Keiko cautiously inquired.

Misato, who had been rummaging through the refrigerator, turned and declared with a smile, "Hanada Kousaku, the Curry General's famous Black Curry!"

"*Gaaaaaaaah!!!*"

And then, she awoke in another world.

After her reawakening as Misato, Adele's consciousness was a mix of Misato's memories along with the ten years of life that she had lived as a young noble girl, both swirled together in a memory stew. Therefore, when it came to Misato's weak points— her inability to deal competently with others—the part of her that was Adele, the ten-year-old girl, and not the part of her that was Misato—took the lead. This girl was far better than Misato when it came to such things, after all...

And if Misato, influenced by Adele's spirit, did things like a ten-year-old girl would, no one would think it strange. The body she was currently in was that of a ten-year-old girl, anyway.

Adele, who conducted herself like a ten-year-old girl when it came to conversation with others, blended right in with her classmates at the academy... Well, actually, she was still a bit young for her age, but the others sensed this, treating her like a little sister. Indeed, there was not a single person there who thought that Adele was more serious or mature than the rest.

And of course Misato, who had led a lonesome, solitary school life the first time around, enjoyed this time to her fullest.

Just as God had wished for her with his final words:

"Please, have a good life..."

Weapons

"**R**EINA, have you ever thought about changing your weapon?" asked Mile one day.

"Huh???"

The other three members of the Crimson Vow appeared bewildered at the sudden proposal.

"Isn't this rather sudden?" Reina asked suspiciously.

"Well, I mean, rather than smacking or jabbing people with a staff, wouldn't some other kind of weapon be a lot more efficient?"

"I mean, I guess you're right..." Reina agreed.

"But," Pauline added, "mages' weapons have always been bludgeoning types since way back when. There must be a good reason for that. Well, that is mages who aren't you of course, Mile."

Pauline did not seem to be in favor of Mile's proposal either, and even Mile had to agree that she had a point. As much as she might call herself a magic knight, or what have you, even with a sword at her side, she was still primarily a magic-user.

"I know that much! I'm fully aware that the incantation is the most important thing for a mage and that they need a weapon they can use to reflexively defend themselves while their concentration is taken up by their spellcasting. It's true that bludgeoning weapons are the best type for that..."

"That, and, with swinging-type weapons, you can generate a lot of force when you swing them. Mages tend to be weak when it comes to facing melee-type weapons, so if they allow even the slightest opening in close-range combat, they're toast. If you prioritize self-defense over toppling your enemy, you create a moment to quickly fire off a spell. That's the conclusion that our predecessors came to, and I'm pretty sure it's the right one."

Indeed, there were some very good reasons for mages to wield the weapons they did. However...

"That's for normal mages, though. I'm sure that you and Pauline could handle something different while casting, no problem! Here, see, try something like this..."

As she spoke, Mile produced a weapon that had three fine blades extending from the hilt of a sword, fanning out at the end—a weapon that looked like it was, well... rather more impressive than practical.

"No thanks! I'm sure that would increase my ability to fatally wound someone, but that would never stop the force of a monster rushing at you, and it would never pierce right through them. Besides, it's not about how badly you can wound your enemy.

A mage's weapon isn't for close-range attack power, it's for getting yourself out of a bad situation. I have no intention of giving up the staff that I've been using all this time!"

Apparently, Reina and her staff shared some memories, and she had absolutely no intention of switching weapons.

"Hm, well then... I'll just install some reinforcing parts on that staff, then!"

"Huh?"

Yet another strange proposal.

However, Reina and the others were already well accustomed to Mile's ways and could hardly be bothered to show surprise.

"What I'm saying is that I can put some metal spikes on the end of the staff that you hit people with. And on the thrusting end, I can put a metal cap for added power and weight balance, and..."

"How can you just pop out literally anything right on the spot like that?!" Reina shouted, though she took the offered parts in her hands and examined them. "These aren't bad. They're a little heavy, but it *would* raise my power that much more..."

Mile nodded approvingly as she watched Reina take forceful practice swings with her staff, when suddenly she heard Pauline's voice softly in her ear.

"Are you sure that's a good idea?"

"Hm?"

Mile cocked her head. She had no idea what Pauline meant.

"I mean, whenever Reina gets mad at you, she always hits you on the head with that staff, doesn't she? Like, *bambambambam*

bambambambam! Now that her staff is stronger, the next time you make her angry..."

"G..."

"G?"

"Gyaaaaaaaah!!!"

And so, Mile withdrew her proposal for strengthening Reina's staff, fully of her own volition.

Afterword

Long time no see, everyone. FUNA here.

We've now reached *Didn't I Say To Make My Abilities Average in the Next Life?!* Volume 6. Volume 2 of the manga is going on sale now as well. Head straight to your local bookstore today!

This volume features a battle with some new enemies: demons.

And, at last, Mavis has a grand awakening, surpassing human limits! It's the first time we've truly seen Mavis in action since the battle against the elder dragons—*ba-bam!*

What? You're saying that she "already surpassed human limits" during that battle?

Whatever! Don't sweat the details!

If you keep picking those nits you're gonna end up bald!

A new encounter, a new burden, and a new adventure!

Here's Volume 6, beaming right onto your shelves!

Lately, I've been busy working on my three series in syndication, as well as working through the publication process. So much so that I've had barely any time for writing thank yous to all the kind messages I've gotten, cooking, reading net novels, or even sleeping... Ah, yes. For the past year and a half, I haven't read any other net novels at all. I figure that's no good, so I've started trying to pick up a few again.

Before, I used to visit izakaya maybe two or three times a week (more for eating dinner rather than drinking), but now I probably only go about once a month, if that. My expenditures have gone way down—it's Engel's law.

MILE: "Oh! Servants of God have started appearing to you at a high frequency then?!"
FUNA: "No, that would be 'Angel's law.'"

FRIEND: "FUNA-san, have you been out much recently?"
FUNA: "More than enough! I visit a fantasy world every day..."
FRIEND: "And as for the real world?"
FUNA: "Once a week, to the local supermarket..."
FRIEND: "............"
FUNA: "................"
FRIEND: "You're gonna die at this rate."

Don't worry though, I only go there late at night, when all of the deli meats are half-off, so I'm safe.

Wait, no. That's not the problem here, is it?

I may be slowly turning to stone, but I'm still a bundle of joy.

"You'd better accept the boss's orders!"

Oh, a bullet for me, then? Thank you very much.

DOCTOR: "When you drink carbonated drinks, it dissolves the calcium in your body."

FUNA: "Gotcha! So I should drink lots of carbonated drinks to get rid of those kidney stones!"

DOCTOR: "No! When the calcium dissolves, that's what passes into your kidneys and *forms* the stones!"

FUNA: "Uh..."

Following the current release of Volume 6 of *Didn't I Say To Make My Abilities Average in the Next Life?!*, along with Volume 2 of the manga, the second novel volume and first manga volume of *Living on Potion Requests!* will be coming out from Kodansha's K Ranobe Books on November 2nd, and the second novel volume and first manga volume of *Working in a Fantasy World to Save Up 80,000 Gold for My Retirement* will be out on the same day from K Ranobe Books as well. Please enjoy these along with *Abilities Average*.

The manga serialization of *Abilities Average* is currently in healthy syndication in the web serial, *Earth Star Comics* (http://comic-earthstar.jp/), while the manga versions of both *Potions* and *Retirement* (the shortened title of *Working in a Fantasy World...*) can be read in the webcomic magazine, *Wednesday Sirius* (http://seiga.nicovideo.jp/manga/official/w_sirius/).

Please look forward to both the novels and the manga from here on out.

And finally, to the chief editor, Itsuki Akata, the illustrator, Yoichi Yamakami, the cover designer, and everyone involved in the proofreading, editing, printing, binding, distribution, and selling of this book; to all the reviewers on *Shousetsuka ni Narou* who gave me their impressions, guidance, suggestions, and advice; and most of all, to everyone who's read my stories, both in print and online, I thank you all from the bottom of my heart.

I hope to see you all again for Volume 7.

I hope that both the Crimson Vow's dreams, and all my hopes, can stick around for a little while longer...

—FUNA

Didn't I Say *to Make My Abilities* *Average* in the Next Life?! ——

AFTERWORD?

JUST LIKE THAT, MISATO-CHAN'S OTAKU LIFE APPEARED! NOW I CAN UNDERSTAND THOSE PHRASES OF MILE'S... BY THE WAY, THIS IS COMPLETELY UNRELATED, BUT... I ONLY DRAW MILE'S ARM GUARDS ON THE RIGHT SIDE. DID YOU NOTICE?

MILE USES BOTH MAGIC AND A SWORD, SO I MADE IT SO THAT IT WOULD BE EASIER FOR HER TO MOVE HER LEFT ARM TO DIRECT MAGICAL ATTACKS.

IT'S LIKE SHE'S A MAGE ON THE LEFT, AND A SWORDSWOMAN ON THE RIGHT.

THOUGH OF COURSE, I GUESS IT'S NOT LIKE SHE EVEN REALLY NEEDS TO USE HER HANDS TO USE MAGIC. BUT THAT'S ANOTHER MATTER...

亜方逸扣
ITSUKI AKATA

CONGRATULATIONS ON THE PUBLICATION OF VOLUME 6 OF *DIDN'T I SAY TO MAKE MY ABILITIES AVERAGE IN THE NEXT LIFE?!*

HOORAY!

I'LL KEEP ON TRYING MY BEST WITH THE MANGA VERSION! PLEASE KEEP AN EYE OUT!

NEKO MINT